Remembered

Yvonne Battle-Felton

BLACK STONE
PUBLISHING

Copyright © 2020 by Yvonne Battle-Felton
Published in 2020 by Blackstone Publishing
Original cover design and illustration by Leo Nickolls
Altered for the US market by K. Jones

Printed in the United States of America

First US edition: 2020
ISBN 978-1-982627-12-6
Fiction / African American / Historical

1 3 5 7 9 10 8 6 4 2

CIP data for this book is available
from the Library of Congress

Blackstone Publishing
31 Mistletoe Rd.
Ashland, OR 97520

www.BlackstonePublishing.com

To my children,
know that you are always enough

The Voice

Sunday, February 20, 1910

Negro Plows Streetcar into C

A night of terror erupted into a morning of much of the same as a Negro hurled a streetcar into dawn and Clyde's Department Store. Barreling down Main Avenue with what witnesses say was a revolver in one hand, the Negro was "hell bent on destroying everything in his path," according to witnesses.

In an evening that has seen hundreds maybe thousands of motormen pulled from streetcars, we can only speculate as to how the Negro came to be operating the streetcar. Our thoughts and prayers are with the unfortunate streetcar operator who has yet to be found or identified.

As the bricks and glass flew, onlookers surrounded the remains of the car, dragging the Negro and holding until police arrived for questioning.

The Negro remains in critical condition.

Rer
foll
imp

The
that
rela
the
beh
of a
exp
in l
its
beh
con
or v

It n
tots

Chapter 1

4:30 a.m.

She's sitting there on top of the chifforobe rocking back and forth, swinging her legs in time to some music she heard ten, twenty years ago. She's like that, Tempe. Gets something stuck in her head and it stays there like a thumbprint in wet cement. I want to ask her what she's listening to, but I haven't let on I know she's there. I can feel her watching me, smoldering. Hating me for ignoring her. It serves her right. It's been nearly a year since the last time she came. She can just sit there brewing and rocking and waiting on me like I been waiting on her since then.

Mama's dead, she had said.

It was fall. She popped up in the middle of the kitchen and plopped into my favorite chair like it was hers. Like she'd been there all along and hadn't wafted in smelling of cinnamon and cedarwood. Always burning. Even on a crisp autumn day. She strummed her fingers on the kitchen table, fingered the cracks. Waited. I turned back to the ham. Had to get supper ready in case Edward came home looking for some little bit to eat between shifts. She didn't care nothing about my ham drying out, my biscuits burning, or my heart breaking. I couldn't think of nothing worse than having my dead sister sitting in my favorite chair talking about my dead mama.

"Mama been dead, Tempe," I told her.

Wasn't no need turning to face her. I knew her eyes would be burning a hole in my back.

She just now died. She snapped her fingers. It sounded like twigs breaking. I wanted to ask her not to do that no more. *You just thought she was dead. I knew she wasn't.*

"If you knew she wasn't dead, why wouldn't you tell me?" I asked. I basted the ham in pineapple juice and honey, put the biscuits in the hotbox, and tidied the tea towels. When I couldn't think of nothing else to do, I turned around. The look on her face said it all. Why would she have told me? We been keeping secrets since we was little girls. Why would death change that?

Beneath the covers, I press my hands together, almost in prayer. She laughs. It's low and hoarse, unused. Whiff of cinnamon. All at once hot air rattles the shade, bumps against the window, lifts the edges of the wall calendar, flips slim pages. Searches. It whips around pictures on the bureau: Edward at six. The house, deed and all, tucked behind a heavy frame. Edward and Lil. It tugs at my bed linen. I tilt my chin. Wouldn't surprise me none if these covers wrapped round my neck. Eyes closed tight I turn to face the wall. How she can whip up a breeze with the window closed I will never know. Wouldn't ask neither.

It's too hot but I won't complain none. Although she don't ever carry nothing but bad news, I'm almost glad to have her home. Lola Mae, Spinner, Mama, Christian: each time somebody close dies, Tempe makes her way back to me. She say can't none of them come theyself cuz of me. "Why you come?" I ask. *Spite*, she said. She laughed. I know it wasn't no joke.

I'm tired. Been tired. Maybe it's time for me to go on home. Don't expect I'm going to Heaven. I can think of some worse who shouldn't be there either. Of course, I would prefer not to go down under. If I could just see Mama and them one more time, it wouldn't matter one bit where I go. But please, don't be coming here for my babies. They too young. Ain't hardly lived yet. Lord, I ain't called on you for nothing else, but please let Tempe be coming for me.

I breathe in her smells and hold my breath.

Hurry up.

I spread my arms and legs wide in surrender. "May as well just take me now."

Who will find my body? It can't be Lil. It wouldn't be no kind of start to her day to find me stone dead, bed undone, nightdress wrinkled. Would she know what dress to put me in? Maybe Sable will come. She'll know how to lay me out just right. She's buried enough people. She ain't been out that house since they killed her boy. Will she come now? What if Edward finds me? He might put me in one of them slack sets he's been eyeing in the catalog.

I know the flowers will be lovely no matter what, but who's going to do my hair? Not one of them can't-wait-to-move-in heifers. I'll just get myself dressed and save everybody the trouble. If I have time, I'll write a word or two that I wouldn't mind someone saying over my body. Don't have to be no church service but a few words couldn't hurt.

Hurry up.

"I'm up." She sits on the edge of the bed. I want to reach out and touch her, to hold her, but she's wispy, like smoke. She's old. What's the use of being a ghost if you still get old? All these years and she's still on fire. "You still mad, Tempe? If I could change what happened, I would, you know I would."

The air crackles. I should have saved her. If I had gone back all those years ago, pulled her out of the house, she'd be alive. Or we'd at least both be dead. A warm hand above my shoulder.

Get dressed.

I pick through dress after dress: *too flashy, too homely, too proud.* "If I knew what I was dressing for, I would know what to wear."

The dresses are segregated by event. I flip through work, visiting, entertaining, and celebrating. Sweat slips down my neck. The room gets hotter. Soon I'll be at the last dress. Please don't let me make it to the last dress.

I skip over consoling. Holding my breath, I reach for the long, thick black dress in the back.

Not yet.

I breathe the thick woody air, swallow the salty lump that rises from my belly, and get dressed. Hope. I haven't worn this one in years.

Downstairs I click on the radio. Jubilee Earle's voice fills the front room. I set the kettle to boil. Nothing goes better with bad news than good coffee. Whatever Tempe has in mind, I'm going to need something warm to deal with it. Neither of us mentions my shaking hands or the water sloshing out of the pot. I still haven't put the woodstove on. I don't expect I'll need to. I peeped into Edward's room before I came down. Still-made bed, clothes neatly hung up, not a speck of anything on the floor. Edward never came home last night. Something's wrong. It's too quiet. My stomach keeps flip-flopping. My chest rattles and tightens. I can't seem to get enough air. Can't smell nothing but death.

I've been staring into the cupboard for the past five minutes. Do I put a cup in front of Tempe or no? I ain't seen her eat or drink nothing since she been dead. I don't suspect she's hungry or thirsty. Mama wouldn't let nobody cross her door without offering them something to eat. What would she think? I grab two cups.

"Breaking news," the announcer interrupts Jubilee. "A collision has been reported on the corner of Broad and Main." My heart thumps trying to drown out the voice filling up my kitchen. The cups get to rattling, the kettle whistle makes me jump. "The late-night Broad Street trolley."

"Ain't been nothing but bad news since them boys started this strike. Ain't safe to be on the streets no more," I say. But I can still hear him talking.

Three months of strikes and now this. Does Tempe know? Don't see why she wouldn't. To hear her tell it there ain't too much she don't know about. What she think about it? Striking over pay. I done plenty of work without getting no pay at all. I ought to go on strike right now. Refuse to take in laundry, clean houses, bake pies, polish floors, scrub windows, clean pots till I get paid enough to do it. They lucky to be getting paid at all let alone paid enough.

I'll ask Edward. He'll know what's going on. Can't seem to get him to shut up 'bout what one side doing to the other. Bunch of schoolchildren. Busting folk up over money. I'll get a nice roast on, he'll like that. We'll talk and eat. What about Tempe? She's waited this long. Don't reckon one supper will kill me. What if that's it? What if she's waiting on me to take a bite of my breakfast so I can choke and fall right down here in the middle of my kitchen? I'll get these cups washed just in case.

"Collided into the window of a corner store mangling innocent bystanders."

Edward will be late for supper.

Edward won't be home for supper.

"According to witnesses, a Negro overthrew the operator, hurtling the trolley into Clyde's."

That's all we need.

"Thrown from the wreck into the crowd."

Things is bad. Union threatening strikes, burning buildings, busting up tracks, beating up drivers, harassing yard workers. Company sabotaging lines, raising fares, doubling hours, cutting pay, bringing in strike workers. Now they crashing up trolleys into stores, killing innocent people? They don't allow no colored folks to operate no trolley. Not even Edward and he been there for years. He's gotta get out of there. They always trying to drag him into something. Laying off hardworking folk to pay new ones less and it's, *Edward fix this, Edward tote that.* Won't let him operate, though. Ain't ready for that. Don't hardly pay him enough to light a lamp. Don't pay him enough to get mixed up in all this mischief either. Next time he brings up getting one of them porter jobs, I'm going to tell him to take it. Just get away from all this. I'll take in tenants. One or two ought to make up for it. He's gotta get away from here.

"Police are questioning suspects."

Questioning? The word makes my stomach drop, my throat tighten, my heart throb. The room swirls. The table, chairs, wardrobe, everything moves around me like a tornado. I can hardly stand. I turn to Tempe. She's the only thing rooted to one spot. She nods, slow.

I snap it off but the announcer's voice still bounces around the walls, glasses, plates, vases, chairs, floors, my heart, and anything else it can find. I pull on a wool cap and thick gloves. The reverend from Second Baptist will be leading congregations of stragglers, his posse of believers, marching to convert me, to lead me through this "test of faith." Edward will be a cause.

Get the book.

I reach for the Bible, thick and unused. What good can it do now?

The other book.

It's foolish to argue with a dead woman. I get the book.

Outside, the streets swell with prayer. Like hisses, voices slip beneath window frames, joints, and cracks. They crowd my kitchen. The book is heavy in my hands. Memories and clippings, pictures and letters, pages stretch the spine. I slip it into my black purse and head to the cellar door. I can climb down the rickety steps, maneuver through the damp enclosure and slip out of the back door, cut through the yard. Forced to use the back entrance of my own home?

I unlatch the bolt and open the front door. Through the wall, I hear Sable knocking goodbye. Forty years stuck in the house. Forty years of being afraid to walk the same streets, see the same faces, hear the same voices and not know which one of them killed your baby. After all this is over, we'll have a good visit. We'll sit in her front room with the heavy curtains drawn and talk about our boys, how they took them and how to let them go.

Outside, a group of men and women, the community grief–birth–death–wedding–new job–new family–justice team, a small congregation of collective faiths, has formed on Twentieth Street. Etta Mae organizes folk into small clusters. In front of Sable's house, a group scrawls "Justice for Edward" and "Not One More"

on the front of handmade signs. Next door, another cluster practices chants: "When one dies, we all weep! No more blood spilled
in the streets!" Across the street old women wrap thick sandwiches
in wax paper. In the middle of the street, men and women line up
to march. They hardly notice me.

Buddy and Franklin stand on either side at the bottom of my
steps. I search their faces; neither brother looks away. They know.
Of course it was Edward.

"Tempe's back," I say.

They stare at me, then past me. They look through her as if
they can't see her. Probably can't. She's stubborn like that. Won't let
anyone see her but me. They nod in her direction. She nods back.

I feel Sable peeping through the keyhole next door. "Sister,"
the reverend calls from the sidewalk.

Sister? Even Tempe doesn't call me that anymore. It almost takes
me back. I smell the river; feel the squishy bank beneath my toes. I
shake my head, clear my throat. Settle down, it's a title, not a name.

"Spring," Buddy corrects.

"Ms. Spring," Franklin adds.

Their voices are deep but soft. The reverend clears his throat
and steps back.

"Reverend," I say. There's no time for polite conversation.

"It's Justice," the reverend interrupts.

"Justice?" I can't have heard him right. My heart's beating, my
throat's tightening, I can't stop opening and closing my fists.

The reverend brushes at the sweat creeping down his cheek.
"My name," he says, "Reverend Justice."

"So it is." Names are coats around here. People try them on.
They slip in and out of them like religion, weather, mood, or
something else you can't afford to count on.

"We don't have much time. They done dragged Edward out the belly of the trolley. Tried him on the streets and found him guilty! If we don't put an end to this injustice, they gonna carry out the sentence right there in the middle of the street!"

Cuz of you, he won't know where to go. Cuz of you, he can't make his way home.

"He'll make his way home to me," I say. Tempe ain't got no right to blame me. I raised him, I near birthed him. I'm his mama. I clasp my hand to my chest. I can tell by the way they look at me, the crowd thinks I'm talking to them.

"Ain't no way Edward coulda done this," Buddy says. "I done known that boy all his natural life. Been there since he was this high." He pinches two fingers together.

The loud snap startles me, reminds me to breathe.

"Edward works on the rails, in the yard. If he was on that trolley, he had a good reason to be there," Franklin says. He nods like that says it all.

"Oh, he had a reason," Maybelle hisses. I can tell it's her without even looking up. No need to see her head-shaking sympathy. "Plowed that Express right in the middle of that high-priced store. No Coloreds Allowed. Serves them right."

"I was there," an angry voice answers. Still out of breath, the man pushes through the growing crowd. He pauses at the foot of the steps then turns to face them. "Seen the trolley damn near flying, sparks and metal everywhere. Folks scattering every which way. Bodies everywhere." His body ripples when he speaks like it can't contain itself, excited. "Edward was where the operator ought to be. He was holding a stick or something in one hand and waving his arms back and forth. Didn't look natural. Didn't seem like he was trying to hit anybody but didn't look like he was trying not to hit nobody either. All around him people running, screaming, but you know what?" The audience gathers closer. "He didn't look a bit worried. Crashed right into the glass storefront. Glass, metal, bodies everywhere, and the look on his face stayed as calm as you please. Even as they pulled him out."

The crowd looks at me for confirmation. My boy wouldn't do that.

"He has been acting strange," a whiny voice offers from somewhere in the back. "Hanging around with them union boys."

"They bound to put him up to it. You know they wouldn't allow no colored to operate no trolley."

"I don't believe it," a voice interrupts.

"Sounds like something he would do," someone else chimes in.

Suddenly, everybody knows my boy. People ain't said hardly two words to him acting like they know what goes on in his head. Everybody knows what Edward might and might not do. I push past the reverend.

"Just wait; things will all die down," Etta Mae says. Even outside of church the reverend's wife sounds the same. Always coaxing, cajoling, cautioning: "wait, wait, wait." Waiting was the best way to make it into Heaven; the only way if your skin was brown. And after all that waiting on Earth, they would finally meet the King and wait on him too. I've been waiting all my life.

Snatches of conversations slap me in the face, sting my cheeks.

"He did it, I know he did it!"

"If he ain't do it, he's sure gonna wish he did."

"Why'd he have to kill 'em, though? Things bad enough without this!"

"They gonna make this black against white. We all gonna look like Edward to them."

"Already do that now."

"I hope he did do it!"

"If we thought things were bad before, just wait."

"Mmmhmmm," they all seem to agree.

Children clamor noisily down Twentieth Street. On Twenty-First, horns honk, heels click, people yell. Quickly, as word spreads through the neighborhood, children are called, doors shut, windows locked. The warning: one of our own has killed a whole lot of theirs.

Hide.

What if he did it? The ground dips. It's a barely perceptible pulse; a movement too minor to fret over now that the stoop has begun to shake. The sidewalk burps and rumbles, the street lurches, houses pitch. The unfamiliar faces of the crowd fade into those of my dear friends Sable and Lillian, Watson, Watson Junior, Edward Senior, both my mamas: Agnes and Ella, Meredith, Myrtle. All the faces of the past stand before me. One face doesn't belong. It's a shadow but I'd recognize him anywhere: Edward. Twentieth Street vomits fragments of the past, spewing bile and memories of Sweetwater, Maryland. Thick green trees, always weeping, leaves interlocking like hands, trunks thick like men you can rely on. Over there the river, rising and falling without mercy, as unfaithful as hymns. There the ramble shacks, makeshift boxes of sticks and gum, leaves, and paper. There the graves, a rock to mark this one from that. All around, straight, long rows of fat-bodied blueberries, thin-skinned and bleeding.

In the center of it all, rapidly taking shape, is Walker Farm. It rises like a bruised, bloated, hissing thing. Smoke pushes through the massive windows and curls around the huge frame, clutching at the wood that's dry like skin. The cherrywood door opens. Tempe, a dark, slender shadow, stares. Behind her, flames beg, *Wait, wait.* Crackling, buckling, smoldering, popping, screaming. Silence.

A siren on the other side of town.

Get going.

"Tempe?" I whisper. I don't trust my voice.

Hush, they hear you. I done told you a hundred times. When you talking to me, use your inside voice.

Don't leave me.

I'll be here till it's done.

I should get word to Lil. She'll be at her day job, washing and ironing for that family just outside of the city. Gideon might be between shifts at the factory. Those two got more jobs between them than other young folk I know. Might be nightfall before they get word. I hope it's sooner. I'd hate for Edward to die alone.

"Buddy, go find Lil. Franklin, fetch Gideon." Buddy opens his mouth to tell me something I already know. The news will get there before he does. "Ain't right for them to hear it from nobody but family," I say.

I make my way off Twentieth Street. I don't bother to turn around to see if the crowd is following. They march, arms laden with posters, fish-fry fliers and cake-sale donation buckets, the other way.

"We need to gather more soldiers," the reverend explains. "It's 1910. It's high time they stop killing our people. If we don't stop them now, it won't ever stop. This here is war."

It is war. Tempe and I march headfirst into it.

Chapter 2

7:00 a.m.

Don't seem like nobody doing nothing but yelling and slowing me down. Their voices take my breath away. Their words run together like one long curse: "One of them Negroes stole a trolley. Damned fool crashed right into the store window. Wasn't no accident, they trying to kill us. Knew this would happen one day. Only a matter of time. Send them back to Africa. Fixed him good; none of them will try that again."

Back to Africa? My boy was born in Maryland just like his mama and papa. And my mama from round here somewhere right in Pennsylvania. How many of them can say they was born right here?

Just eight blocks to go and I want to run. I want to push through these angry red faces, kick my shoes off, and run barefoot down the middle of the street. Fixed him? Lord help us. I march down Beacon, on to Pleasant, and finally to Autumn Lane. Rows of people stacked up on both sides of the street. Union workers in dark-blue uniforms gather on one side. Company men in dark suits on the other. Police guard the middle. Bottles and words hurl from one side to the other. I put my head down, lean forward, and head to the colored entrance of Autumn Asylum Home for the Poor; hospital of the damned.

My feet stop me at the door. I try real hard but I can't remember the face of anyone that's crossed this threshold twice. How many people come with a toothache and come out dead? Headache? Dead. Broke leg? Dead.

Go in.

There's not as many people inside as there are out. I don't blame them. No matter how busted up I was, if I could walk in here on my own, I'd walk to another hospital.

There's worse things than being dead.

You would say that.

Don't worry about that now.

Seems like now's just the right time to worry about it. Doctors have no business experimenting on my boy. Ain't the time to be trying nothing new. Now's the time for something old, something respected. He should be home where I can take care of him. A little honey, onion, lemon, and river grass will do it. Where can I get river grass? Not Schuylkill grass. Lush, down-home grass. If Mama was here she'd know what to do. I look into each face I pass. Are these the victims? Some stare. Others, angry, watch me. Do they know who I am? Do they think my boy's some kind of killer? He ain't. What they think don't change a damned thing. Their pain oozes from bruised eyes, broken arms, busted heads.

Keep walking.

"He can't have visitors," the nurse announces to someone behind me. We've been standing in front of her for five minutes while she flips through charts, adjusts papers, waters a dying plant. She hasn't looked at me yet.

"I'm not a visitor." Her face is twisted up like she don't understand the words coming out of my mouth. "I'm his mama," I say, slow like she ain't from around here.

The nurse looks at the top of my head. Her look could wilt the flower stuck in my cap. Without looking into my eyes, she looks from my dress down to my double-soled shoes and back to the top of my head. She frowns, glances at the chart, flips a few pages, skims a few notes. "It doesn't say except for mothers. It says no visitors." Smug little heifer.

The only thing standing between me and my boy is this little bit of a thing, can't be no more than twenty if she's that. What does she know about dying alone? About a whole heap of people wanting you dead? About ending up in a run-down hospital getting run-down supplies and secondhand care because you colored and been accused of doing something don't nobody care if you done or not? I can push past her and make it to my boy. Just her between me and—

Go 'head then.

"What?" Tempe's always interrupting.

Push past her. She ain't but a little thing, go ahead. What's stopping you?

"What about all these people?"

Couldn't nobody keep me from my boy, 'cept maybe you.

"I ain't keep him from you. You left him. Who'd you think was gonna raise him, if not me?" Tears fill my eyes, spill down my cheeks and splatter on the nurse's station counter. I can't stop them. My shoulders stoop, my body shakes.

"She always like this?" the nurse asks the room.

No one answers.

"This seem normal to you people?"

"Is everything alright? Is she having a fit?" a red-haired nurse asks.

"I just want to see my boy," I say.

"I think she's mad." The nurse nods her head toward me.

"I ain't mad. I ain't. I'm disappointed, hurt, angry too, if I'm honest. But I really just want to see my boy."

"She's not mad," the older nurse diagnoses, "perhaps she's had a fit."

"Does she take medication?" they ask one another.

I shake my head.

"I wouldn't reckon so; they don't usually go to the doctor until they're dying."

"Let's sit this one down. Keep an eye on her. See if she has another fit while I look for a bed."

A bed? First they killing my son now they planning on killing me?

"I don't need no bed. Just my boy. I come for my boy."

The nurses whisper to one another. One points at a chart, flips pages, jabs a pen in the air. "I'll send someone to take you up," she says. For a second she meets my eyes. "Wait in there."

The young nurse turns back to piles of paperwork. The other one marches down the corridor. One step from the desk and Tempe and I are in the waiting room. Wooden benches squeezed into a small space. It would be called a water closet if it was somewhere else.

"I saw the whole thing," a young woman in a heavily creased domestic's uniform, clean except for the blood splatters dried across its front, tells an old man whose arm twists at a peculiar angle. Nothing a little roseroot wouldn't cure.

"Me too," he answers.

"That fool drove right in the store, aimed for it. Didn't swerve or nothing. He aimed." Her bobbing head punctuates each word.

"That ain't what I saw," the man says. "Looked like that boy was propped up, peculiar like, like someone done stuck him there."

"Woulda run me clear over if I hadn't jumped out the way."

"You mean if he hadn't hit a bunch of other people before you," he says.

"Thank God for small miracles," the woman says. The words coming out of her mouth make her whole face look ugly. Shame, too. She almost looks like the kind of gal that woulda been good for Edward. Good job. Home training, maybe not good home training. No sense in her head. Says the first thing that pops into it. Her voice makes my head hurt. I can't stop staring at her mouth.

8:15 a.m.

Just look at the floor.

Every so often my heart stops. The pew-shaped benches, the cold, gray floor, even the thick pamphlets filled with dark-faced patients and white-faced doctors bear worn edges. The room has whittled Autumn's hurt down to patches, splinters, and grooves. My eyes water as bloodred flowers drip onto the concrete floor. I concentrate on my shoes instead. The arch fit special to my wide feet, the thick soles for hours of standing, the tiny holes so my feet can breathe. Something else Edward thought I needed. Eyes stinging, I study the tops of people's heads, walls, the one window, until everything peels into layers. I rock back and forth to keep my eyes open. The bench groans each time I lean back, creaks when I lean forward. Groan, creak, groan, creak.

Stay still!

If I close them quick I can keep my eyes open longer. I try it. I blink. Edward in his work dungarees. Blink. Edward in his army uniform. Blink. Edward in boxing gloves. Blink. Edward at his first colored dance. Blink. Edward's life flashes backward. If I close them too long, he'll be gone. I stare at the wall in front of me. Straight lines turn into squiggles, flecks of paint into people, colors swirl. If it hurts enough, maybe Edward will live. That's silly. I'll hold my breath. My breath for his. Lord, if I surrender, will you spare my boy?

Don't be foolish.

A body slides into the seat next to mine. It smells like fresh earth, sweat, and death. Two long, slender feet, bare. A man-child rubs them together. The *shhh, shhh* of dry feet ignites the room. Small clumps of dirt drop to the floor. People whisper, shuffle. Bodies lean toward the door. No one gets up to leave but they all look like they want to.

"Now look here," a nurse says loudly while rushing from behind useless stacks of paper. "I told you we don't have any more room. We aren't seeing any more patients today. This is the waiting room."

"I am waitin', ma'am," the man replies. I know that voice. He leans into the bench, shifts his weight to one side, then the other, rubs his back against the pine, and finally leans forward, his hands on bony knees.

"He with y'all?" she asks the pamphlets, the stained walls, the dim light and bare floor. Soon she will have to look someone in the eye, to acknowledge the waiting.

Slender feet, bony knees, thick fingers, long arms, and broad chest. He looks older here than he did when he was trying to take over my stoop. What's he doing here now? I wouldn't be surprised if someone had bopped him straight in the mouth. Talking 'bout things he don't know nothing about. Would serve him right.

"I said, is he," she pinches her lips together so the words barely whistle through, "with one of you all?"

Right hand on gun, a police officer, young enough to be excited by the promise of conflict, saunters toward us.

"He's with us," I say. Don't need no more lives on my hands.

The nurse hurries to the sanctuary of her paperwork, the officer fumbles with the button on his holster, the young man settles back into the pine, fidgets.

"You ought to be more careful," I say. "You were about to end up dead."

"I'm in the right place for it," he laughs. "Ma'am, I didn't get the chance to introduce myself properly. I'm Jacob. Jacob Wood. I'm here as a friend of Edward's."

Mint breath tickles my nose; a lie with a hint of sweet. "You ain't sound like a friend when you was on my steps preaching he tried to kill folks," I say. The words and spittle hit his face. Jacob doesn't flinch.

"The truth don't mean he ain't my friend," he says. "I know he done it and meant to do it too, Ma Spring." He leans into me, too close. "It's gonna take more than praying to get Edward outta here alive."

The sweet, salty taste of blood fills my mouth. I turn, slip a handkerchief from my bag, spit, and fold it into little pink blotted squares. "You some sort of doctor?"

"Ma'am, we—my associates and I—have been thinking a lot about Edward's situation."

I can't stand to look at him. All that youth wasted. How is he sitting here, plotting and lying, while my boy, my good, kind boy, is somewhere broke up? Everything about him, from the words coming out of his mouth to his ashy feet, irritates me. I study his feet, thick and naked. Dry as two pickled hams. Toes as plump as figs. Dripping dirt. Dirt. In a hospital. Dirt that black is rich, hearty. Plant a seed in that and anything's liable to sprout up. "You say you can help Edward?"

"My associates and me think we can help you help Edward. All you got to do is remember right. Maybe it was him that come up with the plan to steal the trolley. Maybe he talked about it over supper. Maybe he was working for the Company trying to rile people up by hiring a Negro operator. Had him plow the train into Clyde's to make a point. Maybe it wasn't no accident."

"My boy wouldn't do that."

"You know, Edward ain't no boy no more."

This drumming in my head won't quit. I can't catch my breath. Can't swallow. That boy's mouth is still moving and thank the Lord, I can't hear nothing but this high-pitched train whistle getting louder and louder. Rattling the room, shaking the pews, scattering pamphlets. The only thing it can't do is wipe that grin off Jacob's face. I close my eyes. Blink. Edward leaving for work yesterday. Starched uniform. Glistening smile. A wave goodbye.

Chapter 3

9:37 a.m.

Soft, warm fingers wind around my wrist.

"This way, Ms. Spring. It's just a little piece further." The lie tumbles from the nurse's clenched lips. "I'm sorry. I wish there was a faster way," she whispers.

The colored ward is separated from the waiting area by the women's ward, the men's ward, and the operating room. When it's not serving as a mental health unit, the ward's beds serve West Philadelphia's homeless. When it's not serving them, it serves West Philadelphia's diseased, broken, and dying. The treatment remains the same: colored patients and visitors are ushered the long way round, down the concrete stairs, through the maintenance closet and up again, under the main wing, so as not to disturb the other patients.

"It's just …" she continues.

"How is my boy?" I ask. Ammonia-scented mops and bleach-stained buckets tighten my lungs.

"Careful, that stuff will kill a man. Sorry." The nurse has apologized for the narrow stairs, the concrete floors, the stains that won't fade despite weekly scrubbing with bleach, ammonia, or lye; the patches of bright light filtered in through cracked windows; the stretches of dark not yet granted funding for electricity; and the walk—the need to walk beneath the hospital instead of through it. *I'm sorry* when it's not your fault. *I'm sorry* when there's nothing you can do. *I'm sorry* when you're close to giving up. I'm fed up with I'm sorrys.

The nurse's shoes click against the concrete. My stomach knots and untangles. My mouth sours with thick phlegm. Just a little bit longer. Below the busy main hospital, it's almost easy to pretend nothing else matters.

"He's pretty beat up," she says.

My heart's been racing all morning so I know it when it stops. Where was I when they was dragging him from the trolley? When they threw him to the street? When he cried out for me? When he curled into a ball and they kicked and kicked and kicked? Tempe come to tell me. Did she know before it or not till after? If she'd have known before she would have told me, if she could. Even if there was some sort of rule that she couldn't tell the living, she would have told me. She'd have done it for the boy. Unless there wasn't nothing I could do about it. She would have stopped it, if she could. If she could have reached down and protected him, she would have. Can't tell nothing till it's too late. Can't do nothing about it no how. What's the use in hanging around if she can't do no more than I can to keep him safe?

"We almost there?"

The nurse stops walking. She clasps my hands tight like we're schoolgirls. She bows her head. With no windows it's near pitch black. The grating of air squeezes through a crack and the cadence of her prayer matches my breathing. I time it: one, two, silence. One, two, silence.

"Amen," she says. "You okay? You wheezing pretty bad."

She leans closer.

"It's just my heart."

I feel her fumbling with her stethoscope.

"It's breaking. I just need to get to my boy."

"Has your boy been acting different this past week?" the officer asks. He ain't looking at me.

I've been standing at this very spot since the nurse left me ten minutes ago. *The doctor would like a word with you before you go in*, she said, rushing off like I got time to be waiting on words. This boy done asked me the same questions three times maybe more. Ain't even writing down a word I say no how. I got questions too. You the one that put my boy here? Did you hold him down? Stomp him with them steel boots? "No, sir." If I can just get past him and get to the end of the hall, I can be with my boy.

"Staying out late? Coming home early?" He tilts his head, licks his pink, cracked lips.

What that got to do with anything? "No, sir. Can I see him?"

"Your boy's what, fortysomething?" He taps a black pen on a closed notepad.

Forty-five. "Yes, sir."

"And he's living with you over on Twentieth?"

"Edward takes care of me, always has."

"He have any reason to do what he did today?" He leans close, his hot breath curdles into tiny drops of spit that sprinkle my face.

"Yes, sir."

The officer's green eyes brighten. I must have said no last time he asked. He steps back, flips open the notepad. "What is it?" Words and spit drop from his mouth. He licks his lips.

"Edward works every Monday, sir," I say.

The notepad clicks shut. "Look here, gal, you know they don't allow coloreds to operate trolleys. What was your boy up to? Was he trying to start a riot? Who put him up to it? You could make it easy on him, you know that? Just tell me what you know."

My stomach clenches. My throat tightens. My mouth fills with chunks from last night's dinner, bits of cornbread, a sliver of ham. If I open my mouth it will spill out, soil my words. He'll take my sick and call it guilt, evidence. I swallow it all, hot and slimy, soured. He watches, waits.

"Take your time," he says. Pen tapping against notepad.

What do I know? Who put Edward up to what? What was he doing in the trolley? Was there a reason? Of course there was. As soon as I get to him, I'll ask him. After I hold him again. After I tell him it'll be alright. After I believe it.

"Sir," I say, "seems if Edward was operating a trolley like they say he was, it was a part of his job. Had to be. Edward loves that job and everything about it."

"Enough to make sure he don't lose it?"

I'm nodding my head yes.

"So he would work with the union to start a riot, if it meant keeping his job."

I'm shaking my head no. He's twisting the words soon as they drop from my mouth and I can't do nothing but watch them fall.

"Auntie, how about this, you go see your boy and you see if you don't remember anything he might have said about a job the union asked him to do. If you can remember a name, why that's better. Now what's better than that is if you can ask him who put him up to it. We tried to get him to talk but by the time we got to him, he didn't have much to say."

"Can I see him now, sir?" I'm near whispering. Can barely hear the words come out my mouth but I know they there. In the air, hanging.

You stay here asking permission. I'm going to see my boy.

"Stealing a trolley, tampering with the brakes, murdering innocent folks and all that property damage. Your boy's in a heap of trouble. He couldn't do this without help. If it wasn't the union, it was the rails. They've been trying to force the city to negotiate and this sort of incident is just what they need. Just tell me who he's working for."

"He works on the rails, sir. I told y'all already. He gathers supplies, runs errands."

"You find out who he's working with and we'll make it easier on him. All we need is a name, any name."

They could have killed him. Could have swung him from a tree. Drowned him. Who would have stopped them? "Sir, I'm grateful y'all took it easy on him today."

The officer rubs his chubby fingers along his razor-bumped throat. "He was thrown from the train. If the onlookers hadn't gotten to him first, he might be dead right now."

"I reckon you all saved my boy's life." They could have snatched him up. Locked him away God knows where. I wouldn't never know what happened to him. Never got to say goodbye.

"You could say that." The officer straightens his tie, puffs out his chest. "As soon as your boy wakes up, we'll get him to answer some more questions."

"The doctor is doing rounds," the nurse interrupts. She's out of breath. Must have run from ward to ward. "I'll just get you settled in and then go look again. Y'all done?" she asks the officer while pulling me.

"Bag," the officer says.

The nurse freezes.

"Tell the old girl to leave the bag here. Nothing in, nothing out." I pull the book from my purse, clutch it to my chest. I hold it up, an offering. Engraved, mahogany-skinned cover, thick pages stitched together by hand. Besides Tempe, it's the only thing I have of Mama's.

He nods, takes the bag and plops it down. My good compact rolls on the floor. The nurse is already pulling me down the hall.

"Edward's the last bed on the right. I just want to warn you, he don't look good. He's broke up. His lungs are punctured, his spleen's been ruptured, his—" The nurse stops, stares ahead. "I'm sorry. He's bandaged up, plastered from head to foot. He's in a coma."

She squeezes my hand and slips out the door.

Chapter 4

10:00 a.m.

The room is a lot brighter than it should be. Sunlight streams through the lone window. The gray walls and chamber pots practically sparkle. Tempe's glowing like a campfire. Lighting up the whole room. Six beds. I light-foot past the patients. They don't pay me no never mind. Most of them staring after Tempe. She's standing at the head of Edward's bed, fidgeting. She don't seem to know what to do with her hands, trailing wisps of smoke as she touches his head, caresses his cheeks. "Keep away from my boy." I don't yell it but five heads turn to face me.

Tempe stares at me like I lost my mind. I squeeze past her to Edward's side. I barely feel his warmth. What isn't covered in strips of white gauze and plaster is swollen with purple bruises or hidden beneath a starched white sheet and thin, scratchy blanket. His eyes are swollen shut. His skull, ears, nose, and chin are distorted beneath layers of cotton. His neck is rigged to a contraption connecting his back and legs. I don't know where to put my hands.

He wouldn't be here if it weren't for you!

"Just let me get him home to fix him. You come back some other time, Tempe."

I ain't leaving without my boy.

"What you come for? To watch him die? To watch me watch him die? Save him!"

I can't. She sucks the air from the room. I can't hardly breathe. Beds rattle, charts flip, drawers open and close.

"Ain't got no time for none of your tantrums, Tempe. If you ain't here to help, go!"

I'm taking him home.

"It ain't time. Take me instead."

You? She spits the word like I'm not even good enough to be dead with her. Always second.

"Then let me save him."

Like you saved me? The room bursts into flames. Fire leaps from the walls, the floor, the ceiling. It's hotter than coal in a smokehouse. My heart would be racing if it hadn't stopped. Brick walls slip into dripping wood beams, concrete floors melt into hardwood. Grand windows burst through, leaving Autumn in smoldering rubble. We're back inside Walker's place. Back to the day Tempe died.

She'll kill him and me both. "No, I ain't gonna do it," I say. "I'm staying right here with my boy."

Everything but the smell of burning wood disappears.

He can't hardly hear you over everybody else calling his name.

"I don't hear nobody."

Of course you don't. When it's your time, you won't hear them either. You done forgot all about home.

"You ain't talking sense."

When's the last time you talked about Mama?

"I think about her all the time."

When's the last time you talked about her? Edward know about her?

"No."

Then he can't hear her. That's your doing.

"Then why can't he hear me? He know me."

You think Mama the only one trying to call him?

"Who else, then?"

Tempe stares at me for so long I'm not sure she's going to answer.

All I can do is lead him home. And I can't do that if he don't know who I am.

The room spins round and round. I grab for Edward's hand. "He'll hate me."

Selfish.

"Who want to die hating their mama?"

You ain't no mama if you rather him go to hell thinking you his mama than go home with me.

I put my head where Edward's heart should be. I listen. Nothing.

"I'm going to have to ask you not to touch the patient," someone says.

I put my hand on Edward's chest. "Hold on, baby, I'll be right here. I'm going to talk to the man a moment." The doctor must be about six foot.

"He can't hear you." His crisp coat matches the words clanging to the floor. "He's comatose. Do you know what that means?"

"How long till I can take him home?"

"Ma'am, I'm Dr. Ross. Mr. Freeman is dying. Is he taking any medicines," he lowers his voice, "from a doctor or otherwise?"

"My son ain't need no doctor since he left the army."

"Did he get any pills then?"

"If he did, it isn't likely he's still got 'em. That was years ago."

"Has he ever suffered any trauma to his head"—the doctor pauses to study the chart—"before?"

"I'm not sure what that has to do with him ending up here."

"If we know what caused him to go into shock …"

"It wasn't being thrown from the trolley?"

"Ma'am," the doctor lowers his voice again and places a warm hand on my shoulder, "we want to make him as comfortable as possible under the circumstances. If we can help him make it through the night, he just might make it to morning."

And then what?

"I'm going to look in on my other patients. I'll be back to check in."

"He's gone," I say when he is.

If he live, they gonna kill him. You know that, don't you?

"Maybe they'll leave him be. They'll find out whoever did it and leave Edward in peace."

Even in death Tempe's laugh rattles my teeth.

"Maybe it was that boy, Jacob, got Edward all mixed up in some union mess. Edward didn't want no parts of it and Jacob made him, forced him. That's what happened, isn't it, Edward?" I put my ear to Edward's mouth and listen for moans, gasps, bursts of air, anything that sounds like a yes. Every so often a prick of breath tickles my earlobe. "Probably got wind of what they was trying to do, jumped board that trolley, wrestled it from that no-gooder, lost control and in trying to steer clear of folk, crashed. He's a hero. They can't kill a hero."

Can't they?

If they'd known, they wouldn't have done him like this. "It's cuz they didn't know he was trying to save them."

Why didn't they ask him?

I close my eyes. Edward barrels down the street in a runaway trolley, arms waving wildly. He's screaming for help. He can hardly reach the brake, the controls ain't responding. He's ten, a little boy in a big, flaming trolley wanting nothing more than to go home.

We wait. Around us, patients settle into heavy breathing, some slip in and out of fretful dreams and wake to their own screaming. Nurses jab, bandage, and shift bodies. They note charts, check vitals. Metal wheels squeak as dying patients are replaced with other dying ones. It can't be long past midday but the clouds have hidden the sun. Rain beats down on the roof. Thunder rolls across the sky. Lightning flashes every so often. A thin stream of water leaks onto the floor. A nurse comes in with a bucket. Rain plops and keeps time, tick, tick, tick. Edward does not stir.

What if he didn't do nothing? Will they leave him alone or just put something else on him? If he don't die tonight, will they just kill him tomorrow? Even if he did it, if innocent people died because he was wrapped up in some union dispute over money, he wouldn't deserve to die this way. With no name, no kin, nowhere to go. Whether he's a hero or no, my boy is dying. "I can't save him, can I?"

You can help me lead him home.

I settle down on Edward's bed, lift his head onto my lap.

The weight feels good. I breathe the scent of bleach, soap, ammonia water, the faint smell of death. The book is heavy in my hands. Its soft cover is flesh beneath my fingers. The pages flip rapidly. I turn back to the beginning. They flip again, stopping on articles about the war, the emancipation, the fire. "Tempe, if I'm going to tell this story, I'm going to tell it my way," I say.

You ain't got much time.

"Either I'll tell it my way or it won't get told."

Five stories below, the streets call Edward's name. Tempe huffs but she leaves the book alone.

"Most of what I'm about to tell you ain't in no history book, no newspaper article, no encyclopedia. There's a whole heap of stories don't ever get told. What I know comes straight from my sister's lips to my heart and to this book. Some of it I seen with my own two eyes. Some with hers. You come from free people. From right here in Philadelphia. You wasn't born here. It was me that brought you home."

I open the book and begin.

Chapter 5

The Philade

Friday, April 14, 1843

Whisperings and Warnings

Numerous reports of slave catchers and kidnappers have been reported throughout Pennsylvania, again. As always, travel on the main roads in groups whenever possible. Stay clear of footpaths. There have been reports of possible snatchings and kidnapping attempts at sunset and after dark.

Keep your papers pinned underneath clothing.

Be vigilant and cautious.

Be free.

Ella's neck is stiff but she won't rub it. What's five more minutes of discomfort compared to what other folks have to bear? Has it been five minutes yet? Time doesn't seem to be moving. If it wasn't for the sound of grinding and scraping and now the smell of fresh baked bread, Ella would swear time wasn't passing at all. Maybe not swear. She leans forward on her crate at the end of the row of

West Philadelphia's Third Baptist Church wondering if the sermon would have been over already if she had gone over to East Philadelphia's. With her head still bowed, she peeks. All she can see is a row of shoes, some spit-shined, some lightly dusted, some rooted to the floor, others tapping. None seem to be itching like hers to run.

"God loves even the slaves," the preacher says. His voice fills the small store/pharmacy/church, one of the few places they can speak freely. "Their suffering and pain has paved their way to the Heavenly Gates. Their earthly burdens will be replaced, their souls restored, and they will suffer out of love for our Lord."

Ella shifts her weight from one foot to the other. "By the time service ends today, we'll all be meeting the Lord," she mumbles.

Sister Adelaide, the oldest woman Ella has ever seen, whispers hot and spitty in her ear, "Hushhhhh."

"The life of the heathen is full of despair," the preacher continues, "until our slave brothers and sisters let loose their shackles and embrace the Lord." He pauses and throws off his thin sweater. With the windows shut and the congregation of thirty-five free men and women held captive until service ends, the preacher launches into last Sunday's service. "Won't none of us be free till we all free. Can I get an amen?"

"Amen!" the congregation yells.

One hour later, after slipping the thin pamphlet, *The Price of Freedom: The Guide to the Young Christian Woman's Role in Saving the Heathen, the Slave, and the Less Fortunate*, into the fold of her frock, Ella turns to leave. She has just enough time to get home before supper. Sister Adelaide starts twitching. Unless Ella can stop her, in a few minutes the twitch will reach her bones and her eighty-seven-year-old body will spring off of the hard bench and dance up the aisle for near an hour.

"My God is an awesome God," Ella sings out. Her voice is soft and clear like her mother's. "He's truly amazing. My God gave his Son for me. With my voice I praise him …"

"He laid down his life for me," a deep voice takes up the refrain.

Within minutes the entire congregation rocks and sways to the familiar song of benediction. The collection plate passes around. Folks hoping for an extra blessing surround the preacher. A nickel later, Ella slips out the back.

It's near dark. Mama will skin her alive if she's late again. Now, the only way to get home before sunset is to cut through the woods. The path is short: a thin trail, thick trees. She can cut right through and be almost home. She'll just have to run the rest of the way. If someone sees her she'll be in trouble for sure. Mama's told her not to cut through the woods near a thousand times. Almost as many times as she's told her to say her prayers, set the table, sit like a lady, and act like she had some common sense and home training.

Ella slips into the woods. The path is worn down by feet. Her leather soles barely leave a print. The thin trail is riddled with weeds. In the spring, lush patches of bright colored bluebells, honeysuckles, and cherry blossoms carpet the wood; it would be near impossible to find the path. But today, a breezy mid-fall evening, the brown grass, crisp leaves, and thin branches bow and crunch. Before long the wood thins, the weeds part. Ella can just about see the dirt road. The sky is still light. She can make it. She slips out the wood, shaking leaves and dirt from her clothes.

"What you doing in them woods?" He's not from around here. Thin shoes instead of work boots, the words scattering slow enough to pick them up if she wants to. His mouth twists like he tastes something rotten. He's a stranger, a white one. Trouble.

"Walking," Ella says. She stares at a slippery puddle of chewed tobacco at his feet. His toes seem about to burst through the thin leather.

"Walking, what?"

"Like this." She takes one large step, followed by a larger one, then another.

"Don't walk away while I'm talking to you!"

"I'm just trying to explain what I'm doing," she says. "I'm taking the shortcut from church so I get home in time for supper. Mama gets mad something fierce if I'm late." Ella looks around. Nothing but a lonely wagon stacked with chicken cages, a bureau, and some thick mattresses tied to two horses. Any other time a neighbor or two would be in a garden pulling vegetables for supper, out back taking clothes off the line, walking down the street on the way home from work. Seems like everybody in Philadelphia is shut behind locked doors and here she is talking to some strange white man all alone. Papa will have a fit.

"You supposed to be walking through the woods like that?"

"Like what?" Ella's right eye twitches. Run.

"What's the matter with your eye?"

"Tainted," she whispers. Words seem stuck in her throat. She can't get enough air.

"Damned my luck. First a bushel of broken ones back home and now this. Why me?"

The too-close man's hot breath wrinkles Ella's nose. She steps backward.

"Walker," a familiar voice calls from the other side of the wagon, "will you come on? I got to get back home before it gets too dark."

"Mr. Thompson?" Ella calls. "I'm sure glad to see you!" The words tumble fast, in time with her heart. She catches herself before running to hug him. The last thing she needs is Mama to come round the bend and see her arms wrapped around Mr. Thompson.

"Ella? What you doing out here all by yourself? Your pa know where you at?"

"No, sir."

"You ain't been sneaking round with no boy, have you?"

"No, sir."

"Don't seem like your pa to let you go running around town by yourself. It seems like you're always up under your mama's skirts or running behind one of your brothers."

"Yes, sir, I'm just on my way home now."

"Through the woods?"

"I was taking a shortcut. It seemed like the fastest way to get home. You know how my mama gets if I miss supper."

Thompson smiles. "You should get on home then."

Ella turns to go. She will have to run to make up the time. Won't Mama be tickled when she tells her what a fright she had on the way home? Overreacting, that's all. Just plain imagining. "I'll tell Pa I saw you and Ma that you asked after her."

"Hold still, Negra," Walker demands.

Run. Run. Run. The birds chirp, chickens cluck, wind whispers it. Ella keeps walking. Her heart beats so loudly that she can barely make out Mr. Thompson's words behind her. Walker catches up and grips her shoulder tight.

"Walker, let that gal go!" Thompson yells out. "Get on home, child."

Walker tightens his grip. His thick fingernails dig into Ella's shoulder. "You said if I did a few jobs for you, you'd help me catch one. Well, I caught one. First Negro we seen alone in miles. Must be some sort of sign. Now help me get her in the wagon."

"The Lord is my shepherd ..." Ella prays. I'm going to die. I'm going to die.

"I didn't mean a tamed one. I meant one running around. One I don't know."

"Well, she's one I don't know," Walker says. He pulls Ella toward the wagon. She digs her heels into the dirt. He drags her. Her leather shoes, the ones Mama cured, stitched, dyed instead of buying the ready-made ones in the shop, scrunch and slide off Ella's feet. She fights. She flails and twists her arms, contorts her back. He clamps an arm around her neck, wrestles to pick her up.

"Wait a minute!" Thompson says. "I don't want no trouble with her pa. He's good people."

"For a colored." Walker spits the words with a clump of chewing tobacco on the ground. "Soon you be talking 'bout they just like us."

"Just pick another one." Thompson blocks the way to the wagon.

"Look here, Thompson. You good people. You work hard. Got a piece of land. Do right by your missus. Got yourself a reputation here. You gonna let this fool of a girl ruin all you building up? Don't you care about your family? I care about mine, I do. I don't know what kind of man that makes me, but I can't go home without this gal. I can't do that to the missus. I ain't told you before now but my place is bad off. You know how long it's been since we had a young'un? Something ain't right there. Need to start over. Build from the dirt up. Need a gal like this to break the curse."

Thompson laughs. "A curse? You talking just like them. There's no such thing as a curse."

"No? Then there's no harm in taking this gal, is there?" Thompson stares at Ella, wriggling in Walker's grasp. "Ain't nothing wrong with what we doing," Walker continues. "What you think gonna happen to her if she keep running around with her uppity ways? Talking to folk any ol' kind of way? You want her pa to have to bury her cuz she don't know how to talk to white folk? And her ma, you want her ma to be chasing round trying to make her do right? Won't be long before some boy's in her skirts. She won't bring nothing but shame."

Walker's hands fumble over Ella's body as he tries to haul her into the wagon. Her pamphlet falls to the ground. She kicks hard like her brothers taught her and runs without turning to watch him double over.

"Call the law! Call the law!" Walker yells. "You seen it. She attacked me!"

Ella's arms and legs pump as she runs down the road. Just a few strides more and she will be at the bend. Behind her someone stumbles, the earth crunches beneath the weight of too-tight shoes. A slippery hand tugs at the back of her dress. Thompson.

Wheezing, he grips a handful of cloth and hefts her off her feet. "Stupid fool," he whispers. "Wouldn't none of this have happened if it weren't for you."

She's dying. The high neckline Grandmother had sworn by and insisted upon clings to her neck like stingy hands. Between the biting lace, Thompson shaking her so that her head rattles and her lungs refusing to breathe, Ella's world turns black. She almost doesn't feel it when Walker hits her in the head with the side of a pistol.

It's dark when she comes to. Her head throbs. Her heart hurts. Her arms and legs, tied, are sore. Her throat is dry. Her tongue's thick. The drying vomit under her nose, around her mouth, covering her chin, suffocates her. Her head thumps against wood planks each time the wagon bumps, swerves. I want my mama. She lays on her side in the back of the wagon tied hands to feet under a thick row of scratchy blankets and smelly chicken crates. The squawking and scratching of the chickens muffles her screams. The wagon bounces for hours. Days. It is dawn when it finally stops. Shuffling feet, hushed voices and then Walker's voice, angry and short.

"Just tend the horses and unload the chickens. I'll get the rest."

Ella screams.

A sharp bang on the side of the wagon is the only response. The horses are unhitched. The crates unloaded. The blankets lifted. A flash of light. Fresh air, dark-brown eyes staring into hers. Ella jumps.

Quickly a brown hand releases the blankets. Darkness.

Ella's heart pounds. Her clothes stick to her skin. Her skin sticks to the wooden wagon bottom. The ropes cut into her wrists and ankles.

Hours later she's dragged across the wagon floor, dumped to the ground. She stares up into an older version of Walker.

Walker joins them. He spits near her face.

"Sir, there's been some mistake," Ella says. Don't look them in the eye. Lower your voice. Be respectful. Her throat is hoarse. "If you would just cut me loose, I can get back home."

"What's she talking about?"

"Damned if I know," Walker Junior says.

"Would you shut her up so we can get down to business?"

Ella closes her eyes in time to see the sole of Junior's shoe before he kicks her in the face.

Chapter 6

For three days Ella is chained naked to a wooden beam a little thicker than she is. Her legs, arms, neck, and every piece of flesh ache. Flies buzz and settle in her hair, on her legs. Her muscles flinch; the flies, undaunted, lap at streaks of urine that dry down her inner thighs. A barn. The air is hot with the stench of manure, pee, sweat, and hate. The smells sizzle, filling Ella's nostrils. She had been left alone the first two nights. No food, no water, no answer to her screaming or begging to be set free. No glaring eyes. She is almost thankful. Ella has heard stories about robbers creeping in through windows and snatching up colored children who didn't mind their parents or clean their plates. But she wasn't a kid anymore and these weren't googly-eyed demons. She hasn't been snatched from her bed. For as long as she can remember she's been warned of the dangers the night brings. There were stories. Always don't do, don't do, don't do, or they'll snatch you. But in the broad daylight? Who warned her about that? She prays. Please Lord, let me see my papa again. Papa must be worrying a hole in the porch by now. Most likely he's rounded up the boys and the men from town, hitched up wagons and corralled horses. He's armed with loaded rifles and unleashed hunting dogs. Right now Papa's on his way with his men and his guns and his fury. Just wait and see. Just wait.

For three days the cows stare—bored.

When they come, they come carrying candles. Two shadows circling, watching, appraising; casting lines.

"How much she cost?" the old one asks.

"I negotiated some good terms, you'd be proud."

Sweat trickles into Ella's eyes. Her body burns all over. "I've been stolen!" she screams.

The back of a hand cracks her dry, swollen lips. "She ain't got no papers, son?"

"I am free!"

Hot fire presses under her arm; her skin burns. Ella screams. The candle flickers.

"What's the matter with you?" Thin hands press cloth on her skin. Smells of skin, lilac, and turpentine swirl as the old man prods the fresh burn and stuffs the rag in Ella's mouth. Ella bites hoping for bone, flesh, or blood, instead she holds a mouth full of fraying dirty rag and screams. "Won't get near as much for her if she's scarred up."

Fingers part folds of flesh, pinch. Ella writhes and squirms, twists from hands that are soft like pincushions.

"Look at her, heifer must be in heat."

"You only got a few weeks to break her in. If you can't, I'll do it."

"It won't hardly take that long, Pa. She's mine now."

Ella's stomach spasms. It constricts and tightens. I am not a slave, I am not a slave, I am not a slave. The dry cloth smothers the words before they can leave her mouth.

A few hours later, stars pepper the sky. It's not the carefree breeze of a Philadelphia night. The air is crisp, cold. Inside, candlelight flickers. In gentle voices the men worry over the loss of appetite of a milking cow. Hay rustles. A sweet scent. Cows cull. Heavy boots stomp, wood slides across cold floor. The men settle, wait. Their voices echo. She feels them, knows they are close. Soon Papa will come with her brothers and shotguns. The white men will be sorry. Will Papa kill them anyway? Probably.

But when the killing is over she'll get a whupping. It's her fault she's here, chained to a beam in a stinky barn, and not home. It's her fault she's been stolen. Something in her eyes, her walk, her voice. Whatever it is, it was in the way he looked at her. Like she was the devil. Soon as she gets home, she'll go to church, twice on Sundays. And no more sneaking out the house like she's been doing. From now on she'll do as she's told. She'll finish her chores and wait for her mother or grandmother to walk the five miles to the big church clear on the other side of the city. She won't complain about passing at least ten churches just to get there or being forced to sit through the children's service even though she's nearly twelve years old. She'll mind the young ones with their dirty hands reaching for her ribbons and just smile when they beg for sweets, even though they know better than to ask for something before the bell rings. She'll smile and sing and tell stories and let them climb all over her and miss the service and ask Mama and them what the preacher said. She won't even think of sneaking back to her own church with the smell of warm bread where she sits with the grown folks and is chair of the Adult Reading Group. If she's good, maybe Mama will let her go back to her little church even though there's "hardly any prospects there worth considering for a young lady," even though she's not even considering. If Mama does let her go back, for as long as she lives, she will never take another shortcut home.

Splinters pierce her skin clasping her to the beam. The chain winds around her neck, snakes across her belly, wraps around her thin thighs. It is old. It digs into her flesh, leaving flecks of rust and blood on her skin. Heavy on her soul. As the air cools and the night thickens the men talk numbers, coins, pounds, percentages. They count cows, berries, acres, slaves down to the last penny.

"Hips wide for breeding. What you reckon she's good for—ten, twelve?"

"One a year for," Walker Junior taps his fingers loud against his palm, "that sounds about right."

"We should have a healthy stock in just a few years."

"You sure she can birth?"

"I don't see why not."

"Nothing else grows here. Ain't no young'uns been born here for over—"

"—Don't start talking that curse nonsense. The only thing keeping these Negroes from birthing is the devil. They're just too evil to birth babies."

"It ain't just them."

"Son, your wife ain't nothing like them. She's delicate. Give her time. If there's any wool to that curse yarn, this new gal will change it. Start afresh. And if there isn't, well, she didn't cost you much."

Sour phlegm bubbles from Ella's stomach, floods her mouth, saturates the cloth, seeps down her chin. She will die here. Of all the ways Ella has imagined dying: flattened by a runaway cart, trampled by an ornery mule, beat to within an inch of her life by Mama's switch, choked by a rag full of throw-up wasn't one of them. Ella M. Clarke, twelve years old. Dead.

"The damned fool's choking. How you choke on your own spit?" The old man yanks the rag from her mouth. He folds the cloth, wipes streaks of vomit from her face with a scratchy patch of it and shoves the rag back in her mouth. "The way I see it, you done her a favor. Roaming the streets, clothes torn off like a hussy? It's a wonder no one took her sooner. She coulda ended up dead."

"Sure coulda."

Ella bangs her head against the solid wood. If she can get it to crack, she can wake up. There will be blood, maybe a knot on her head, a headache. Even if her head splits wide open, it will be better than this. When she wakes up, maybe all this—the strange look in Thompson's eyes, being stolen, soiled—is a touch of wine, Christ's blood, sipped from the bottom of a jelly jar. She'd known better than to dip from the grown folks' Communion glass. Any minute she'll wake up and find herself lying in the middle of the cornfield out back of the church or swaying on the path through the woods, cocooned, safe. Her skirts might be damp, a bit muddy. She'll have to run home for sure. If she can wake up, she'll get home.

"Stop it, you damned fool!" Sweaty hands around her waist. Senior tightens the heavy chain links. "Since you're worrying about it, we ought to see if something's wrong with her," he says. "I'll do it." He unbuckles his belt.

"No, Pa, what if she's got something? No sense you getting it too."

"What you wanna do? Send for Doc? By the time you get him to come over here, he'll be too full of drink to think straight."

"No need to get him involved. I'll get Little James, he'll do." He's out the door before his father can answer.

Before it stops, Ella's heart beats so loudly it echoes in the beam, the shutters seem to shake, the floor trembles. Her body shakes.

The old man runs dry, thick fingers across her skin. He presses, pinches, slaps, twists. She worries his sandpaper fingers rubbing against her flesh will start a fire. Ignite them both, she hopes.

"Ain't nothing wrong with you, is there?" he asks. He probes, sinking his fingers deep inside her.

A few minutes later, Walker returns with Little James. He hangs a lantern on a nail. Nods his head in Ella's direction. "Do your business," he says.

James unhitches his breeches. "Don't do this," Ella begs through the rag. Her head barely reaches his chest. Little James is at least two heads taller and nearly as old as Papa. Without looking at her, he spits on his hands, rubs them together, spits on them again and pushes two fingers inside of Ella. She shrieks. James smothers her screams with his chest, he enters her. He ruts inside her. His cold sweat drips down her skin. She shivers.

"That's it," he coaxes.

The beam wedges into her back. Splinters dig into her skin. Her body burns from the inside. James's body shakes. He grunts. A warm glob drips down Ella's thigh.

"Sorry," he whispers. He pulls up his pants.

"Well?" Senior asks.

"Sir, sure don't feel like she tainted," James declares. He adjusts his breeches.

"Good, good," Senior says, reaching to unbuckle his belt. James rocks back and forth on his heels.

"Would you stay still?" Walker asks.

James fidgets. He rubs one thigh, then the other. Soon he is frantically rubbing them both. "I'm burning! I'm burning!" He screams, flinging himself to the floor. "Master, please take that rifle and shoot me." He crawls on his knees toward Walker. "I ain't gonna be no use to you at all." His eyes roll in his head. Tears drip down his face.

Ella, Walker, and Senior stare.

"Pull yourself together," Walker demands. "Go down to the old woman see if she ain't got something to keep it from falling off."

"That's a damn shame," Senior says. "Thought for sure if there was a curse, and I ain't saying there is, but if it was, wouldn't expect this gal would already be touched."

"She was probably worn down when I got her. Damn Thompson sold me a rotten one."

It's nearly light when Walker returns. Ella whimpers. "Don't you worry none," he says. "You still good for something." He unlocks the chains letting them clang to the floor around her feet. Before she can run he forces his fingers inside her—slaps her for being "dumb enough to let a buck take her and for not having the decent morals of the lowest farm animal"—pulls her to her knees, yanks the rag from her mouth, and forces his man part between her teeth. Words flash behind her closed eyes. Slave. Breeding. Papa. God. Home. She bites down.

There isn't nothing else to do but hold on. Junior howls and bucks. His fists crash into Ella's head. Even as she lets go, the sides of her head, her mouth, her eyes, her chest, her belly, her legs, her special places crumple beneath the blows. Barefoot, he gives a final kick to her mouth. Teeth give way. She swallows them—eight teeth gulped like dreams.

Walker grabs her feet, drags her across the barn, across planks, nails, manure. He lifts her up high and tosses her into a mushy pile. If she hadn't rolled off she would have died there, buried in a pile of dung. Darkness fills her head. Pain swirls into a melody. Tiny sharp rocks bite into her back, her arms, her legs. They dig into her cheeks.

Moving hurts. Not moving hurts. She measures short breaths: in, out, in, out, with long pauses in between. The motion makes her sides hurt so she stops. Something inside is broken. Her eyes are puffy and sore, her jaw aches, her head rings like a church bell. She flicks her tongue along the oozing holes in her mouth. Gone. Her mouth is heavy with dirt and rocks, her tongue slippery with seed she will not swallow that thickens and mixes with spit and tears. Her flat palms press the cool earth. Her dull nails filled with dried slivers of skin and flecks of blood dig into the ground. Ella's lips are raw, swollen, and blistered, gummed shut. She moans in a rich baritone that would have been the envy of all the girls in the choir.

A deeper voice joins in. A girl with hair thick and matted, clothes thin and worn; a voice sweet like love, forgiveness, peace, joy, and anything at all worth having hums Ella's song.

Mama?

Ella lays naked, surrounded by trash, leavings, and dirt at the bottom of a hill. Her arms and legs twisted, her body bruised, sore, broken; her soul stolen. Through squinting eyes, the girl's smile is the last thing Ella sees. The darkness takes over. Ella Mae Clarke is going home.

Chapter 7

Ella wakes to warm hands and cool water dripping over her body. She's still alive. Damn. The touch is gentle, loving. The hands move in circles, kneading and cleansing. Ella's skin is raw. It flits and jumps.

"Way you was carrying on, thought you'd be all busted up," a girl's voice says. Smelling of sweat and lilac, she's kneeling just beside her. Too close.

Ella tries to open her mouth.

"Don't try to talk. I haven't tended your mouth. Probably a good thing too. Youse a screamer. I'm Agnes," she says as if she isn't wiping blood and seed from between Ella's thighs. "And don't you even think about running. You hear?" Agnes lays down her cloth and scoops up a rusted rifle. She points it at Ella's head. "Massa say you even look like you thinking about running, I shoot."

Ella flinches. Shoot me then.

"I'm hoping I don't have to shoot you none. Who you think gotta clean all that up?" Agnes laughs, settles the rifle beside her.

It takes three trips to get enough fresh water from the river to clean Ella's body to Agnes's satisfaction. Agnes's job is to tend the sick until Mama Skins gets around to them. She just moves the aches around to different places, but Mama Skins is a healer.

When the sun goes down, Agnes pushes and pulls Ella across the pasture. How can it take so long to drag one little dainty gal home, Agnes thinks. Not like she's helping neither. They've been moving forever and they aren't even to the halfway post let alone to the gate. She'll be late. If she doesn't get back in time to feed the animals, Mama will kill her dead. And it will be her own fault too. If she dies tonight Mama will have no one to blame but her old fool self. *Agnes, boil the meat. Agnes, keep the gophers out of Master's garden. Agnes, keep the chickens out of Missus's drawers. Agnes, bring me that colored gal.* Like all she needed was one more thing to do. She props Ella up to see if she can stand. She slumps over and slides to the ground. Her head thuds softly on a bed of grass.

"You'd think you'd have sense enough not to fall down," Agnes says, staring down at her. She's already had to leave her good bucket and cloths behind the barn, now she'll have to leave Papa's busted-up rifle too. This gal sure is a lot of trouble. "I'm gonna leave this right here. So's you know, I can run faster than a cow at a barbecue. You start to look like you running away and I'll come right back and blow your head off. Clear off." In case she doesn't understand, Agnes waves her hand in her best "your head rolling away" motion. She puts the rifle down. With her hands beneath Ella's armpits, she hoists her up again. She lets Ella lean against her. Agnes studies the small frame. Ella's hair is thick and matted, her arms and legs are bruised, and her lips are busted up. She looks like a hen that got caught out in a real bad storm. "What if I just pick you up?"

Ella moans.

"I'll be careful."

Ella moans louder.

"Suit yourself." Agnes pushes her through the high grass of the far field. The grass stings her legs. If she'd only move those big feet. "If you'd walk, we'd get there faster," Agnes says.

Ella shakes her head hard. Agnes waits to see if it will pop off. If it does, Mama Skins will just put it back on.

"Mama Skins is going to make the hurt stop. You'll see. It won't be so bad round here after that."

Ella keeps shaking her head.

"She gonna look after you."

More head shaking.

"You ain't gotta like it. This is home now."

The head shaking is joined by Ella rolling her eyes.

"See that fence there. We make it to there, we can rest a spell."

Ella digs her feet into the soil.

Still pulling her, Agnes plods ahead, ignoring the tufts of dirt and grass she'll have to replant. "Look, past that fence, we going through those woods, by the river, and when we get to Mama Skins you can moan and twitch all you like, hear?"

Ella goes stiff. She even stops that annoying sliding motion she'd been getting away with.

Agnes has a good mind to slap her across the face. She stops pushing, twirls her around, puts her face close enough to Ella to breathe the same breath. Hand raised, she looks deep in Ella's eyes for a long time. They are brown and wide, filled with fear, anger, hope, and staring back at Agnes. Agnes turns away first. She lowers her hand, unwraps her shawl—old even before it was handed down from the Missus—and loosely hangs it on Ella's thin shoulders. "We rest when we get to the woods. Then we head home."

Just beyond the fence, Agnes lays Ella down in her favorite spot under the copse of willow trees. Above them, thin branches

interlock and embrace, sway and create a gentle breeze. The droop-
ing leaves weave a canopy. Agnes wants to tell her that nothing bad
happens here. Knees on the hard ground, she stretches her arms
wide. "All this," she says instead, "is Walker land."

"Hmmphh."

"It is. Them fields, that barn, those pastures—morning and
evening one—these woods, that river stretch from one end of
Walker land clear to another and farther too. And you know what?"

"Hmmphh."

"It's cursed."

Ella tenses.

"Got our own haints right here. I ain't never seen nor heard
'em but everybody know it. 'Cept you. Course you wouldn't
knowed it. But you should have felt it. First time they step foot on
Walker land most folk say they feel something pushing them right
back off. And you know what again? They don't allow nothing to
grow here that they don't want to. Them haints is stingy. Onliest
thing that grow here is blueberries and carrots. That's it. Plant let-
tuce, know what spring up? Blueberries. Plant good ol' mustard
greens. Know what spring up? Blueberries. Mantha and Meredith—them's the cooks up at the house—got so good at making
blueberry cakes, blueberry pie, blueberry tea, blueberry stew. They
got everybody fooled into thinking they like blueberry. And if you
don't, there's carrot cake, carrot pie, carrot tea, carrot stew. Like
you some meat? A good ol' hog bone or calf foot? Don't even look
at them cows out the pasture. Each and every cow on this place
got a number and if one missing, there's hell to pay. Ain't no baby
cows here, count of the curse. No baby nothing. No baby chicks,
no baby pigs, no baby slaves. Only thing allowed to grow up on
Walker is me. Know why?" She lies down next to Ella, buries her

fingers into the dirt, breathes slowly as if she's fallen asleep. "It's cuz they choose me. The haints do. Couldn't be no babies born on this place before or after me. All of them born dead. Mantha and Meredith babies died fore they was born. And after that, Missus's baby. And after that no more baby cows. And after that no more baby nothing. The haints sent Walker to find me. Told him exactly where to go to find my other mama dying in the woods, running off, I suspect. Walker saved me. Brought me back to Mama Skins. I wasn't the first. He brought other ones home and you know what they did? Died." She snaps her fingers, grins as Ella jumps. "Wasn't nothing wrong with them till they got here. Haints ain't want 'em. Tried a few more after me. They died too. I'm the onliest one growed up here. I sure hope you don't die." She jumps up and brushes her scratchy gingham dress off before nudging Ella with her bare foot. "Think you can get up?"

Still on the ground, Ella folds her short body into a ball. Her bony knees bend into her little chest. Her thin arms wrap around her long legs. Her feet tucked beneath her, she cries. For a while Agnes watches her back shake. "You want to die here, fine." She walks slow enough to give Ella time to change her mind, pull her body up, drag her feet in that slow walk she has and catch up. She counts the trees: beech, beech, oak, oak, pine, pine, pine. What's taking her so long? She probably got lost. Even though the path is clear as day and Agnes hasn't even gone that far, the poor little dumb thing is probably all turned around and scared she won't find her. Fine, she'll save the gal. Just one more thing to do.

She turns slowly, half expecting to find Ella right behind her. She searches through the wood to the left of the path. Then to the right. Mama Skins will kill her if she's let the girl get lost. What if something has gobbled her up? Agnes hopes it will try to eat her too. Not a hungry bite but a little taste; maybe a nibble of foot. Mama Skins can't be mad if the thing takes a bite of her too. Just in case, she tiptoes back to where she left her. Ella lies there with her legs crossed ankle to ankle and her arms laced across her chest.

"Hey there," Agnes whispers, "you dead?" She lightfoots close enough to see Ella's chest moving. "No? Well, I can't let you die in the woods, Mama Skins will kill me." She stoops down close, whispers: "If you dead when your papa come, what you want me to tell him?"

Ella twists her lips but holds her arms out.

"I heard you carrying on about your papa coming to rescue you. I expect they heard you clear up to the house and back down to the fields. I don't mind telling you, all that screaming set my spine to shivering. That's why Mama Skins sent for me. 'Go get that gal before she get herself killed,' she said. Mama Skins probably saved your life." Ella doesn't say so much as a thank-you, no smile or nothing. Agnes hefts her up, positions, and push-pulls her through the thick woods. Every few trees Agnes catches herself humming. No, if she wants silence, I can be silent. There's the rock Little James fell from last planting season. That's where mamas go to pray for babies that ain't never been. There's where babies lay while they wait on their mamas to join them. Won't tell that haughty gal nothing. Let her stew in her own breathing and that loud beat-beating of her heart. Her chest hardly moving but her heart pounding like a dying calf. Nope, won't tell her one thing.

The scent of the river fills her. The promise of washing away dirt, hurt, and anger flows over rocks, through passages. It bubbles and swirls. Invites. Halfway between the house and the cabins, the river is a meeting place for Walker's slaves. The Washing Up place where pots and clothes from the house and pots and clothes from the cabins are scrubbed, soaked, boiled, and seasoned. The only place slaves from the house can talk freely with field hands.

"This where I go to be free," Agnes says. She can't stop the words from coming out. She's just not selfish like some folk, stingy with words. She sits down on the edge of the riverbank and lets her feet dangle in the water.

Ella slumps down beside her.

"This river comes from up north," she continues. "If I sit right here when the moon is bright and the river is high, the water from the north mix with the water from the south and in that very spot, I'm free."

Ella's laugh, a low rumble, pierces the air.

"That's one ugly laugh," Agnes says. "You ought not to do it too often." She crosses her arms, tilts her chin, purses her lips and thinks of all the things she will never tell Ella. She turns her back on her. At the edge, water laps at her toes. Dried leaves tickle her fingertips. Above, blue sky peeks through tangles of branches. Animals scurry all around. Bunnies, a deer or two. Nothing to be afraid of. Lessin you wasn't from around here. How far is this gal from home? Who'd she leave behind? Did she have a mama like Mama Skins waiting on her? A papa like Papa Jonah, quick with a laugh, a kind word? Is she supposed to share them? She'll help in the fields, maybe the house, Master Walker had said. Just like that. Agnes is supposed to be the one to go to the house. Mama Skins had promised. Who else but Agnes can carry two pots of boiling water from the river to the house faster than it can cool? She can carry more firewood than Little James, polish longer than Meredith, scrub as hard as Mantha, cook better than them too if she has a mind to it. Now all that means nothing. She'll be back in the fields soon as this gal learns her place. This girl's grating on her nerves. She isn't nothing but trouble.

"If you was free like Mama Skins and them says, what you doing here?" she asks. "You here to take my mama and papa, you gonna have a hard way to go. You think you gonna come here and work in the house and leave me to the fields, I'm gonna stop you right there. I'm the one gonna work in the house. You hear?"

Ella moans.

"Good. Mama Skins and them says you here to birth babies, seeings none of us can."

Shaking her head, Ella sits up too fast, clutches her side, rises to her feet.

"They say the ones Master keeps is gonna work in the field soon's they can walk. But they'll be yours. Unless they get sold away."

Ella doubles over.

"No, wherever they be, they be yours."

Sobs ripple through Ella's body, pouring out of her mouth.

In her fourteen years, Agnes has seen a lot of pain.

"You don't want to birth no babies, do you?" she whispers. Ella slides down to the thick grass, she crawls to the riverbank. At the edge, she slips her feet into the water. Her body rocks back and forth, back and forth. The river ebbs and flows, swells and rises. Over there a leaf swirls in lazy circles.

A ways off a thick branch is swallowed whole.

"It ain't deep all the way through," Agnes says. "I studied it. Know its dips and turns like I know my own." She places a hand on her hip.

Ella leans forward.

She wouldn't jump in. Only a fool would jump in the middle of a river buck-naked in broad daylight. Agnes leans back to make shapes with the clouds. "See that fluffy one over there?" She raises one hand to shield her eyes and points with the other. "That looks just like a bushel of apples from the Missus's garden. You try it. What that one look like to you?"

With hardly a splash Ella slips in.

That heifer better can swim. The tide pulls her to the middle of the river. Her arms and legs go every which way. Agnes doesn't know whether to laugh or jump in after her.

Ella doesn't holler or ask for help. She just flops there like to drown in knee-deep brackish water.

"You trying to kill yourself?"

Ella's arms and legs flail. Water rains fat droplets onto Agnes's good dress.

"You gonna have to try harder than that you want to get somewhere," Agnes says. She scoots closer to the edge of the bank.

The river sucks and pulls at Ella. *Mama*, Agnes practices, *I was sitting there and she was sitting there and then she wasn't. I only got the one good dress and with it being three days till the next washing day, I couldn't get it dirtied up.* Agnes inspects her dress. She fingers the streaks of mud and grass stains.

"Stand up, you fool girl!" she yells.

Can she even hear her over the splash she's making? Agnes watches Ella's tiny chest crumple in and out. Now she's gone and made herself cry. She slips off her shift, steps out of her underthings and slides in the cold water. Agnes lets the water pull her down to the clay bottom. The sand sucks her skin and squishes beneath her feet. She holds her breath and counts to ten. She keeps her head underwater and lets her body rise to the surface. The sun warms her back as she breaks through the water's skin. Slowly Agnes lets her feet sink to the bottom and stands up.

"You go out too far the river will suck you clear through the bottom. I seen it happen. Swallowed whole men. What you think it do to a gal like you? It ain't gonna carry you home if that's what you thinking and I can't let it take you nowhere no how. Mama Skins said bring you home. I'm gonna bring you home. After that, we just have to wait and see."

Wait and see. Ella lets the girl drag her from the water. Though she can't read her face, Ella half expects Agnes to slap her. Her movements are quick, she already has Ella propped up as she drags her across the dirt. Her hands are gentler this time, which is good since she doesn't seem ready to let go anytime soon. But she's in the way. If it comes to it, she'll have to knock her in the head with something. Can't take her in a fair fight. Not with them strong arms. She's the fastest girl at the schoolhouse and could even take some of the boys, but Ella can't outrun those long, muscled legs. Least not with her side burning up. If she can get to that shotgun she can scare her off, maybe. With the girl holding tight, she won't get far. Maybe if she talks to her, explains that she hasn't come for her mama or her papa, that all Ella wants is to go home, she'll just let her go. Let go, let go, Ella thinks. She closes her eyes. The girl's smooth hands are still stuck fast to Ella's shoulders. If she lets go, Ella won't have to hurt her. They're moving farther and farther away from where she left the shotgun. The trees here look like the ones before it; the fields, even if the girl calls them by different names, look the same, the stories about who did what where sound like one long eulogy. Nothing good has come from this place. Why would this girl be any different? She'll have to kill her, later. Until then, Ella marks the way tree by tree.

Going around it will take hours. Instead, they cross the river at the shallow. On the other side, the grass beneath her feet is springy. Even for this time of year, the clumps cushion and soothe Agnes's cracked feet. Soon as they get home she'll rub them in sweet balm. Might even use some on the gal. Her skin is bruised from head to foot. What could she have done to deserve that? Nothing. Agnes would bet that busted shotgun on it. Mama Skins said she'd brought it on herself. Papa Jonah didn't say much of nothing 'cept, *Be gentle. Be quick*, Mama Skins had said. It was the closest thing to them arguing that Agnes had witnessed. Sure, there had been slamming pots, stomping feet, and if he was real mad, an untouched plate. Mama Skins wasn't no stranger to anger either. Summer squash when she knew it backed him up, tea leaves instead of tobacco, and if she was real mad, silence. But Papa and Mama didn't argue before today. Even if the words were curt and whispered, things were different. It was all because of this gal.

Agnes knew enough to know there was something they weren't letting on about. Good thing Meredith and Mantha didn't feel the same. Soon as he could get clear of the house, Little James had told Agnes everything the two said. She still didn't believe it. This gal was gonna make life a whole heap better for everybody on the farm? Lessin grown folks sprung out from her belly ready to pick, plow, and do all that needed doing on this place, Agnes didn't see how. She can't help but smile. Little James's liable to tell her anything to get her to run off with him. The bottom of her feet start to tingle.

"This poison," she says. Ella stops moving.

"No sense standing still. It's all around here. Right there." She points to white-tipped bushes. "There, there, and right there where you standing? It's all up in there. Squeeze some of that juice from them leaves between your legs and any man who touch you will go crazy with itching and scratching." She breaks off a fat leaf and snaps it in half. "Rub some on you, see for yourself."

Ella takes the leaf. She watches the clear, sticky goo drip out. "Just a drop now," Agnes coaxes. "I heard you done met my James."

Ella's fingers tingle. She rubs the liquid between her legs. Fire. She's sure she's on fire. Burning from the inside out. Sweat pours down her forehead, under her arms, down her legs.

"It'll cool down. Just takes getting used to. Think about something else. Take your mind off of it. It just takes a bit of time for it to work." She smiles, hums. "Now you won't have no baby, least not by my James. Stop fidgeting!" She taps her foot, kicks up soft tufts of dirt. "Just a little while longer." She watches the clouds scoot across the sky. "You thinking 'bout something else? Good. Don't think nothing about no itching, no burning. Don't scratch it! It'll take your skin clear off. Then what? Just let it be. I like to die the first time Mama Skins put it on me. Had to be five, six. I scratched and scratched. Still got the marks. Now, I hardly notice it at all. Just used to it. You didn't use too much, did you? It'll kill you. First it dries out your mouth."

Ella tries to swallow.

"Then your heart get to boom, boom, boomin' and your eyes get to going every which way, and everything inside, well, it ain't in there no more."

Ella sways.

"Next thing you know, you dead. Just like that." She claps her hands together. "Mama Skins got something she can give you in case you took too much. Just be sure to stay away from James."

Ella's stomach clenches. If she wasn't about to die, she'd kill Agnes.

It is nearly dark by the time she finally pushes Ella through the slight frame of the small cabin she shares with Mama Skins and Papa Jonah. Inside it is dark and cool. Any cracks or holes had been patched with gum to keep the rain out. The floors are swept and smell of fresh lemon rind. In the center of the room a steel pot glows. From the corner, Mama Skins unfolds herself and stands. Standing, she is smaller than she looks. She is head to head with Agnes. Her arms are thin and bare, smooth except for pockmarks. Her legs are hidden beneath layers of a frock made of patches of fabric, fur, and animal hides. Dark patches scatter her forehead and cheeks. Wrinkles frame her mouth. Her thick gray hair is plaited and adorned with tiny pebbles and shells. Strung into necklaces that hang loose and woven into a belt wound around her slim waist, shells and stones clank together as she walks. She jingles over to the girls and even though Ella pulls away, she gathers them both in her strong arms. Her eyes glisten.

"Rest," Mama Skins commands.

Although she's shaking her head no, Ella falls asleep standing.

I can run. Knock down this spicy-smelling, sing-song-talking, shell-clacking old woman, straight out the rickety door, back the way we come. Find my way to the poison patch back to the river, cross it, follow the path to the big willow, get the shotgun, go through the field and go where? Back to the barn? The river. I can follow the river. Sooner or later it's gotta cross the ocean. From there I'll make my way home. Ella lies on a thick blanket on the floor, pretending to be asleep. What she wouldn't give to be in her own bed, piled high with old mattresses or curled up in a home-made quilt lying on her own wooden floor.

"I thought you were planning to sleep clear through the day," Mama Skins says.

Ella opens her eyes and glances up at the woman's mouth then concentrates on her fingers instead. Legs crossed at the ankles, she's sitting next to Ella, elbows resting on the thin pallet, fingers deftly sewing swatches of cloth. Her slim fingers glide across the fabric, stretching then binding with precision. She stitches without looking down. Mama would be envious.

"My teeth?" she asks. "Knocked out long ago." She runs her tongue along her gums. "When I was young I had a lot of mouth. They thought knocking out my teeth would make me keep it closed. It worked. But not how they expected." Her laugh is like piano scales, practiced, beautiful.

Ella tries to sit up. Her back, arms, and legs are sore. Her skin is covered in large black-and-blue bruises and red welts. What will Mama say? Tears slide down her face.

"You ain't as broke up as you think you is," Mama Skins says. "I had to rub some of them herbs to get you blistered up. The worse you look, the longer they'll leave you be." She tucks the soft covering, a blanket of animal hides stitched together, tight around Ella. "Agnes told me she gave you some of that goo. She ought not to give you that. I don't suspect it was enough to stop no baby coming. No need in making it any worse than it's gonna be." She moves closer, leans forward. "It's done now. Just need to wait for it to wear off. Before you know it, you'll be having babies. Sooner you start, sooner you be finished."

Ella can't feel her legs. If they were shaking like the rest of her body, she'd know it. Her teeth rattle, her head throbs, her whole body is in motion, except for her legs. No telling what they're doing. She pictures them already gone.

Mama Skins marks the cloth with a needle. "Settle yourself down. It could be a lot worse. Just one, two, three babies at the most. Thanks to the curse, you'll get to keep them." She holds the piece up. "It's for you," she nods at Ella, "a dress of your very own." She lays the garment on the end of the bed. "These yours, too." She holds up a set of grinning teeth. "Jonah's been working them since you came. Whittled a year's worth of wax. Now you be all pretty. Try 'em." She pries open Ella's mouth, slides the grin in place. "There." She leans back, admires her work, squints. "They'll take some getting used to."

Ella presses her swollen tongue along the waxen grooves. The teeth, some large, others small, crowd her mouth. They force her jaw to shift, her cheeks to spread.

"See, I knew you'd be smiling before long," Mama Skins says. "Walker likes pretty little smiling faces around here. You'll be just fine."

I want to go home! The words bounce around in Ella's head, rattle in her heart.

Laden with cream, eggs, and cornmeal, Agnes tiptoes into the cabin. "This is from the Missus," she says. "For her." She nods her head toward Ella.

Mama Skins stares at a spot above Ella's head. "It's the Missus's way of saying sorry," she says.

Agnes puts the cream, eggs, and cornmeal next to jars of pickled carrots, glasses of blueberry jam and stacks of peppermint soap. For supper, Mama Skins makes carrot mash with roasted blueberries. She leaves the cream to curdle. Ella doesn't so much as taste the sweet carrots or nibble the crunchy berries.

Agnes watches Mama Skins and Papa Jonah fuss over the gal at supper. They try to coax her to eat like she's a stubborn cow. She thinks she's too good for us, Agnes thinks. She reaches over to pluck a morsel from her plate, but the look Mama Skins gives her forces her to change her mind. Fine, I'll wait, she thinks. She finishes her own supper and clears the plates. Mama Skins tells her to leave the gal's plate so she can eat it later. Fine, one less plate to clean. Agnes does the washing-up and puts out the fire.

Later, because there is nowhere left to sleep, Agnes pulls her bedroll next to Ella's. Ella has been scrubbed and rubbed with so many ointments and herbs, leaves, and berries that she smells like one of Missus's sachets. Her sweet scent tickles Agnes's nose. Her breathing is shallow and fast, like deep water. Agnes tries to match it. Her head is light. Her body is weightless. She floats above Ella to the top of the cabin. Her fingers, wisps of gray smoke, peel back the thin layers of the roof. There are no stars in the sky, there is no moon. Freedom. If Little James come tonight talking about "run away with me" she just might listen. "You awake?" Agnes is close enough to touch her. She listens to the young girl's labored breathing. She's been crying, again. "Ain't really no haints here," she says. "No magic, hoodoo, nothing to be afraid of." Walker, Missus, overseer. "Nothing that ain't living." Ella's breathing turns to light snores. "I know you ain't sleeping." Agnes pokes her in the ribs. "Know what else I know?" She pauses, swallows, whispers close to Ella's ear. "I don't care what my mama says, when you run off, I'm leaving with you."

Chapter 8

Agnes pulls clusters of carrots from the earth in angry clumps. The girl's hardly been here a week and they're already rushing her out the door. There's no way that gal's making life on Walker's better for anybody. She's been here nearly seven days and hasn't lifted a finger to help. She hasn't cleaned the cabin, picked one carrot, plucked one berry. Has she helped in the fields? Not one bit. *She's too weak to be out in the sun.* Nobody rushed her then. Why's Mama Skins so bent on rushing her to do this now? Glaring at Mama Skins's back does nothing to stop the woman from washing Ella. Mama Skins pulls, prods, dresses, oils, all the while cooing, "Won't last longer than it has to. Don't you look pretty? Ain't no use in crying, be over soon enough."

Thick-braided hair, skin rich like firewood, voice soothing like a summer bird. She looks like the same Mama Skins but the woman readying a shaking bit of a gal for plundering ain't her mama. When Mama Skins is satisfied that she's ready, she pulls Ella toward the door.

"I might as well take her myself," Agnes says.

Before Mama Skins can respond, Agnes is up. She wiggles between the woman and the girl, then pushes, pulls Ella out the door, through the wood, toward the river. Ella fights her. She digs her heels into the ground, her nails into Agnes's arms. Agnes drags her. They slip, stumble, fall. Each time they fall Ella picks up something to hit Agnes with. A handful of rocks, a thick branch. She isn't going to let Walker anywhere near her, doesn't matter what that crazy old coot or her crazy daughter says.

"I said I'd take you to the barn and I'm taking you to the barn. But first, we gonna get you some of that goo. Can't do nothing about him touching on you today but put enough up in there and he won't be bothering with you no more anytime soon." Agnes leads her to the sweet-smelling patch of poison. "Myrtle done got it in Walker's head that maybe ain't nothing wrong with you. That ain't nothing wrong with James that 'a little time in the well' won't cure. As if soon as he got out she wouldn't be fussing over him."

Ella's feet dig into the ground. Planted, her body goes rigid. She opens her mouth but instead of words, she speaks in guttural growls and wheezes. She spits. Drops of red and yellow sprinkle the ground in front of Agnes's feet.

"What's the matter with you?" Her words are like a hiss. "I told you," Agnes says, "Little James don't want no parts of you. Only reason he done what he done was he had to. If it wasn't for James, Walker and them would be laying up with you way before now. Just like you to think he'd choose you." Agnes scoops a handful of flowers, plucks the leaves off, squeezes the stems and drinks from the stalk. "When he was in you, you know what he was thinking 'bout? Me. He told me so. Now Myrtle trying to mess it all up. Got Walker thinking my James is lying. Can you believe that? Walker got to beating on him. Beat him so bad even

Myrtle got to saying maybe she was wrong. James say hearing Myrtle say that almost made it worth it. But Walker act like he ain't hear her, though. Said he gonna find out for his damned self. If ain't nothing wrong with you, there ain't nothing wrong with James. And if ain't nothing wrong with James, soon as he heals up, Walker's gonna sell him. You ain't gotta like him but he helped you. Now you gonna help him."

She watches as Ella's lips twitch, her eyes squint. The hairs on Agnes's arms stand up. She's got something on her mind. Agnes steps away, turns her back to the girl. She listens as Ella moves closer. Her feet barely make a noise in the soft grass. Her breath is hot on Agnes's neck. She cocks her head to the side, tosses the words over her shoulder: "Maybe you won't. Maybe you'll go in and tell Walker there ain't nothing wrong with you. What do you think will happen then? James will be sent down south. What about you? As soon as he knows there ain't nothing wrong with you he'll be on you like bark on a stick. First it will be Walker, then Old Walker, overseer, who else? They'll get to bedding you all the time. Well, guess that's up to you too. But you right, you don't have to help James."

Ignoring the burn, the girls slather the grainy mixture anywhere they think Walker might touch.

Five minutes after Agnes pushes her in the barn, Walker, still cursing, storms out. Agnes creeps from her hiding place and rushes to find Ella. Blood trickles down the side of her mouth.

"Seems like you tainted just like the rest of us," she says. Agnes slips down to the floor next to Ella. Puts her head in her lap. Smooths her hair. They sit until their hearts stop racing, until swallowing no longer hurts, until breathing steadies. "Soon as James can walk without that limp, we leaving. Walker ain't gonna sell him over this but if it ain't this, it'll be something else. Ain't gonna wait to find out what that something else is. Don't see why you can't come too."

"Why can't she come?" James asks for the third time. "Because she don't do nothing for herself. She would slow us down."

It's early in the morning, before the sun is up. Agnes and James lie side by side, her head touching his, in the tall grass.

"Ain't nothing wrong with her legs," she says, "she'll be plenty help when we get to town. We can all work. Besides, she can read."

"How do you know? She can't even talk."

"She can talk, just ain't got nothing to say."

"She's got plenty to say from what I hear."

"Not when she's awake."

"What if one night she gets to talking about us running away? Then what?"

"Even if she do, at least my mama ain't gonna tell nobody about it."

"Myrtle doesn't mean any harm."

"Well, my mama wouldn't do what Myrtle done."

"Are we going to sit here arguing about old women or are you going to hold me a spell before I have to get back? You know how Missus is if I'm late."

Agnes nestles in his arms, breathes in his scent of furniture polish, lilac water, and ash soap. "She still coming," she says.

"I know."

Later, when Agnes tells her, Mama Skins says nothing. She has already heard the rumors: that gal ain't no savior. She murmurs, gestures, grunts, but the yelling Agnes expects doesn't come. The silence is worse. Agnes can feel Mama Skins watching her as she lays Ella down, washes and clothes her. The woman's stare bores holes in her back as Agnes tidies the small cabin, taking care not to get in her mother's way. She'll tell her about the leaving when Mama Skins is ready to listen. Until then, the women move in silence with Agnes mending, scrubbing, dusting, polishing, and touching every tin cup, wooden plank, worn hide, or frayed cloth as if she was saying goodbye and Mama Skins watching her doing it. Keeping secrets don't come easy. Agnes moves outside on the step to settle next to Papa Jonah; she feels the woman's eyes even then.

"Wasn't nothing else I could do," Agnes says. "I had to use them herbs. She's one of us."

Papa Jonah chews on his empty pipe. For a second, his warm hand presses into hers before letting go.

Evenings with Mama, Papa, and even that girl give her something to look forward to during the long days. But picking, even if it is for her own supper, is still picking. The slave gardens behind the cabins are the coarsest on all Walker land. Still, year after year, Mama Skins's patch grows blueberries and carrots that taste like green beans, squash, onions, and anything else that was planted and never grew. Her coveted concoctions are a natural delight. Agnes looks back at the tree Ella props up. She claps the vegetables together and watches the dirt rain down over gaping holes before snatching up another clump.

"I don't know how things work where you from but here, if you don't work," she calls over her shoulder, "you don't eat."

Ella shrugs.

"Mama Skins said youse supposed to help me pick these vegetables for the circle." She snatches a carrot up, curls her fingers tight around its hard flesh and shakes it like it's Ella. "You ain't fooling nobody, we know you can talk if you want to."

Ella turns her back.

"Can run too."

Ella straightens.

"All night long you screaming, *Papa! Papa, don't leave me!* and kicking them legs like a mule on fire. That's the honest truth. That's why I had to move my roll from next to yours. I was afraid you'd kick me clear in the head. And you know what else? When you ain't screaming, you mumbling all the time 'bout grabbing that rusty rifle and shooting somebody clear through the head. Shooting us that done helped and cared for you, mended you. Even worse, you talk about leaving us where we lay, not even stopping to bury us, and drowning your fool self in the river. Why I gotta be dead for you to kill yourself? When you ain't busy killing us or you, you talk about running away. Can't seem to get you to shut up lessin youse awake. Some nights I just pray and pray, Please, Lord, let that gal wake up so I can get to sleep!"

Ella snorts.

"Just so you know, that rusted heap couldn't shoot clear even if it did have gunpowder. So if you planning to kill us, you gonna have to find another way. Way I see it, there's the poison down by the river. What's to stop you from slipping a leaf or two into the pot when nobody's looking? Time? Nah. Got plenty of that. Any chore Missus and them want doing, I been doing so you don't have to. Who gonna see you? Field hands got better things to do than to wait for you to drag yourself cross the floor, down the step, through the grass. If you could find your way there. Laziness? Well, I ain't one to say nothing about your mama but …" She lets the words linger.

With one hand holding on to the tree and the other reaching for Agnes, Ella stands.

"Only thing wrong with your legs is you. You want to get off this land? Run. Run as fast as you can because you know what? You ain't gonna get nowhere dragging your legs behind you. You afraid? Got every call to be. You don't know where you at. Don't know how to get where you want to be. If you don't know where you going, you ain't never gonna get there. You want to get back to your people? You better get yourself to the circle. If anyone can tell you what you need to know, it's them women. And if you want them to give you something, you better not get there without offering something in return." Out of the corner of her eye she watches Ella stomp over to a ripe row of tangled vines and stems, bushes overgrown to bursting. Ella pulls, trying to rip up a tender carrot from the ground, root and all. Agnes grins and slows down her picking. Now she carefully lifts leaves and delicately pinches buds while Ella tears and rips. Agnes fingers the shell within her pocket. She wouldn't miss the circle because of that heifer.

"I ain't going to fight you. Come if you want to come, don't if you don't. But if there's news about your people, don't expect me to come running to find you."

She gathers her vegetables and walks away. Ella follows.

The women arrive after sundown. They arrive, some from miles away, laden with slivers of meats, bits of breads, chunks of sweets, slices of soap, and other snippets that can be spared, will not be missed, or have been saved for the special occasion. Every full moon since Agnes remembers, the women of her life gather round to share stories. This will be her last one. When she runs off with James she'll miss the circle most of all. She won't let that gal make her miss this. Agnes is too far ahead. The sounds of hushed laughter and lilted voices guide Ella's steps toward the circle. She whispers her name. A hoarse moan from deep in her chest makes her jump. It's been weeks since she's allowed herself to speak. She tries again. A raspy, grating cough bubbles up, fills her throat and echoes into silence. Stumbling, she heads into the dark.

The women make room for her to sit next to Agnes. Agnes squeezes her hand. As they talk, the women weave and plait, knotting vines in intricate ropes.

I can't talk, she mouths to Agnes.

Agnes nods to the side where Mama Skins and a young pregnant woman argue in hushed voices. "That's Grace," she whispers. "She wants Mama Skins to give her something to stop the baby. Don't look over there!"

Ella looks away. She points to her mouth, slowly mouths, I've lost my voice.

"She says she don't want her baby born a slave. Mama Skins says she waited too late," Agnes continues.

Mama Skins joins the circle. Grace follows, slow and empty-handed. The circle makes room.

"Missus still mumbling about not getting this one." A woman nods her head toward Ella. "Walker done told her time and time again, she for breeding. But Missus say she want a city gal to show off to her friends. You sending Agnes in her place sent Ol' Missus to spewing and hollering about insolence and whippings."

Ella's skin prickles. Breeding?

The women laugh.

"I knew Agnes would satisfy the Missus," Mama Skins interrupts. "It didn't matter which one they got."

"Sure do matter to Walker, though," Myrtle says. "Walker got plans for that one that don't have nothing to do with talking proper or impressing guests. Who she gonna breed with? Little James?"

Agnes stiffens.

"You got a name?" Samantha asks. She jabs a finger at Ella.

Ella nods her head.

"She don't say much of nothing," Agnes says.

"'Cept how she gonna kill us all?" Samantha asks.

"Mama!" Agnes shoots her mama the closest thing she dares to a dirty look.

"Ain't heard that from me," Mama Skins says.

Seem like the only time that Little James can keep his mouth shut is when he's kissing. "She don't mean nothing by it," Agnes says. "She only talk like that when she sleep."

"I'd sleep with both eyes open if I was you," Myrtle says. She frowns at Ella.

"Why don't you give her one of them special sachets, Meredith?"

Even Ella stares at Grace.

"Wrap it up real tight, put a pretty bow on it." Grace's voice is deep, low. She glowers at Mama Skins across the flame. "Dead by morning. Isn't that what you said?"

Mama Skins tosses a twig in the fire.

"I'm still here. Baby's still here," Grace pokes her belly. "I ain't wake up dead."

"Don't always work. I told you that too. Ain't gonna be no more talk of that tonight. I said no."

A chill plays up and down Ella's spine. How will she ever see Papa and Mama again if one of these heathens kills her?

"Iola," Mama Skins calls to a young woman. "It's time." The women, even Grace, stand. Ella readies herself to rise.

Agnes shakes her head no, grabs her hand and holds tight. "They took my babies," Iola says. Her words are mixed with old, deep sobs. "I'm bringing them home."

The women nod as some strip Iola. Her clothes are tossed in the fire. They rub her pocked, bruised skin with soothing oils. With deft fingers they wrap bundles of herbs and twine around Iola's calves and thighs. They wind the knotted vine around her belly, over her breasts, around her sinewy arms and tie it around her neck.

"It's to throw off her scent. To give her time," Agnes whispers.

Mama Skins unrolls a stiff dress made out of animal skins and cured in skunk essence. The garment's musky scent makes the air bitter.

"For the dogs," Agnes says.

The dress of skins makes Iola look wider, heavier. Weighed down like she is, she won't get far. Ella looks around the group. She can feel the cool certainty of Iola's failed escape. Iola slips into the night. The women resume their places around the fire. Ella jumps up to follow. If she can catch up with Iola, the two can help each other get away.

"Let her have her chance," Myrtle says. Her annoyance clips the end of her words like teeth. "You'll get your own chance."

"Hush," Mama Skins warns. "Ain't nobody going nowhere."

Ella rubs her hands together to stop them from shaking. "Walker set out to steal folks because he can't afford to buy no more," Samantha continues.

"And on account none are born on this place," Myrtle adds.

Ella stares at Mama Skins. She stands up, trembling and

pointing. If the old woman hadn't been poisoning them, they'd have babies of their own and Walker wouldn't have stolen her.

"Walker had a mind to do it and he did it. From the way I see it, you here now," Mama Skins says. "If you have babies and break the curse while you here," she shrugs, "so be it."

"What if she don't break the curse?" Samantha asks. "You gonna give him what he wants?" She nods toward Agnes.

"He ain't got no call to want Agnes."

"If this one can't have no babies," Myrtle asks, "what's gonna happen to her?"

Ella doesn't wait to find out. She stands, turns her back on the circle, and slips into the waiting darkness. If only she could wrap her hands around Mama Skins's neck. She would shake and shake until the old woman begged her to stop, then she'd shake some more.

"He took you because he wanted to and wasn't nobody with a mind to stop him," Agnes says. She plops down next to Ella. "Mama Skins ain't have nothing to do with it. Walker probably figured on getting you with child so he can afford all he's missing out on like shoes and tobacco. Mama Skins is the only thing standing in the way between you and that." Agnes points toward Grace.

Ella hasn't gotten as far as she thought. Nearby, the fire's glow casts shadows on the women's faces.

"Well, the Missus is hopeful," Samantha says, "seems folks stopped talking about the doctor and before long Mama Skins can be hired out again."

While they talk, Mama Skins passes a bursting basket around the circle. Whoever wants something is free to take it. If someone else wants it they can share it if it's enough or barter if it isn't. In this way meats are exchanged for fur scraps, vegetables for clay, and slivers of soap for hope. Only Grace and Ella take nothing.

With a bundle of damp skins, Mama Skins smothers the flames. The smoke smells of cherrywood and sassafras. As the women chatter, Grace gathers her belly and leaves the warmth of the group to follow the soothing call of the river. With each step she takes, she puts a pebble in her mouth. She reaches the slippery bank and keeps walking. There is a soft splash as the water welcomes her. She walks to the middle of the river. The tide sucks and pushes her in deeper. She stops, as if uncertain. The tide pushes her on.

Ella watches the woman disappearing as the river swallows her a bite at a time. She shakes Agnes, points to the river, mimes jumping in.

"You thirsty?" Agnes asks.

Instead of watching Grace, the women watch Ella watching Grace. She'd rather do it herself than ask the old woman for help. Following the light from pale stars, Ella makes her way to the edge. The river rushes and bubbles, swirls.

Grace smiles, waves.

In her mind, Ella screams, *Help her!*

"She don't want no help," Mama Skins says. "She waving goodbye."

On the shore, the women wave heartily, silently. In the river, Grace sinks beneath the waves. Before the feuding starts, the women know there will be no more circles. Two in one night? Even if they didn't believe it before, no one will deny Walker's place is cursed. No owner would allow a slave to set foot on Walker soil. When they hug, they squeeze tight, linger. They settle their stories: some sort of spirit reached up and snatched Grace to the bottom of the river. Didn't they try to help her? Yes. The women slip into the woods one by one, leaving Agnes and Ella to stare into the water.

"I ain't leaving here like that," Agnes says. She crosses her arms to stop them from shaking. "When I leave this place, I'm gonna be alive. You stay here waiting on somebody to save you if you want to. I'll be long gone."

The next morning word filters down from the main house through Little James's lips. The sun hasn't been up a good ten minutes. The air is cool. The water, ice cold. It's Sunday, Agnes's favorite day. It's the only day she can sleep late. Still, Agnes has been up since dawn. She likes to slip out of the cabin, a biscuit in each pocket, before Mama Skins can get started with her list of things to do to occupy Agnes's time. As soon as she finishes the wash, beats the rugs up at the house, and does the ironing, she can have the rest of the day to herself. She doesn't count on Little James interrupting her washing. She has already gathered firewood to set the pot boiling. She strings a line of clothes to soak. The branches crackle like footsteps. She wades knee-deep into the water, a trail of underclothes behind her. She half expects to see Grace staring up at her.

"Ain't none of y'all allowed to set foot off this property," James calls from the river's edge. "No walking to town, visiting neighbors, evening strolls, or trips to market." He raises his voice above the lapping waves.

Agnes rolls her eyes and keeps walking. The water swirls and foams around her. She steps through nibbling fish and over slick grass.

"Not that any of y'all been allowed to leave since Mama Skins was accused of killing the doctor. No telling what would have happened if Old Missus hadn't convinced the sheriff your mama was too dumb to mix up a concoction that would have done it.

Master says none of you will ever set another foot off this land without his permission, ain't anybody allowed on it either. That means no more circle, in case you wondering."

Agnes stops walking. For a second she bobs along with the water before diving beneath the surface. She touches the soft bottom with her hands, plants them in the dirt, extends her legs and unfolds into a handstand. She wiggles her toes at James. Upside down, her tears drain into the river. When she returns to the edge, her arms piled high with the washing, she puts the clothes into the pot to boil and sits, arms crossed, under a copse of trees. James joins her.

"The first thing I'm going to do when I take you away from here is build us a house near the water."

"That's the first thing?"

"You already mine."

Agnes nods.

James puts his hand on Agnes's stomach. "Soon as we free, we can start a family."

"You all the family I need. I don't want to birth no babies until my babies can be free."

"So we aren't ever going to have a family?"

"Can you promise me they gonna be free?"

James stares into the river. He slips his hand into Agnes's. Their feet dangle over the edge.

Later, as Agnes gathers the drying clothes, James tells her stories.

"The horses are still galloping and Doc Sampson comes jumping out of that buggy before it even stops. Walker Junior meets him before he can get to the ground. 'Don't you come here looking for no handouts,' he says. James runs from the left side to the right. 'Handouts?' Sampson asks in that quivering voice of his. 'You owe me one thousand dollars for ruining my I-Oh-La. I come to collect it!' He jumps back to the other side. 'A thousand? She wasn't worth that much alive. I tasted her cooking!' He puffs to the other side. 'Don't think I won't get the sheriff. I'll do it! This whole damned place is cursed!' Sampson says. You know Walker Senior don't like to hear talk like that so Junior gets to trying to whisper. Doc ain't having no parts of it. He's nearly yelling. 'Don't see why I allowed that visiting business in the first place! Bunch of Negroes gathering to do what? Share recipes and cleaning tips? More likely trying to figure out how to kill us all and you just setting there letting them! No more. You done cost me two heads.' 'Two?' Walker says. 'That crazy girl of yours walking off cost me my best hounds. You ought to be paying me!' 'Your best hounds chased her clear over that blasted ledge. Don't you send none of your people on this land no more. Ain't none of y'all welcomed here!' 'Welcomed here? You don't have to worry about that. Next time you see me, it will be with the law!' 'Gentlemen,' Little James says. He spreads his palms, wide. 'Let's settle this indoors, like neighbors.'"

"Let me guess, that was you?" Agnes says. She folds the linen in tight squares and sprinkles them with dried herbs. Jasmine fills her nose.

"Who do you think kept them from killing one another?" James laughs.

"What really happened?"

James frowns. Stares across the river.

"I ain't mean nothing by it," Agnes says. "Tell it like you want to."

"It ain't that," James says. He stands behind her. Pulls her close. A sheet slips from her hands. He breathes in the smell of her hair. "Things gonna get a whole lot worse around here."

"What you mad for?" Agnes asks. Later, Ella sits on the step whittling away while Papa Jonah whittles at his pipe. Even layered in skins, her bones poke through the garb. The rise and fall of her back is the only sign she's breathing. "No more circle? What that mean to you? I'm the one been suckling on them stories since before I could walk. What you think I grew this big on blueberries and carrots? Them women are my family and I don't get to see them no more till Walker and Sampson make nice or die. You don't see me burrowing a hole about it." Ella hasn't looked at her since supper. She'd sat there not even pretending to eat the steaming plate of coon tail and smothered carrots. Stood up before Agnes had even finished the telling and sat on the porch, without asking Mama Skins if she could leave the cabin.

"Come on," Agnes says, slipping beside Jonah to stand face-to-face with Ella. She doesn't wait for Ella's silent response but drags her around the back of the cabin, through the garden and into the woods. The trees here are taller than any on Walker land. Agnes drops her hand. She wraps her arms around a thick tree. She wiggles and stretches them but still, her fingers do not touch. "Go around the other side," she commands.

Ella rolls her eyes, drags her feet and faces the tree. She looks up and up and still can't see the top of it. The bark is smooth in some places, worn in others. Here and there scars and holes dot the thick trunk. It oozes sweet-smelling sap. Sniffing, she leans closer.

"It ain't gonna bite." Ants scurry up and down the thick bark. Patches of moss and clusters of leaves barely conceal knotted wood, holes, and burrows. Sap slides lazily from seldom used holes. The tree tickles her cheek, but Agnes waits. Finally Ella's hot fingertips press against hers. "The end of the circle don't mean we not gonna get out of here. Just mean none of them can help us. All I need you to do is hold on and I'm gonna hold on just like this," she says. "We keep holding on just a little while longer, we gonna both be free."

That evening the girls sit with their backs pressed against the rough bark. The cool night air wrinkles Agnes's nose. "Don't nobody out there care nothing 'bout how you feel 'bout being here," she whispers. She breathes deeply so the air fills her lungs. "Just do what you told and don't end up dead. You better start eating too."

Ella snorts.

"I mean it. I ain't going to do all this planning just to end up carrying you. You heavier than you look. I swear them bones got to weigh more than a head of hogs."

Ella giggles.

"It ain't gonna be long, you'll see." No sense talking about bringing James. He's coming no matter what.

Agnes is up before dawn the next morning. Before sunrise she has done her share of picking, washed the windows up at the house, soaked pots, and scrubbed the front room. By noon she has washed the steps and beat the dough for supper. Grinning, Samantha hands her a full chamber pot. She whispers above the stench, "James heard that gal's pa is looking for her. Folks in town talking about a gang of black men heading this way. They gotta be her peoples. Sheriff sent them every which way but here. He told them this place is haunted but they heading here just the same, should arrive just before suppertime."

Agnes nearly drops the pot. Its contents swirl and slosh like her stomach. Come to take her home. Agnes's hands tremble.

"Go tell your ma," Samantha says. "She'll know what to do."

Chapter 9

Samantha and Myrtle hear them first. Trotting horses, stomping mules, murmuring voices, and one lopsided cart clomping up the path. Tufts of dirt and pebbles fling as they pass. Somebody's going to have to clean that up, Myrtle thinks. Black men tall as trees trail behind the sheriff and one of the reverend's boys. This ain't no coffle. The men dismount. Clutching the reins in tight fists, they stare. With sweeping gazes they take in the chipped paint, missing planks, coarse lawn, bare fields, and slave hands dotting the fields. Myrtle wishes they had come ten years ago when the grass was thick, the house freshly painted, when the manor was plump with flowers, vegetables, cows, and slaves. Young ones fetching milk, grabbing reins. Older ones watering horses, shoeing if need be. Fields covered with slaves picking, pulling, mending, fixing, plowing, maybe even singing. One or two babies underfoot. Myrtle would have looked at these men and known they appreciated all she did for the place. That was before Meredith come, before the fields were full of nothing but graves.

Walker Senior sits in the parlor, his legs crossed beneath his writing desk. Every once in a while he leans forward, spits a wad of snuff into a kerchief, refolds it.

"What they doing now, James?" Walker Junior asks from the chair across from his father.

Big James parts the curtains wide enough to peep out. "Sir, they've dismounted. It looks like they're just huddled up in front of the door. One's looking right at me through the window and pointing up here. Should I invite them in?"

"No, you damned fool! Not till I tell you to," Junior snaps.

"James, tell Myrtle to get supper going," Senior directs. "Son, that ain't no way to treat company. Go see to the door," he says. He stands with his shotgun behind his chair and his pistol on the blotter.

James pushes the kitchen door open. "Master Walker says y'alls to start supper to cooking," he says. Before the door clicks shut he whispers, "Send James to fetch Meredith."

"Come in from that heat, Sheriff," Walker calls from the top of the porch.

The sheriff climbs the steps, finds a patch of shade and leans against the railing. The rest of the party is left to wait out in the Maryland sun. "Been some time since I been up here. I'd say ten, eleven years?"

"Sounds about right," Walker says.

"Not since—"

"The plague?" Senior interrupts. He settles down in a wicker rocking chair, shotgun propped against his leg.

"Weren't no plague I can remember," the sheriff says. "Only hit here. Folks got to saying only thing growing here is ghosts."

Senior laughs. "Folks liable to say anything."

"I ain't here to tell you how to run your affairs," Sheriff says, "but that gal's pa been told you snatched her up in Pennsylvania. She's free."

"I was in Pennsylvania a few weeks or so ago, wasn't I, Pa? I'm sure quite a few people was too. I ain't buy no slaves. I saw plenty of Negroes just running around the streets. I couldn't say for sure I seen one in particular. It's his word against mine, ain't it?" Junior asks.

"His and Mr. Dwight Thompson's. Thompson's a business-man, much like yourself far as I can tell. Sheriff up in Philadelphia sent this boy down here with papers and testimony and asked me to help him look around and send him on his way. Says here Thompson don't usually go about telling tales. But now since Mr. Thompson ain't here, I reckon Thompson ain't sure what he saw if he saw anything at all."

Myrtle slips out the back to look for James. That gal leaving sure is gonna undo all Meredith's fixing. All that scheming to save Agnes from Walker. All them dead babies scattered across them fields. When Walker find out she 'bout the only thing not dried up round here she'll be birthing babies aplenty. What Meredith gonna do then? She can't kill 'em all. Myrtle finds James cleaning out the barn. "Your pa wants you to go get that gal. Her folks come to take her home."

"Can I offer you another glass of tea, Master?" James asks the sheriff. His hands shake. James stares just above the sheriff's head. What's taking that boy so long? Probably fiddling in the woods with Agnes. Like nobody knows. That boy could take any house slave from almost any neighboring plantation, any one Master Walker is on good terms with, and he chooses a girl headed for the fields. He's probably rolling around in the dirt with her right now. What else could be taking him so long? He couldn't be still trying to come up with a plan. James had thought of at least ten, three of which seemed less likely to end with one of them getting killed. One even ended with the pa and them carrying her off alive. If she just come running along the fields like she was running from someplace else, why it wouldn't even look like Walker had set off with her. If it did, wouldn't nobody say it did. Happy to have found her, her pa would just leave. Walker would be madder than Old Missus in a rainstorm but things would settle down soon enough. If they said she'd escaped, maybe knocked one of them out, it might not be so bad after a spell. The sheriff shoos him away.

"If it gets to court, Thompson's word against yours, I don't know whose side will hold up."

"Sheriff, the only young gal I got on my property is Agnes," Walker says. "You met her yourself. She was born right here."

"Rumor is that no children were born on this place, cuz it's haunted," the sheriff says. "Boy, give me some of that air."

James waves a hand-folded fan in wide arcs.

"The place is a bit haunted, as you say, Sheriff. Just the other day a darkie was fished right out the river with rocks all in her mouth. They say she was held down by a big hand from the sky but I don't believe it. They liable to believe anything, you know. Another one was found strung up like a tree with vines and twigs all round her body wrapped up in animal fur. She turned on three tracking dogs, spooked them. It took three rounds of buckshot to take her down. It's getting dark but if you want to look and see if that gal done found her way down to my grounds some kinda way?"

"I hardly think that's necessary," the sheriff says.

Thick clouds pass overhead. The wind swirls leaves in quick moving patches. Below, the men shift from one foot to the next. It's time to go.

"Agnes was born right before we started having all them

troubles. Back then we had all sorts of things growing here. She the last one, though," Walker says. "She's down the river right now, down the very spot where Sampson's gal got snatched up. You all are most welcome to go down there and have a look around. That would satisfy all sides, wouldn't it?"

By the river, sweat drips down Agnes's forehead, into her eyes to her chin. It wouldn't take this long if she had someone to help. She's hauled three rocks and two logs and can still see the worn edges of the circle plain as day. Walker will kill her if Mama Skins don't do it first. Mama Skins won't have nobody to blame but herself. *You get started, I'm gonna take this one for a little walk*, Mama Skins said. As if Walker hadn't said he'd skin them all if there was anything left of the circle. She was lucky he hadn't already taken the whip to her. The way he'd come storming down after the men hauled Grace out of the water. Made them all watch as they slit her belly open in case the baby had survived. Had them carry mother and son to a ditch behind the far field, throw them in. They'd still be wandering Walker's if Mama Skins hadn't gone back late that night, said words over their graves, told stories of rising up, being together in Heaven.

Agnes's back and arms ache. Down yonder, field hands trill like doves. Closer, a familiar trill rings—James. Agnes trills bluebird in response. Listens. His response is clear. She trills robin, listens for Mama Skins's response. Trills again. Silence. Where could they have gone?

Deep in the woods, past the river, beyond the far field and the ditch, Mama Skins whittles a pipe out of a fresh stripped piece of bark. "This is just the wood I've been looking for. Couldn't have found it without you," she says. "Jonah will be tickled."

Ella sits on a large rock. Her feet dangle down the sides. Her fingers trace its cracks. The forest is alive with birdsong. She stops to listen. Is that a robin?

"Damned birds," Mama Skins says, "sounds like they eating up Master's crop. No sense in hurrying home. We'll head back when things settle down a bit. All this walking got me to thinking." Mama Skins pauses, tilts her head, listens. From between the layers of her garb she pulls out a bundle made of sewn hides. She unties the large bow. A bright green apple, a lemon, strawberries, and a beet roll out. From another fold, she pulls out a blunt, rusted knife. Without looking up, she saws at the lemon. Bits of yellow skin sprinkle the rock. When she finally breaks through, she puts the lemon to her lips, sucks the juice out in quiet slurps. She wets a fingertip, gathers the scattered flesh before popping her finger into her mouth. "I hear you and Agnes thinking about running off. That true?"

"What we gonna do?" Little James asks. He's out of breath from running to the circle and out of breath from pacing since he's been there.

"I don't know," Agnes says for the third time. "Done looked everywhere they could be."

"They gotta be up to the house, then. Your mama know they was coming. Coulda took her up there, handed her over to her pa. Think he bought your mama? Give her her papers as a thank you? Your ma wouldn't go lessin she could take you. Walker wouldn't allow that. She would expect you to take her place. Why, you could be free this very minute!"

"You know Walker better than that."

"Why wouldn't her pa at least buy you? You the one been taking care of her."

Would Walker really sell her? Her, the only child from this place in a lifetime of dying babies? Would he sell her away from her mama and papa? From James and them? He could use the money but would he take it? If he did, would that make her free? Not quite free, sold to a free man. Would she be that little gal's slave? What would happen to this place if she wasn't there? Would Mama Skins keep doctoring? She'd probably kill Walker. Less he's dead already. If that gal's pa is anything like she say he is he could be halfway to jail right now. Less he killed the sheriff too.

"We gotta get to the house!" Agnes yells. She's already sprinting through the grass. If he hadn't killed anybody, if that gal's pa is gonna buy her, Agnes will come back for James and Mama Skins and Papa Jonah. But she won't be left behind.

Junior and Senior sip iced drinks on the porch. Below, the men gather around the sheriff in a circle. James catches tails of words: "lies, guns, cahoots." The sheriff's "Watch your mouth, son," rises up to the porch.

"He's a good sheriff," Junior says.

"Not as good as the last one, though," Senior says. "Last one woulda come in, took off his hat, sat a while, then asked 'bout that gal after supper. He knew how to be respectful."

I'm ready if they storm the house, James thinks. The circle

seems to tighten up, to close in on the sheriff in ripples. Can't hardly see the deputy over the broad backs and long necks of the gal's kin. It's the sheriff's thin, whiny voice that wafts up in snatches. James can't hear the men's deep voices. As one, at least when he tells the story later, they tense, spread their feet, reach for guns in holsters. James shivers. He'd hate to harm young Walker but he wouldn't mind knocking Master Walker upside the head once or twice. An icy wind blows. A crack of thunder, followed by another and a flash. God don't like this. Ice-cold rain pours over the men, the fields, the lane. Even as they stand there it washes away their footprints. The men mount donkeys and horses. Before they've even left the lane, all traces of them are gone.

Agnes, with Little James behind her, slips and runs through the rain, down the path, around the field, to the back of the house. Myrtle, Samantha, and James sit in the kitchen praying.

"She gone? I miss her?" Agnes asks.

Agnes will never forget the looks on their faces and the shivers up and down her spine as they turn to stare at her.

12:30 p.m.

Why you stop? Tempe asks. She's got her legs crossed like she's sitting, only ain't no stool there.

"You hear that?" I ask.

She shrugs. Around the room bedsprings creak. Patients moan. If I listen real hard, I can hear Edward breathing just about.

Wish that was all I heard. The window's open but it don't carry no breeze. Only thing blowing in is the sound of angry voices from the streets. Raised voices chanting so fast it sounds like a mumble. Don't matter, though. I know what they saying. They want my boy. If I could look out the window, I would see miles and miles of pitchforks and torches. Every so often loud cheers break the chant. I sure hope they ain't hurting nobody. That mob's liable to do anything. Glass bottles and rocks soar past the window, crack against the wall outside. Sirens start the same time the screaming does. I try to drown it out so it don't worry my baby none.

I'm patting his hand. With my eyes closed I picture him the last time I seen him.

Spring.

"Not yet," I say.

Open your eyes, woman.

"Tempe!" I'm about to say something I'll wish I hadn't. But I hear it. Music playing on a phonograph. Before I can say anything, day turns into night. Sunshine turns into candlelight. The hospital beds turn into couches and crates, a cupboard turns into a table, and my Edward is standing there, in my front room, dressed for work. He's grinning, sharp even in his wrinkled trousers and sweat-stained work shirt. Them boys there too. Instead of laying up hurt, they sitting on my good furniture, their work boots on my hardwood floor, beer jars on my table. I don't mind, though. Without bandages and bruises I recognize them. Neighborhood boys that went to school, war, and now work with Edward.

There's Jacob, a fresh-rolled cigarette hanging off his bottom lip.

"Don't you smoke that in here," Edward says. "My mama doesn't stand for that in the house."

"Man, your mama got a rule for everything. Take your shoes

off in the house, put the cup on the saucer in the house, don't light up in the house. She ain't gonna know nothing 'bout it," Jacob says.

"You've broke all the other rules already. Just don't light it. I'd hate to put you out before we even get started."

"When you gonna get your own place?"

"I have my own place. My own room. Use the kitchen when I want. Come and go as I please."

One of the boys laughs.

"Alright, almost as I please," Edward whispers.

He's smiling but lines crease his forehead. All the windows are shut and he's sweating despite the cool night air.

"Man, what you worried about?" Jacob asks. "Your mother ain't gonna wake up. We been meeting here for weeks and no amount of noise gonna get her out of that bed. Only sound that wakes her is that drawer full of money sliding open. Besides, long as the music's playing, she'll think you're down here with the future Mrs. Edward Freeman. She don't want to interrupt that, that's for sure."

Except for Edward, everyone laughs.

"What future missus are you talking about? I don't have my eye set on anyone."

"You don't need to," a boy from down the street says. "Your mama got five, six set of eyes doing the looking for you. Every time I see her she's talking to some girl about Edward this, Edward that. That's probably why she stopped going to church in the first place. She run out of girls to talk to about you."

"That's not why she stopped going," Edward says.

"She still seeing ghosts?" Jacob asks.

I feel my cheeks burning.

"She doesn't talk about it, but I can tell. She needs me here."

"She doesn't seem to think so. She's really trying to get you hitched."

"She'll have to wait a little longer. Right now, my mama is the only woman for me."

Tempe grunts so loud I'm worried Edward will disappear. She's glowing like there's a piece of coal in her chest. His body starts to waver.

"Tempe, stop that right now," I say.

She glares at me, then at Edward. For a moment he seems to look right at her. The heat, her anger with it, fades. I don't know how much time has passed. Edward and the boys are back in the front room sipping beer.

"It isn't my mother I'm worried about," Edward's saying, "least, not like that. What's gonna happen to her when I'm gone?"

"You ain't going nowhere," someone says.

"I can't come back here. Not if I go along with your plan," Edward says.

"The plan," Jacob says. "Not, your plan or his plan, the plan. You gotta come back here. If you don't you'll be the first one they suspect. That right there is suspicious. A mama's boy not going home to his mama? They'd snatch you and her right up. What your mama gonna do if she locked up somewhere? No, come back home. Go about your business. Go to work like nothing happened. If you want to keep your mama out of this, come back home."

Edward paces the front room. A couple of times he nearly walks through me. "Baby, don't do it," I say. He don't hear me. I reach out to touch him. My hands pass through him. He shivers.

"Who's going to look after her if I don't come back?" he asks.

"Why you keep saying you ain't gonna come back? Where else

you gonna go? You ain't gonna hop on no train and leave your mama to fend for herself, are you?"

"Man, I'm talking about dying. You're talking about hopping on a train."

"Nobody's dying. Least of all you."

"And if something goes wrong, who's going to take care of her?"

"It's just cutting a few wires."

"Who is going to take care of my mother?"

"It's just a warning. Nobody's getting hurt."

"Who?" Edward asks.

He's in front of him before Jacob can move.

"I will," Jacob whispers.

None of them will look Edward in the eye.

The men disappear, leaving the scent of spice, soap, and sweat behind.

First Tempe and now this. I add Edward's name to my list of sins. Tempe's settled on the bed like she ain't never left his side. She's tapping her foot.

Want me to tell him? she asks.

Before she can start telling it her way, I get the book and pick up where I left off.

Chapter 10

It feels like days. The sky turns from black to pitch black and black again. Ella runs from tree to tree feeling for landmarks. Is this the tree she had sat under with Agnes? Is that? Thin, thorny branches, thick sap-filled cones, dry-rotting tree limbs; in the dark, it all looks, smells, and feels the same. Ella runs through the night. She tumbles through woods and gets tangled up in briars and weeds. She hears dogs and runs left. Footsteps and runs right. Even with the bright light of the moon, the only thing she can see is that she's lost.

The rain has stopped but the air is still thick with it. Her feet sink into the mud, slip and slide on leaves and rocks. If only that whistling would stop, Ella could clear her mind enough to figure out where she is. But it's closer—the whistling. It echoes her breathing, a raspy hiss that rattles. She tries to outrun it. It gets closer, louder. She collapses in a mound of leaves and sticks. Her lungs burn. Out of breath and panting, she picks herself up and lumbers on. Her body is soaked in sweat. She knows the dogs will pick up her scent soon if they haven't already. Her own smell of fear and sweat burn her nostrils.

Papa had come for her. Just like she knew he would, he had found her. But she is still here. Why had he left without her? No matter what Agnes, Mr. Jonah, Mr. James, and them thought, Ella didn't believe that witch hadn't planned it from the start. *How was I to know?* Mama Skins had said. And them just standing there like they believed it or like they couldn't believe it. Couldn't believe after all these years the woman they trusted to run the plantation, to decide on the planting and the harvesting of the land and the people, couldn't do nothing to save one little slave girl. Why couldn't they see? If she'd wanted Ella saved, she would have been saved.

Wasn't that basket of food proof they were paying Skins to keep Ella a slave? They all sat there eating up them lies and that food. Ella's stomach grumbles. When nobody was looking, she had been picking at crumbs, pinching the crusts of bread. But not today. She refuses to sneak even a scrap of that *you done good for keeping a slave* basket. She'd rather die. She'd only been sneaking food to be ready. Just in case Agnes kept her word. How could she, though? With her mother bent on keeping her around, Agnes couldn't get her own self free let alone help Ella. The look in the old woman's eyes when she asked if it was true she and Agnes were planning to run away was enough. Ella's silent "no" didn't even feel like a lie. Not then, not when the old woman said, "Good, cuz I don't plan on losing this baby," and not now.

Fresh dung clings to Ella's foot. It's been miles; she might even be in Pennsylvania by now. Her legs ache, the soles of her feet sting. It would be nice if Agnes could have come with her. But she's probably still huddled over her mother whispering, "It'll be alright," as if her life had been the one galloping down the road. As if it wasn't her fault Papa left. Them whispering and poor-Mama-Skins-ing drove Ella to slip out of the cabin, down the mud path, through the woods, and finally to start running. Poor Mama Skins? What has she lost? Some magic she ain't never had? With everybody crowded around the old woman like she was a broke-up doll, no one seemed to notice her go. Ella had never wanted to hurt anybody as much as she wanted to hurt Mama Skins. With all of them standing guard, she couldn't get close enough and she had no intentions of staying one more night even if it meant waiting to kill her in her sleep. *Please, Lord*, she prays, *strike that crazy old devil woman dead right now.*

She pictures Agnes bent over as the old lady's body goes rigid. Mr. Jonah and the Jameses will probably carry her to the pit. Walker will say a few words, slice her open to make sure she's dead. Toss her in. Agnes and James can run off. Will she leave her pa like that? Alone? Please Lord, maybe don't kill her, just let her get hurt up real bad. If you're going to kill anybody, let it be Walker, the old one too.

Just a little while longer and she'll be able to soak in a long bath of salts. She'll even suffer her grandmother's cure of castor oil, lemon, and onion stock. She just has to make it home.

There are no stars.

Her lungs fill with the heavy musk of animal. She's close to a farm or field and if she keeps low and creeps through the tall grass, she might find a quiet place to rest for the night.

Before long Ella reaches a barn. She slips through a low opening, scraping a thigh on a splintered beam. Her feet give way underneath hay and feed. She crawls across the dirty barn floor to huddle behind a stack of hay. She'll just rest her eyes and be gone before morning.

She wakes to mooing and shaking. Her whole body rattles back and forth. The strong hands gripping her arms feel like one of her brothers trying to wake her for lessons. Home! Finally. Rapturous joy, sweet like molasses, fills her throat. Sleep crusts her eyes, gluing her lashes together. She reaches out to touch the heavenly face in front of hers. If only he'd stop shaking her.

"Gal, gal! Hush all that noise!" he whispers.

What's James doing in her bedroom? Mooing cows, sharp hay, dirty floor. She wipes the sleep from her eyes. Walker's. All that walking, running, and sliding, all that praying.

"Better get you back, been hours since you left the cabin. Agnes been worrying all night. Ain't you hear her call?" He pulls her up, shakes his head. "Thought for sure you'd be gone by now. I tol' Agnes, I says, 'Agnes, you just watch, that gal done took off after her pa and left you and me both.' And Agnes says, 'No, she wouldn't leave without me.' And I got to thinking, would you? I would. If my pa come, if my pa was free and if he come for me and somebody kept me from him." James stops, watches her face.

For a second, Ella reaches out to him. Her hand hangs in the air. It's still James. No matter what Agnes said, he raped her. He's no better than that old woman. He'll still get what's coming to him. She prays she isn't there to see it. She clasps her hands together, nods her head, mouths the word *yes*.

Finally, someone understands her. If only she didn't hate him. It's a momentary joy. Tears clog her throat.

"Agnes won't believe it. Ain't no way Mama Skins ain't know your folks was here. Samantha told Agnes to tell her they was coming day before last. She tell you?"

Ella wishes she was like her pa. No matter how good or bad the news, her pa's face won't give nothing away. No expression at all. His body either. He stands more often than not, feet firm on the ground, back straight. It's all in his hands. Ella and her brothers got good at recognizing the signs. He reacted to news in three ways: a hand under his chin, on a belt loop, or fingering a holster. She's more like her mother. Her eyes, mouth, the lines on her forehead; her face reflects everything she feels. Her stomach curdles at bad news, her heart stops beating. Now, heart breaking, she crumples to the floor.

James kneels beside her. "I told her to tell you. Her mama said she'd take care of everything. Don't blame Agnes for believing her. We gonna come up with a plan to get Agnes, me, and you gone. We can part ways after that if you want to. You can't get your way off here by yourself and we can't get around out there without you. Way I see it, that makes us family."

Ella's body shakes. She doesn't trust James any more than she trusts Agnes but unless she can find another way, she'll have to make do.

Agnes spoons a thick stew of mashed carrots and rabbit into a gourd. "Frown your face up all you like," she tells Ella, "ain't nothing wrong with the way it smells."

The smell of roasted meat mingling with the aroma of carrots and spices fills the cabin. Ella goes outside. Even sitting on the lone step of the porch, it's overpowering. Eating her food don't make us friends. Agnes sets a bowl on the porch. Ella takes turns staring at it, the sky, the trees, the scatter of slave cabins of people she's never met, and back to the bowl. Ella slips a fingertip into it. The warmth feels good. Ignoring the muck underneath her growing fingernails, she sucks stew off her finger. Mama would kill her.

"We got spoons," Agnes says. She plops one down on the porch.

Jonah must have made it. The careful grooves, smooth wedge

and thick handle feel like him. Patient and biding. Like the porch. Hardly more than enough room for two people to stand side by side, Ella can picture Jonah whittling it out of some rotted tree trunks, discarded planks, throwaway pieces. Ignoring the spoon, she picks the bowl up between both hands. The warmth of the gourd, the steam of the stew. She puts it to her lips and sips. Her stomach growls. And sips. Her stomach lurches. And sips. It is her first meal in weeks. She wipes her mouth on the back of her hand.

Agnes squeezes in beside Ella. The night air cools. Agnes shivers. She eats slowly, humming between spoonfuls, as if each one is better than the last. Ella gets up, leaving the empty bowl behind. She walks round the back to the garden. Sits on a patch of packed earth. Watches the clean sheets billowing on the washing line. Dancing like ghosts.

"That's where Mama Skins's babies buried," Agnes says.

Ella half expected Agnes to follow, still she jumps at the sound of her voice.

"You can sit there, they don't mind."

She won't give her the satisfaction of thinking she's spooked. No such thing as ghosts. And if there were, first thing they'd do is get far from here. Only thing haunted is her and her mama.

"Don't you think that 'bout my mama," Agnes says. "She ain't want to kill them babies!" Agnes leans against the wash line.

Ella closes her eyes, pictures Mama Skins wringing baby necks.

"Used to have to birth it first. She'd clean it, dress it real warm, love on it and by night, she'd smother it. Not in its sleep. While it was awake, so she could talk to it, tell it she loved it and how killing it was the most merciful thing she could do in this world. By the next morning she'd be back at Doc's birthing babies for the farmers' wives, merchants, anyone who could afford it. Was a time

Mama Skins was sent for at all hours of the night. First one too. Before they even called the doctor, they'd send for Mama. He'd taught her 'bout how mixing this with that could save this one, soothe that one, still another one. For long she was doctoring, just about. Then Doc up and died. You know how folks are. Ungrateful gossips. They got to saying she killed him. My mama. As if she'd do that. Walker put a stop to all that talk. Stopped hiring her out too. She been doctoring here since."

A sprinkle of poison in his tea, some of them itchy flowers on a roll, a rusted nail? Ella wonders how the old woman killed him.

"I wish I could take her with me when we go."

Though she hasn't moved, Agnes is too close. Her voice stings Ella's skin like bees. Her words scatter from her mouth, buzz across the sky, attack. Ella scrambles to get up, to get away from Agnes, her foolish words and her pretend ways.

"You right," Agnes calls to her back, "she's too frail. The trip alone could kill her."

That night Ella curls up like a cat, half on, half off the porch. In her head she recites her favorite prayers, practices hymns, lists names, birthdates, and faces so she does not forget. She tries counting the days she's been here, forty-seven, but that makes her cry. So she counts the days until she goes home. One. Before long, she is asleep. Tomorrow she will follow the river's bends clear off Walker land. She will find a path and stay clear of it like the runaway slaves used to talk about during testimony. She will pack enough food for seven days. No meat, meat attracts dogs someone had said. She will bundle breads, carrots, and blueberries while

Agnes is in the fields and Papa Jonah runs around trying to keep the farm alive and Mama Skins runs around killing it. She will find a church and they will help her find her way home.

Mama Skins stands at the cabin door listening to the girl's dream planning. Inside, Agnes lies alone on her pallet watching her mother's silhouette.

Ella wakes to the cold early morning air. The sun is not up. Just as well, she thinks, she has to get ready. Her eyes aren't open a full minute when she feels someone squatting too close next to her.

"Master wants you down to the fields to help with the clearing," Mama Skins says.

Slaving. She hasn't planned to be here this long. Forced to bend and break for the man who kidnapped her. Not able to speak up and if she could, what would she say? You know you wrong?

"Ain't gonna be no more nothing less you earn your keep. You gonna have to take your hand to something just like the rest of us. No sense sulking 'bout it. Sooner you get started, sooner you get done."

"Leave her be, Mama. I'll help her," Agnes says.

Ella follows Agnes to the river. Agnes points out markings along the way, she has a story for each one. That's where so and so broke his neck, that's where so and so got bit by a snake. Not one good thing happened on the whole place. Now's as good a time as any to get going. No food. She'll have to live off the water, maybe catch fish or something. She ain't been eating much anyway. The morning's near as dark as night. Once she gets to the river, she'll run. The fresh smell fills her nostrils. Not far now. A few steps more and she can hear it. Her heart beats in time with the rush of low and high tide meeting, swirling.

Agnes stops a few steps ahead. She clasps Ella's hands tight like a schoolgirl on the playground. "James got a plan," she says. Her words come out in bursts. "Been waiting to tell you till it gets set but now's as good a time as any. Walker hired a hand!" She throws Ella's hands in the air. "Coming here!" She twirls in a circle, her arms outstretched.

Ella resumes walking toward the river. What does one more set of hands have to do with her?

"A free black hand. Someone to help with the hauling and clearing. Somebody who knows following that river is a sure enough way to get caught or killed or both."

Ella stops walking.

Agnes talks over bathing. A few minutes later they set off for the fields. "Remember, all we got to do is be nice to him," Agnes says. "Not too nice. Let me see you smile. Oh Lord, no. Don't do that no more. Like to scare him for days. Just let me do the talking and the smiling for both of us."

It takes longer than Ella expects to get Bird, the hired hand working his way up north, to trust her. He spends most days not looking at her. Not looking into her lost brown eyes, not thinking about her broken spirit, her long legs. He's been warned by the locals in town not to trust a soul on this place. But James and Agnes seem alright enough. They don't look haunted. He feels bad about not accepting any of their food or drink, feels rude not to. But even if he hadn't been warned "not to put so much as a crumb in his mouth lest he be tied to the place forever," he won't take the little bit they have. He eats supper with them. Clears and hauls side by side with them. At the end of each day he goes home to the boardinghouse he shares with ten other laborers, tumbles into bed and gets up before dawn to haul, lift, and not look at that little bit of gal wasting away.

It takes ten days for the overseer to stop watching her, whip ready, waiting for her to walk too fast, haul too slow, carry too little. Agnes had told her how much to lift, how far to haul, how fast to move to satisfy him. Too fast got everyone else in trouble. Too slow meant the lash. It only takes once. One crack of tight wound leather heavy on her small back sends her crumpled to the ground. The other slaves, including Agnes, keep working like the whoosh hasn't sliced through the air and her skin and her scream and flesh haven't torn from her body. But Bird drops his load of broken branches and stumps. He walks quickly, stepping around bent backs, over tangled roots to get there before the second lash.

"I'll teach her how to untangle them roots without messing with the crop," he says. He's already scooping Ella up with one hand, picking up her hoe in the other. His body is a short wall between the overseer and Ella. Before the overseer can answer, Bird is leading her off, talking about berries and branches. He spends the next seven days teaching Ella to uproot bushes without killing the roots. He spends his nights thinking of ways to get her free.

"Bird's sweet on you," Agnes whispers on the eighth night.

The girls lay on the edge of the riverbank. Despite the cold, they sleep here most nights "to be closer to the fields," Agnes had told her mother. Mama Skins fussing about it didn't stop Jonah and James from building the girls a small cabin near a copse of trees. Long as the girls took their supper at the house, Jonah didn't "see a dang thing wrong with it." He lined the roof with hides and furs, stuffed a fresh mattress with feathers and hides.

"He's been asking Little James about you. 'Tell me 'bout that gal,'" Agnes whispers in her best Bird voice. "You know that's as good as him asking if youse taken. James got to talking 'bout what a shame it is you been stolen from your people and if you could get up north, anywhere up north, it would be a miracle. He ain't say nothing else about it. Few days later, Bird come saying he didn't see why a gal like you should stay here. He said he thought he could buy you free."

Ella's heart gets to beating out her chest.

"Why, James liked to die. Ain't no way Bird can afford to buy us all. No, James tells him, Walker wouldn't sell you to nobody, least of all not to no black man who was just gonna set you free."

Ella's throat closes.

"James left it at that. Today, Bird come up with a plan. Walker ain't got to set her free. Just need papers that say she free."

Ella's stomach goes one way, her head the other. She waits. "Bird's gonna buy passes soon's as he saves enough. Got a friend to write them and everything. Just a little while longer. We'll be free before you know it."

A few weeks later, Samantha, Myrtle, and Mama Skins gather at the river over the soapy undergarments and work-stained dungarees of the field slaves. The monthly washing is one of the few times the friends can talk openly. Mama Skins stirs a large boiling pot of clothes as the other two women dip them in the river and wring them out. When they finish they will call Agnes and Ella to hang them on makeshift lines made up of vines and rope.

"What you know about Bird?" Mama Skins asks.

"Not much," Samantha says, "hardworking. Don't talk much 'cept to Little James, Agnes, and that gal." Her thin fingers pinch each drop of water from the worn fabric between her palms. After inspecting and wringing them again, she puts the breeches on the pile before scooping another from her woven river basket where they cool.

"I think he sweet on her," Mama Skins says. "Could be he come and steal her away."

"That mess up all your planning, though, wouldn't it?" Myrtle asks. "All that working to save Agnes go soon as that girl go." She grins. "Isn't that what you want? Save your gal?" It's in her voice, her eyes, the set of her mouth, the way she holds her head. Even if Mama Skins didn't know her like she does, she'd recognize Myrtle's jealous ways.

"What you talking 'bout, Myrtle? Turns out, when that gal go, she gonna take my Agnes right on away from here. And if Agnes go, Little James gonna follow right on behind her." Mama Skins lets the words hang in the air with the soap bubbles.

"But if she goes, who's gonna be here for you? Who you gonna have left?" Samantha asks.

"Me and Jonah and of course you and Myrtle and James and Little, no, not Little James. You practically raised that boy, ain't you? Had your heart set on him and that gal from up the road getting together?" Mama Skins shakes her head. "Well, soon's they hit freedom, first thing he and Agnes probably do, I imagine, is get married." Hot soapy bubbles splatter Mama Skins's skin. She doesn't seem to take notice. She hums and stirs and waits.

Myrtle thrusts a work shirt underwater. She holds it under like it's fighting back. "Be back, need to get something up the house." She's already moving before the two can respond.

"Oh, Meredith," Samantha says. "Why'd you say that? You know how Myrtle gets herself worked up."

It's got nothing to do with Agnes and nothing to do with that bit of a gal either, Myrtle thinks as she trudges down the path. If it weren't for Meredith convincing them all to take that stuff, none of this would be happening. Her girls wouldn't have been sold off for being barren, her brothers wouldn't have been sold south to pick cotton, her friends, most of them gone now, wouldn't have buried baby after baby after baby. She stares straight ahead. She won't look at the heads poking up through the ground, blooming like spring flowers. Why should Meredith get what she wants? How many women come to her to keep their masters out of their beds at night? How many had she given a little bit of this to? How many times had that little bit turned into a whole heap of that? When they were all shriveled up inside and Walker started buying babies, wasn't the pact to kill them? Won't be no more slaves after us, the women swore on it. When Walker brought a little baby, they all hugged on it, loved on it, and in the morning, one of them would love it to death. Love it to freedom. How many was it?

They'd taken turns. She had Jebediah with the bright-green eyes, Every with fingers long like vines, Shy with the pink lips. She can still see their faces, their eyes big with shock, the questions in their eyes. She told them stories, all of them, of who they were and who she was and where they came from and where they was going, all so they could make their way home. When Agnes come, Meredith said the baby didn't need killing. Said Walker was convinced the place was haunted and one miracle baby wouldn't hurt nothing. Walker brought two more. They

died the same day. Wasn't even Meredith's turn. "Babies sometimes die," she said, like that was that. No more babies come
until that gal. Shoulda been Myrtle's turn. That gal didn't need
killing neither. Myrtle would have loved on her, been her mama.
But Meredith fixed it so she'd go down to the cabins.

No more. Just a whisper in the Missus's ear, a question: What
do you think that laborer talks to the field hands about? That's
all it would take to get Missus's imagination to running. Before
long she'd conjure up worse than Myrtle could say and that hand
would be on his way north, alone, and that little gal would be up
the house, scrubbing and cooking and mending. She'd teach her
who to look out for, how to make the days pass like lightning,
how to stop hearing the whispers of the dead.

Voices drift through the woods.

"How we gonna put three people on one pass?" Little James.
If he'd been born after Meredith come, there wouldn't be no Little James today.

"Can't. This pass says I got one slave, one. I told you I was
coming for the gal. Now it's all mixed up," another man says.

"But my woman and me, we're planning on leaving together."

"Ain't trying to stop you, just can't do it on this pass."

From behind a tree, Myrtle watches the silence settle like
smoke between the two men.

"Whole lot easier for two to get free when one's already free,"
the man finally says. "You can come back for one, both of them,
or all four of 'em."

"Four?" James asks.

"They both with child, ain't they?"

Could they be? Meredith hadn't given Agnes anything to dry
her up and she sure didn't give that gal any, although she told

Agnes she would. There was no doubt Meredith had given Agnes something to keep Walker off of her for all these years. Agnes might have slipped some to that gal, but babies? Meredith sure hadn't counted on this. Two of them? After all this time? James's hemming and hawing could get them all left.

"Seems like you would have mentioned she was with child before now. Unless you didn't know. But, I can't be toting no pregnant gal. What happens if we get found out? She ain't gonna be able to run. Get us both caught. Either you go or no. I ain't gonna make up your mind for you."

"I am," Myrtle says. "Ain't I been a mama to you most your life?" Even though she's stepped in front of the tree, both men jump like they've seen a ghost. Bird looks like he wants to run one way, James the other. "You gotta leave here while you got the chance," she continues. "Come back for Agnes when you get yourself set up. Get you a job, a place for the baby, her. I'll take care of her and the other gal and her young'un too."

"What about my pa? He'll die without me," James says.

"You so full of yourself," Myrtle laughs. "He'll be sorry you ain't gone sooner. You think he want you to be a slave your whole natural life? Your mama wouldn't want that neither."

James shifts from foot to foot. Bird shifts from foot to foot. "It ain't like you leaving us. You being free is like us all being free, one step at a time," she says. She wraps him in her arms, holds him tight like she held all them before him.

Loving him to freedom. She lets go.

"I'll be back for y'all," James promises. "Tell them for me. Hear?"

Myrtle nods, takes a breath and almost skips to the far field. She hasn't been there on purpose in years. She sits among the graves, chattering and laughing and singing. She's still singing when the overseer finds her the next morning, singing and chattering about babies and graves. Walker drives her five towns over. He comes back the next morning with twin calves.

Agnes knows James is coming back for her. She feels it. Walker rallies a search party to save James from Bird "the slave-charming-abolitionist-thief." Damned Bird done tricked James into leaving. Soon as he can break free, James will be home. Agnes waits. Days pass, then weeks. Blueberries peek then burst through. It's planting season. Just like James to make the most of things. He's probably got himself a job, saving up to buy her. Hope he make enough to buy the gal too. If not, they'll come back for her before long. Might have a room somewhere but more likely James done built a little something somewhere near the water, he likes the water. Agnes bundles clothes, shells, things she can't stand to leave behind, wraps them in skins and buries them. She'd fold her mama and papa up too if she could. The hole is shallow. Buried in Mama Skins's patch with the babies so they can keep an eye on it till it's time. Won't take a minute to scoop it up. James will be in a hurry.

Since Bird run off, Ella's been waiting. Instead of counting days, she focuses on voices. Mama's singing geography lessons: "The Monongahela through and through, river flows from me to you." Papa's, "Oh how it glitters, oh how it shines, when dirt turns to soot, look out for the mines." Pastor's, "The Heavenly star, that shines clear and bright, leads straight to God's North, keep freedom in sight." But the voice she hears most often is Hazel, a runaway slave she'd made a shawl for: "Stay clear the shallow, stay clear the wide, cross at the rapids, where dogs fear to stride."

She'll need to be ready for when he comes back. Most likely Bird will know the way, least to Philadelphia. She can do the rest. Mornings she hauls and plans and waits, no Bird. Weeks pass. She's hungry all the time. When she's not throwing up yellow bile, she's eating dirt, bark, starch, carrots. Her arms are lean, her legs strong, her belly round. Agnes's is too. Must be all that good eating. Deer, possum, raccoon. Agnes can catch anything. Agitated, Ella is waiting on Bird when it's time for planting. When grass and flowers sprout. When bushes and trees bloom. July brings hot sun and bursting blueberries ripe from the bush. They stain her fingers, her arms, her legs, her patience.

Mama Skins has been waiting too. Ever since Walker sold Myrtle off, the air has become thick. It stinks all over. Most days, she can hardly breathe. Fresh rain does nothing to wash the smell of rot from the dirt, the trees, her skin. Even if Agnes and that gal can't smell it, Samantha, Old James, and Jonah do. They don't talk about it, don't need to. It hangs between Samantha and her like a pair of soiled undergarments at the river washing. Between Old James's words on the few times he brings news from the house. In that space between her and Jonah where she used to put her head on his chest at night. It's only a matter of time before Walker gets to selling other folk. She will never see Agnes again. Never hold her grandbaby. The baby will grow up a slave, just like Agnes, just like her. If she ain't never gonna see her again no how, Agnes may as well be free. She won't get far without that gal's book smarts. But two little gals won't get far weighed down with babies.

If she slips a handful of ground herbs into Agnes's stew, the baby won't be born at all. Mama Skins has been up since sunrise gathering and grinding herbs from her medicine garden. Some for Agnes, some for the gal. The carrots are slow cooking with rabbit and onions. In a small iron pot, the bitter herbs simmer. As it cooks, Mama Skins makes up memory bundles for both babies. She whispers stories into shells for safekeeping and to guide the babies home when they pass. She wraps the shells in fabric, a pocket from Agnes's dress, a torn ribbon she'd been holding on to since the gal came. She wraps these small treats in stolen scraps of newspaper, tufts of fur, hides. She rocks the bundles in her arms, kisses them. She has supper on the table. For the girls, two black gourds; for her and Jonah, two brown.

The sun set hours ago. The day's been so long the moon doesn't even bother to come out. The sky is pitch black. Not one shining star. The stew has been heated twice. The herbs have steeped too long in their own juices. Picking season. As the summer air cools the few borrowed bodies Walker can afford make their way back to the shacks to live side by side with the few slaves left. After hours of waiting, slippery with sweat, the girls and Jonah plop on the porch.

"Y'all gonna wash before supper?" Mama Skins asks. No one stirs.

Just as well. They'll have to wash all over again once the blood starts flowing. "Supper's on the table," Mama Skins says. She paces inside the cabin. Comes back to the door, waits.

"Meredith," Jonah says, "I ain't got no intention of getting up no more tonight. If that supper want me to eat it, it's gonna have to come right here for me to do it."

"I'll get it, Mama."

From the sound of her voice, don't sound like she could get up if she wanted to. "I'll get it." Mama Skins squints, fingers each gourd for nicks and grooves. She can't see the colors but knows each by heart. Satisfied, she balances one in each hand, elbows pressing the other two, one each to either side of her body. "Huhn," she says, delivering Jonah's, then Agnes's, then the gal's. She stands in the doorway, the black bowl cool between her fingertips. "I been thinking. Won't be too long before Walker get to selling again," she says. Sips deeply. "We gotta make sure you two is gone before he do."

There are four soft thuds: Agnes's sleeping head against the wood step as untouched stew slides to the porch and the brown bowl falls from her fingers. Papa Jonah's seizing body on the ground as poison ripples through his veins, turning his stomach against him. Mama Skins's insides pouring from every orifice of her quickly bloating body. Ella's feet running through the soft grass.

The overseer finds them the next morning. Agnes, still sleeping, on the porch. Her parents, one slumped over, one standing stock straight, both dead. Samantha and Big James come for her. They lead Agnes to her little cabin. Hush her screaming. They tell stories of Meredith before Agnes, before she became Mama Skins. Stories of a wild-eyed slave girl smarter than a soul for miles. So smart she got her learning from the good doctor. Learned her everything he knew. Meredith with a voice so strong she could sing the skin off a coon. The Meredith they remembered laughed and sang. The Meredith they remembered didn't kill babies.

Agnes hardly recognized the Meredith they described.

While James and Samantha split Meredith's story in two, her body was dumped in the pit with Jonah on top of her. On account of the oozing, Walker had the pile set on fire. Contractions hit the moment the flames roared. At the same time, Ella's body came bobbing to the surface. I was born headfirst in the bottom of the river. Tempe, my sister, popped out of Agnes's belly just one minute before me. To hear her tell it, she's the one that broke the curse and I'm just the one who broke the curse's sister. She never lets me forget it.

2:01 p.m.

Hush.

Tempe's whisper, hot like the whistle of a tea kettle, sends chills up the back of my neck. She's always trying to boss me. I tuck the yellow newspaper article, *Philadelphia North, November 28, 1850*, into the middle of the book. I put it in front of Tempe and put Edward's bandaged hands in between mine. "It's gonna be alright, baby." The lie springs to my lips before I can stop it.

The door clicks. A rush of warm air. The soft thump of the door, humming, and the smell of lilacs lift the stale air. "I'm going to need to check vitals," a nurse announces to the room. A chart slaps against her hip. There are two of them. Accosting one patient after the other, they slip behind patient screens. Their shadows lift, turn, tug. Moans and grunts accompany orchestrated movements. The snap of rubber gloves. The stench of alcohol, urine; the slosh of a bucket. They make their way to Edward's bed. I glance at Tempe.

Told you so.

"We just need to check on Mr. Freeman," one says. Staring at the chart, she nods her head at Edward.

"Just be a moment," the other says. She's already got one hand clutched around my arm, pulling on me and the other reaching for my book. She's so close I can read the name, Bernadette, on her tag.

"I'll get it," I say.

We grab for it at the same time. My hand on one end, hers on the other. Years slip from the pages. 1855, 1860, 1865, 1880, 1901: scatter like june bugs. *The Emancipation* slides onto the floor followed by *Missing Girl; Reward for Runaway Slave; Lost: Woman Missing, Answers to Mama; Found: Baby, Six Months Old*, and *No Coloreds Allowed*. Damned fool. She lets go of the book. I clutch it tight but that don't stop it from shaking none. It's warm and throbbing like to jump right out of my arms. My arms get to shaking and my legs too. Tempe's rolling her eyes, shaking her head at me from the corner. Spiteful words gurgle in my throat. *Toe stomping, speckled heifer* is pushing its way pass my tongue. Bernadette holds the clippings clumped together so that *Lost* is on one end, *Found* on the other. She gives them to me gently, and ushers me away from the bed.

"How long they gonna keep him?" the younger nurse says. She lifts and prods.

Bernadette peels one of Edward's eyelids back, stares, writes. Peels the next. "Why, till he gets better, of course."

"Expect that's possible?"

The look the older one gives her could stop a heart. She puts her head down, scribbles notes.

"I wouldn't be surprised if Mr. Freeman got up in a few days ready to shake all this off and put the past behind him."

"I would," the young nurse whispers.

"Excuse us." Bernadette pulls a curtain attached to a metal frame around the bed. The contraption rattles and clinks into place. As soon as the starched, thin piece of cloth is in place, she starts talking. "What ever made you say that?" Her body casts shadows across the screen. Her hands are on her hips. She leans forward, bends almost double. "I've told you a thousand times: don't talk like that in front of them."

"I didn't mean nothing by it. I been hearing 'bout this case all—"

"Patient. Out there, it's a case. In here, he's a patient."

"I been hearing about this all day. I'm surprised he's still alive. Soon as I heard it on the radio I just knew he'd be here and that I'd be one of the last people to see him alive. I just knew it. I said, Maddy, you gonna be the last face that ol' colored boy see."

"Will you hush?"

The hiss of words is replaced by the whoosh of ripping gauze as they remove and replace strips of fabric with new ones. Through the curtain, they roll and unroll, measure, snip, and tuck.

"I left soon as I could. Mama was all: 'Where you going so early?' And I said, 'Mama, I'm going to work, they need me.' I couldn't get out the door without her fussing and packing supper in case I had to work through the night. Can't be fooling around with no bus or trolley today. And wasn't I right? Wasn't off my porch step when people came running up the street asking me if I heard the news and in the same breath saying stay indoors. They was gonna go round up the coloreds so there wouldn't be no trouble till it was all over. That sounded like trouble to me so I said, 'Don't you do that. Don't you go riling them folks up. It'll all blow over.' And they said, 'Damned right.' Just like that. Folks standing round waiting on the Broad Line or the Vine Express like it didn't matter what time they showed up. Mother Matthews would have me scrubbing chamber pots for a month, two if I was that late. I walked clear here." Her hands are moving at the same time her mouth is.

"I've been here since first thing this morning. Buses have been tied up ever since it happened."

"You walk her up?"

"Oh, heavens no, Maddy, Claudine did that. Seemed like she was hoping to stay around. I don't blame her. I wouldn't want to be walking out there right now if I was her."

"All she has to say is 'I'm a nurse' and they'll let her right through."

"Who will?"

"The police. They all around the hospital. So is the Klan and everyone else. Tell me you can't hear people chanting, 'Throw him down, throw him down!' I swear it's like they right outside the window knowing exactly where he is. I feel like they're watching me right now. Who do you think is keeping them from coming right in here, dragging him from this bed and tossing him out the window?"

"Well, it'll all be over soon."

"How do you figure? The police can't figure out if he was pulled or did the pulling. And just what was he doing operating the trolley anyhow? Is he working for the strikers or the rails? Ought to be ashamed. Ramming into a heap of—"

"—Wasn't a heap. Shop wasn't even open yet. It couldn't have been more than a couple of people in there."

"That's not bad enough?"

"A few is less than a whole heap. Ones we getting are from after the accident."

"A certain amount of violence is to be expected after events like this," Maddy says. She puts her hands on her hips, shakes her head.

"Don't you sound just like that man from the radio?"

"Mama loves when I do that. Says I got it just right. I said it to the officer by the door earlier. He didn't smile or nothing."

"Of course not, he's been there all day. I'm sure he can't wait until it's all over. Did he say how long he'll be out there?"

"Wait, let me do it like he says." She tilts her head, puts a hand up to an imaginary cap. "Till it's all over, ma'am."

"Then that won't be much longer now."

"They'll move on once he's gone."

"Don't see why folks stick around. Even if he did do it, he won't be able to tell them nothing about it."

"When I came in the police were calling on the coloreds to go home peacefully. I could hear it before I even got here. "Just go home and you won't get hurt." They didn't listen, though. Some of them started singing and praying and chanting. Then people and water came gushing down the street. I just stopped. Right there. When it turned to a steady stream of pink, I come on through. Seen a whole heap of them—no, a few—police had arrested a few. Seem to think they must be in cahoots or something. I hope one of them confesses soon. We don't have that much room to take many more."

"I don't think he did it," Bernadette says.

"I don't see why not. He was in it, wasn't he?"

"That's what they say."

"A whole lot of folks say that."

"I heard they're already questioning somebody else."

Maddy sucks her teeth.

"A union boy from up north sent down to get the strikers worked up."

"Don't need much riling up. They been at it since they got fired yesterday. Been boiling over before that, if you ask me."

They tuck the covers tight around Edward.

"Don't much matter now, does it?" Bernadette asks.

I don't realize until the curtain starts billowing that I've been holding my breath ever since they started talking. My chest hurts. My mouth is dry. The curtain flails and rustles. It slaps against one's back, creeps against the other's legs.

"Oh, my!" Their mumbles grow louder as wind presses the cloth against them.

Tempe. She's standing right next to me, red-faced, huffing

like an old freight train. Hot air streams from her mouth, blowing the curtain, rattling and shaking the thin railing. I didn't know she could do that. Edward. I know she can hear me, so I just mouth the word. She stops blowing. The curtain stops moving. By the time the nurses, flustered, can pull it back, I'm standing below the window. Tempe done blown it shut. Even with it closed I can hear faint noises outside. A horn wailing. People chanting. Anger rising. With their backs to Edward, the nurses straighten their clothes, fix their hair, gather the charts.

"All finished, Mrs. Freeman," Bernadette says. She plasters a smile on her face. I ain't never seen two people in such a rush to get from a place.

"Tempe?" She's faint. I can just about see through her. Seems indecent being able to see sunlight streaming clear through her head. I don't turn away, though. She's huffing like she can't catch her breath. "You need something?"

Hurry up. There ain't that much time.

The pages flip through the years. Tempe ain't never had too much patience.

Chapter 11

March 11, 1855

Tempe pokes out her bottom lip, letting it droop while staring down at the bare wood floor as if she's lost something important but can't remember what she's lost.

"Like this, Mama?" she asks. She slowly raises her eyes. Her lips part innocently.

"Not quite, sugar." Mama shakes her head so even the shells in her hair clatter with exasperation. "Let me see you walk."

Tempe stomps across the floor with long, wide steps. She swooshes her imaginary layered skirts as her arms swing up, then down, then up in unison. It takes Mama a while to recognize the airs and when she does, she holds her hand to her chest and laughs with her mouth wide open. Mama has the most beautiful laugh in the world.

"You shouldn't poke fun at the Missus," I say. "She's sickly."

"It's not my fault. That's how she walks." Tempe scrunches her face up like she's trying to hold her laughter in her chest, but it bubbles out before she can stop it. She parades around our cooking/sleeping/visiting/sewing room. Her bare feet slap against the wood floor. She pretends to inspect and poke pots and pans, boxes and cases. "What's this? What do you call that?"

"She's just curious. You stop that. She don't mean no harm," Mama chides.

"Okay, how about this one?" Just like that, the Missus is gone. Tempe smooths her thick shift, two old dresses sewn together, and stands with her head up high. She unbinds her plaits, letting her hair fall around her ears in thick, chocolate curls. Licking her lips she raises her eyes level with Mama's before cocking her head to the side. Before Mama can stop her, she's sashaying across the room, long legs and hips slowly swaying with each step.

"Where'd you learn to walk that way?" Mama asks.

"From you. It's how you walk when you think no one's watching."

"Don't walk that way, people will stare."

"I don't walk that way, Mama, I walk like I got good sense," I say. Mama smiles, nods without looking at me.

"So?" Tempe puckers her lips in the nasty way the hired hands taught her.

Mama stares at Tempe's feet, slightly dusted as if they never touched the ground for long. I know she's looking at her golden brown calves and up to her thick waist. Mama's been fooling herself if she thought that scratchy yard frock hid Tempe's long arms and slender fingers. Maybe she ain't notice it till now. Eleven years old and Tempe's filling out. And if she's been around them hired hands long enough to pick up their ways, it's been long enough for them to recognize she ain't gonna be no little gal for long. Her body might be that of a woman, but it will be her eyes, wine colored in the light, or those lips, full and sculptured, that will ruin us all.

Tempe looks at the floor while Mama stares. She shifts her weight from one foot to the other then rocks back and forth while idly tugging at strings on her dress, fidgeting. At least she's got the good sense to look shy.

"Okay, how about this?" Tempe hunches her back as if she's carrying the Missus's packages, weighed down with gifts for this person or that but never for anyone else really. Her body looks heavy. Her walk is slow and clumsy and a bit unsure. Mama watches her walk the length of the cabin.

"Perfect, you look just perfect," Mama says.

"I can do it too, Mama. I can look ugly."

"Of course you can, Sister," Tempe says, "you don't have to try near as hard."

Mama grabs her bony arms and shakes her. Tempe's little head rattles and bobs like to fall right off. "Don't you ever say nothing like that again," Mama hisses. "Them words sound ugly coming out of your mouth. I ain't raisin' nobody to be mean to nobody else just because. Nary one of y'all are ugly on the outside and I won't let you be ugly on the inside neither."

What if Mama kills her? My sister will be buried around back with the bunny we tried to save last winter and the frogs from before that. Will Mama find the critters when she digs the little hole to dump Tempe in? Will she split her open like James say they used to do? With Tempe gone, will I have to do her chores? "She didn't mean it, Mama. She says stuff like that all the time and she don't mean none of it."

Mama pinches Tempe's arm. Tempe whimpers.

"There's plenty enough people to be nasty to my girls. I won't have one of you being mean to the other."

"Mama, Master's all the time saying how ugly she is—"

"—Don't you bring nothing that man says into this house."

"Master says it's his house—"

"Mama said don't go repeating anything Master said." I put my hands on my hips.

"Take your hands off your hips, you ain't grown," Mama says.

"Yeah, you ain't grown. Mama, Sister's got her fists balled up like she's gonna hit me again."

"Tempe, you lying! I ain't never hit you—"

"—Have never," Tempe says.

"See, she's lying!"

"Spring, Tempe, why don't both of you go out back and fetch something for supper?"

"Cuz ain't nothing out there," Tempe says.

"There's greens and radishes and onions and potatoes," I say. Mama's garden is almost better than Walker's.

"Ain't no ham, no thick pork chops, no plump roast." Tempe runs down the list from memory.

"Just pick something we do have," Mama says in her *don't push me* voice.

Tempe ain't but two steps behind me when we run out the door. She pushes past me when we get out on the small, rickety porch, leaving me to trail behind. I run round back and start pulling beans and potatoes and sprouts. My peach crate's almost full before I notice Tempe hasn't put a thing in hers.

"Mama's gonna get you if you don't start filling that crate."

"Why Agnes always get so mad anyway?" Tempe whispers.

Running around calling Mama by her given name. Least she's got sense enough to lower her voice. I keep picking.

"She's almost as bad as overseer," Tempe continues.

"How you even know? You ain't supposed to be out in the fields."

"Overseer ain't tied to the fields."

"Where you go that he go?"

"Sometimes I see him when I'm running errands to the house or out by the barn. I see most everybody on this place."

"Well, I've seen him too."

"Know what else I seen?"

"What, Tempe?"

She twirls and dances, tiptoeing her way through the rows of Mama's garden.

"Mama's gonna get you," I yell. But I know Mama won't. Tempe can dance up and down these rows without stepping on anything she don't want to. I put down my crate, pick hers up and start tossing in leaves and clumps.

"Meet me by the river, I'll tell you then."

"But Mama said—"

She's already gone.

She's naked as a bluebird when I catch up.

You'll die. The warning catches in my throat. How many times has Mama said to stay away from the river? Tempe slips in. I wait for her to come up. I watch the sun shining on the river skin. Leaves float on the surface. What if she dies? What will I tell Mama? Tempe jumped right in the river and it swallowed her up, just like you said it would. I tried to help. I look at my dress. It's my favorite. A few splashes of water won't hurt it none. Will she float up like a fish or get tangled in the weeds? Who will cut her out? Mama? James? I bet I'd have to do it. I look for something to cut the reeds. My hands will have to do. Lord, please let her rise to the top right here on the bank. Then I won't have to go in after her.

"Tempe!" I yell.

"Hush!" Her head breaks through the surface. "Sister, you sure are a worrying somebody." She laughs when I jump. "I wasn't gonna drown. I ain't the one 'fraid of the water." She bobs near the middle of the river.

"I ain't either."

"Then come in. Just a little. Just poke your little toe—"

"So what do you see?"

"Come closer and I'll tell you." She opens and closes her arms like a starfish. The river moves in little ripples with her. I know better but I go to the edge. She moves her mouth but I can't make out the words. I scoot closer to the edge. She's whispering so I have to lean over to hear.

"Up at the house they got so much food they can't even eat it all," she whispers. "Roasts, ham, chicken, taters, pies, fruits; and that's just for supper. Ivy sends plates piled this high with all sorts of juicy stuff and most times plates come back with food still on 'em. And no one can touch none of it till Missus say she had her fill and what's to be kept for when and who."

"If they got all that food, why are we hungry?"

"Cuz we black."

"Being black don't have nothing to do with being hungry."

"Master say we always want more than we need and it's up to him to make sure we don't get nothing we don't need."

"When he say all that?"

"When he was hitting Rose in the mouth," Tempe says.

"When was that?"

"I don't know, musta been the other day. I was waiting on Samantha to finish packing supper for the hands so she could get me the fabric to take round to the sewing shack and Rose was carrying trays stacked with plates and saucers and cups this high." She points to the sky. "When she went back with the after-supper coffee, Master said he smelled meat on her breath. Rose said she hadn't eaten any meat and maybe some spilled on her from cooking out back all day and Master said she was calling him a liar and Rose said she hadn't called him any such thing and Master got to screaming that she had called him a liar twice and he hit her, pop-pop, in the mouth." Tempe splashes water with each pop. "He told her don't take nothing without asking and no one said nothing about it after, but I hope Samantha said something cuz Rose didn't eat no food off no plate. I did."

"Tempe!" I yell.

Water covers her chin. It swallows her mouth, her nose and eyes—still open—and finally her head.

"Why do you keep your eyes open?" I ask.

Laughing again, Tempe jumps out of the river and twists into her shift. Now she lies with her wet hair on my back. I'm drenched. I don't move.

"You can't see 'em with your eyes closed," Tempe whispers.

"Can't see who?"

"The dead."

"Then how do you know they're down there?"

"I can just tell. You know that spot where the water goes ice cold for no reason? The sun will be hot as a skillet. Water almost boiling when you get in. You wade in deep. Just go where the water takes you. It's just you and the river pushing and pulling you where it wants you to go. You let yourself be; you just let the water do what the water's gonna do. You know?"

"What do you see?"

"Souls," Tempe answers.

"How do they look?"

"Mad. I'm hungry."

"Mama will make something good—"

"I know, but let's go up the house first."

At first I think she's talking about the old shack Mama lived in before, back when she was just Agnes. Even though Mama don't like it, Tempe and me play there all the time. The busted-up roof and sides 'bout to lean in make a cave. Just me and Tempe and them bundles of shells and stuff Mama don't think we know about. To Mama and them, it's a shack. To me and Tempe, it is home. But Tempe ain't talking about home. The House. I follow. I have to. Tempe runs down the trail through the woods and instead of going around the fields like we've been told a thousand times, she runs straight through one. It's harvest time but everybody's down the main field. Not a soul around for acres. The forbidden dirt feels softer. Even the air smells sweeter. We race. I would have won if I had known where we were going. If we were just running up to the house to slap the old girl like we usually did when there wasn't anybody around to tell Mama, I'd have won. I'm about to smack right on a smooth beam when Tempe runs toward the back. She's going to knock on the kitchen door! If she finds out we went knocking on the kitchen door begging Samantha for food, Mama will be madder than she was the time Tempe threatened to tell Walker on her if Mama hit her again. I don't want to see nothing like that again. I run around back to catch up.

"You'll get them in trouble if you go begging for food," I say. I'm out of breath. I hold my side and lean against the cellar door.

"I ain't asking them." She darts past the side to the front.

"Tempe!" I whisper but I know she can hear me.

The back door swings open. Rose stares at me.

"What you doing hollering back here?" Her rich voice is warm and deep.

I don't mean to but I smile.

Tempe reaches the front of the house. She skips up on to the large, white porch. By then Rose, Samantha, and me have reached the side. Tempe knocks on the door. The wind carries James's surprised voice and his attempts to shoo Tempe off the porch. Master Walker comes out. I can tell by the way she's standing, she wasn't expecting him to be home. Serves her right.

"Oh no," Samantha moans.

Instead of knocking her down like I expect, Walker stoops down to talk to her. Whatever he says, Tempe shakes her head no. He says something else. She shakes her head yes. A few minutes of headshaking and she's inside. The door shuts behind her.

It's almost dark before the back door opens.

Tempe ain't said nothing since she come out the back door cradling that hunk of ham between her hands.

"What's wrong with you?" I ask. Mama will kill me if something happened to her.

"Nothing."

"Something happen in there?"

"Nope."

"Somebody hurt you?"

"Nope."

"You ever gonna tell me what happened?"

"Nope."

She never does. Instead, she grabs my hand and we run through the woods till we get home. We let the door bounce against the frame behind us and tumble onto the floor. After pulling them from under the planks, we unwrap both bundles. Tempe rubs the stones against her face, kisses a smooth lump of hide, breathes deep. She splits the hunks of meat in two and puts one in each satchel *for later* before wrapping them back up.

"Why'd he give you that?" I ask.

"Did you know ain't no babies born here 'cept us for years and years and years? Not one. Not even Agnes."

"Mama will kill you if she hears you calling her that."

"That's what Master calls her."

I give her my *you know better than that* look. "Besides, Mama was born right here on Walker Farm."

"Was not."

"Was too. Lived right here with her ma and her pa since she was born."

Tempe's already shaking her head. "That ain't hardly true," she says. "Agnes lived here with a mama and a papa. Walker gave her to them. He's gonna give you and me babies one day too. In about a year when we older. Walker bought her when she was a baby. Bought plenty of babies too. Even bought one wasn't a baby."

She's staring at me like she's gonna be sick and throw words up all over the floor. Sweat starts beading up around my forehead then popping up under my arms. I'm holding my breath, waiting. "If he bought babies here, where they at?" I ask.

"Dead."

"All of them?"

"'Cept Agnes. Walker says the whole place was cursed. Wouldn't nothing hardly grow. Then Mama's folks died and the curse was lifted. I popped out and then running behind me, you. Walker says I'm a miracle."

"You?"

"He said you and me both. He meant me cuz I was first."

"Then why ain't no babies come after me?"

"Maybe you brought the curse back with you."

Later, when Tempe tells Mama, she leaves out the part about Walker buying her. She don't call her Agnes neither. Mama doesn't listen anyway, not after the part about giving me and Tempe babies. I want to ask her if I'm cursed. I don't, though. Even though I tell her I wasn't in the house Mama scrubs us both with every sliver of homemade soap she can find. When that's used up she uses lemon peels and tomatoes. She scrubs until my skin tingles. Then she says our insides need cleaning. We drink four jars each of "inner ointment." The smell of lemon and onion and the thick gooey tree sap is enough to make you sick but I don't dare drop a drip. Tempe lets a dollop fall to the ground and has to drink a whole other jar to replace it. I drink mine fast so I can't taste it. We do our business out back downwind from the house. By the time it runs through us, we're tired, sweaty, and empty. Our stomachs rumble when we finally lay on our thin bed of stuffed skins. Tempe shakes next to me. For months Mama makes me and Tempe drink that concoction. I drink mine every night. Tempe dumps hers in between the floorboard underneath her pallet. I watch her do it. As we get older, Mama adds a cream to rub between our legs, some herbs to put on our tongues. I do mine every morning. Tempe stands right there and watches me wiggle and squirm and pretend my insides ain't burning up. She watches and shakes her head. She don't wiggle or squirm except when Mama's watching. When Mama's there, Tempe dips her hand in the jar, rubs her fingers between her legs and then jumps and hollers like she's on fire. Mama stands there telling her it'll be okay like she believes it. She tells us the cream is like medicine. When Tempe says we ain't sick, Mama says you take it before you need it. Then come the herbs. Mama dips into a satchel and measures out a pinch each of bitter herbs. We ain't supposed to swallow them, just suck on them until it tingles. Tempe never gets it right. Because she's the oldest, Mama puts the herbs in her hand and lets Tempe slip them on her tongue. She don't do it, though. Soon as Mama turns to give me mine, Tempe slips hers into her pocket or scatters them on the floor. By the time Mama turns back, Tempe's pretending her mouth is on fire. Sometimes I make her wait. I hold them on my tongue until my eyes start to water and my throat burns. The juice burns going down. It's worth it, though. Mama smiles, relieved that her girls are safe. She gives us pressed blueberry syrup to drink after. The dosing becomes a routine, every morning before sunrise. Now that Mama stopped watching us do it, Tempe don't bother to pretend.

Chapter 12

August 17, 1857

"Why do we have to go, Mama?" Tempe asks. She sits cross-legged on the floor, stuck between Mama's legs. She squirms and yelps like Mama's killing her while she gets her hair plaited. A preacher's coming. Walker's taken to going to church and having preachers, reverends, and ministers for Sunday supper but this is the first one I will ever see. Walker sent down new dresses for the women and dungarees and shirts for the men.

We all got hats and headscarves and new shoes. He called for all the slaves, even them from the house, to worship.

"We're going to hear the word," I say. Mama done my hair earlier. I stand on the porch, careful not to lean on the new rail Mama built and careful not to dirty my new dress or sweat out my puffs.

"The preacher is going to talk to us about God," Mama says. She twists and pulls Tempe's thick hair. Tempe jumps. "Sit still."

"We already talked about God. What can he tell us that you don't know?"

"What's God look like?" I ask.

"Us," Mama says.

I picture God, his brown face and eyes lit up like stars. He's long-legged and tall, taller than any man I've ever seen, with arms as long as trees stretched wide enough to hold me, Mama, and Tempe too. He's standing there smiling, with a smile so bright it's like looking into the sun and he's waiting, just waiting. "Does God's Mama make him sit still while she pulls and yanks on his hair too?"

"Tempe!" Mama yells. She laughs. "Ask God yourself."

"I ask God a lot of things but he don't never answer," Tempe says.

It's hot. Including the hired hands, there are only fifteen or so of us here, but it's boiling. The preacher wants to hold the service in the barn. Even though it's warm as could be outside, he got the door shut and the shutters closed.

"Y'all ought to be thankful to Master Walker for allowing me to spread the Lord's Good Word to you lowly heathens," the preacher says. His face is pink and shiny. Even worse, he's a whisperer. We have to lean in close to hear him.

"What'd he say?" someone asks.

"He said we ought to be thankful to the Lord for heathens," someone else answers.

Darned hired hands mock everything. The way Tempe milks a cow, the way I walk, and now this. And on Sunday!

"That ain't what he said at all," one of them says. "He said we should be thankful heathens."

"I said—"

"Well, why's he yelling? Lord got him all enraptured already?"

"Praise Lord! Hallelujah!" Rose gets to singing.

"Amen, amen," someone says, "that was a right good sermon." The hands turn to go.

"We ain't finished!" The preacher's pink face goes red. "I'll say when it's time to go!" He fans himself with one of them wicker fans Rose uses to cool the Missus. "Now the Lord in his infinite wisdom has seen to it to give you all to Master Walker for his care. The burden of responsibility is lifted and all you have to do now is serve your Master on Earth and serve your Master in Heaven and—"

"What he say?"

"Repeat after me," the preacher says. He wipes his face. "Y'all are heathens sent to pay for the sins of your father."

"Y'all heathens sent to pay for the sins of your father," the hands repeat.

"No! Say I'm a heathen damned to—"

"What he say?"

"He's damned! He's damned!"

"Oh Lord Jesus, save us, save us, Lord! He's damned!"

"I'm not damned, you all are damned!"

Don't seem to be nothing he can do. Them hands hightail it out of there like the barn's on fire. Door not even shut good and I can hear them laughing out there in the cool air. It's just Mama, James, Rose, Samantha, Tempe, and me left.

"You sent here to save us?" James asks.

The preacher looks relieved. He taps on his Bible and straightens the brim on his hat. "I am here to save you, with the word!" His voice bellows. I jump. "That's right, heathen," his eyes burn into mine. "God knows you evil. He gave you the mark of the devil."

I look at Mama. If he's right, I ain't the only one cursed.

"It's your skin, your skin!" he yells. He waves his Bible

frantically. "The mark of the curse is the black of your skin. God made you in the devil's image."

"Have you seen God?" Tempe asks. She steps closer. "Everyone knows what God looks like." The preacher waves her back with his hand. "He looks like me and like Master Walker and—"

"You and Master Walker don't look nothing alike. How your God look like you and him both?"

He paces the length of his imaginary pulpit. "It isn't my God and your God. There's only one God. God has seen fit to yoke your people with the chains of slavery and it's your job to uphold those chains until God sets you free."

"Freedom? God's going to set us free? Hallelujah!" James says. Tears stream down his face.

"When you die," the preacher raises his voice, "you will shake off the chains of slavery and serve your new Master in Heaven."

"According to that book you got there, I'm called to hold the chains up and you called to lay them on?" James asks.

"That's one way to look at it," the preacher says. His head bobs up and down. "Escaping your obligation to the Lord is a sin. If you were to cast off your chains without God or Master Walker setting you free, you'd go straight to Hell and live a life of eternal damnation."

"What's Hell like exactly?" Mama asks.

"It's fiery hot with no cool water to drink or cool grass for shade. Nonstop work. The devil's work is never done from sunup to sundown. Nonstop pain too; whipping and harsh words. The burden is never lifted. And if your family isn't there with you, but then, you wouldn't want your family there with you, would you? Well, if they aren't then it's you all alone with no one to love you. Can you imagine? Being separated from your loved ones for eternity?"

Samantha, Rose, Mama, and James look at each other.

Preacher must feel it. Anger. Blood rushes in my ears.

"How about a song?" the preacher suggests. He starts to hum a fidgety tune as he edges closer to the barn door.

Samantha picks up the tune and adds a melody. I still don't know the words but the rest of us join in.

"Amen, amen," the preacher murmurs as he ushers us out.

"I don't believe in your old made-up book," Tempe whispers on the way out.

The preacher grabs her by the shoulder and lifts her off the floor.

"She don't mean that," Mama says.

Tempe reaches out her hand to Mama. Mama don't move. "What you mean, child?" the preacher asks.

"I don't believe no God would make one group to be better than another and expect them not to do nothing about it."

"You are an ignorant little thing, aren't you? Your Mama believe it, don't you, gal?"

"Yes sir, I believe there are words in that book that I never will understand."

"And you believe youse all put on this Earth to serve white people, don't you?" Preacher asks.

"We all believe it, Master," James interrupts.

Samantha and Rose stand close to the preacher. Fiddling with tools, the nearby hands watch.

"You gonna lay hands on us all, sir? So we all get saved?" Samantha asks.

The preacher stares down at his hand and at Tempe fastened to it. He drops her. Mama scoops her up, walks away. The preacher looks at me. "You know that little gal is going to Hell and if you don't watch it you'll go right along with her," he says.

I run to catch up with Mama and them.

"Mama, is Tempe really going to Hell?" I ask that night. It's so hot we're all sleeping out back right in the summer grass.

"For what, angel?"

"For not believing we damned."

"Don't you go mistaking anything that preacher says for the truth," Mama says.

"Will I go, then? Since I'm cursed?"

"What kind of curse you got?"

"Don't know. Why weren't there no babies born here after me?"

Mama don't answer.

Chapter 13

September 23, 1862

It's early. The day hasn't even started and we're already preparing supper. It's like this every Dehaunting. The whole plantation is up hours before dawn preparing for the evening's celebration. It's the one day Walker allows us to do nothing at all. If only Mama would allow the same. Just like they been doing every year since we been born, Samantha and Rose have probably been up all night baking pies and cakes. James is off readying the new slaves, though there ain't but two of them and they been here for years. The three of us sit on the porch gathered around two baskets: one brimming with green beans, the other with a smattering of tips. If Tempe did her share, we'd be finished before now. It seems like we've been snapping beans for days.

"Tempe, you and Spring keep the little ones out of trouble," Mama says.

Like this year would be any different than the year before. Seems like Tempe and me do an awful lot of work for a day celebrating us being born and lifting the curse. Please Lord, don't let Tempe start complaining.

"What you think gonna happen to us when Walker dies?" Tempe asks instead of shucking.

"Hush, don't talk like that."

Mama don't like talking about the dead.

"He's bound to die one day," Tempe says anyway. "It ain't natural for nobody to live forever. Even white folks face their maker." Tempe crosses her arms.

"You think Walker Senior's in Heaven serving the Lord, Mama?" I ask.

I picture angels with fluffy wings and a smiling God surrounded by shiny faces filling goblets and emptying chamber pots and scrubbing those golden floors and polishing those iron gates. Angels dripping rivers of sweat with their sweat-soaked angel wings: perspiring for the Lord. This time, instead of picturing them white, I picture black faces staring up at God. When my eyes blur from not blinking I see a God with a face as brown as mine staring back.

Mama looks down. "It ain't likely." She wipes her hands on a scrap of newspaper.

It leaves streaks of black, like words, on her palms. The paper was worn before we got it. Between chores, the hired hands give scraps to me and Tempe. Presents with pretty squiggles from all over the world. News they been saving or thinking on, traveling with. Most of them can't read neither but the stories they tell! Get them filled up on some of Mama's good supper and they get to "reading." This here say so and so did such and such, one will start up and get to saying who done what. That ain't the whole truth. Let me tell you what really happened, another will say. That's my favorite part. I could listen for hours. We not supposed to but me and Tempe find reasons to be around the men. Mama don't seem to trust them but since Samantha's getting on in age, we bring supper, wait for jugs and jars, wash 'em and carry 'em back to the house. Mama can't find cause to complain in that. Of course, she still do.

"Don't trust them papers any more than I trust them hands," she says. She rips one in half and throws it to the floor. "Lies and liars." Tempe rescues what she can. What she can't save lays scattered like a rug beneath Mama. Mama slides her bare feet along smudged pages. I wonder if she has the words *Freedom* and *Emancipation* rubbed into her soles. I know better than to check.

"What if you wrong, Mama?" Tempe asks for the hundredth time. "What if freedom is coming this time?"

"According to them papers," I say, "freedom comes every few years and then it don't. Don't see how this time is any different than the last." I sound just like Mama.

Even if I can't read her lips, the look in Tempe's eyes hushes me.

"When the families get here, go off and take care of the kids," Mama says.

Seem like Mama don't want to be around them children any more than I do. The celebration always seems to make her sad. I pinch the ends of each long, green bean, one at a time: plink, plink, plunk into the slowly filling tub. Just last week me and Tempe had been young enough to play Gotcha; a few days ago we were too old to roughhouse like that and now we're too young to listen to grown folks' talk. We grown older and younger in the same week.

"I don't mind, Mama," I say. A trail of heat rises from the middle of my chest to the top of my head. Tempe's stare can take the hot out of fire. I concentrate on snapping beans and the soft plunk each one makes as it glides slowly to the pile.

"I suppose that means you don't mind either, do you, Tempe?"

Plink, plink, plop; plink, plink, plop; head, feet, spine; head, feet, spine; Tempe snips the head off of each thin string bean, two at a time like each one has my name on it. "No, ma'am, I don't mind. Just seems like you could use a hand around here. Dehaunting Day always seems to make you sad. Don't you wanna remember the day me and Sister was born?"

Even though James told us don't never bring it up, I know Tempe's about to ask.

"Two little slave babies. Ain't we the best thing that ever happened to you?" she asks.

The look on Mama's face scares me for just a second. Her forehead wrinkles, her eyes darken. She's Agnes. Young and hurt and angry. Agnes stares at us from behind Mama's eyes. She don't come out often. Only when Mama's real scared or mad or when we talk about her mama, the babies in the backyard, or the list of things Samantha and James told us not to talk about. Me and Tempe both run to her. We wrap her in our arms, pet her hair, shush her crying. We rock and wait. There's nothing else we can do.

The smell of neckbones and simmering beans fills the air about the same time as the families arrive. Every Dehaunting Day slaves from as far as Sampson's place travel to Walker's for the festivities. It's like the whole world's celebrating me and Tempe. Soon as they drop off their passes at the house and get counted, women in colorful dresses made of cloth, sacks, hand-me-downs, and scraps of other garments; men in pressed shirts, dungarees, and boots if they have them; and children with scrubbed faces arrive laden with offerings of meats, vegetables, drink, sweets, and news. This is the last of the large gatherings. Will Watson come? I wonder.

Today, women rush out back to the cooking pot with meat in need of a few more minutes over the fire, collards almost done, and biscuits that are near ready. Jars and jugs of tea are placed on chips of ice, a gift from Walker, to chill before supper.

"It never fails," Too-Wide John remarks after being told where to put this, where to prop that, and then sent, with a kiss on the forehead, to the small porch to help the men set up the crates for the food. "This time every year Glenda Mae gets up first thing and you know what she does?"

"What's she do, John?" Samuel asks.

"She starts cooking!"

"Noo!" A deep chorus of male voices grumble in practiced disbelief.

"I ain't lying. She cooks. In between boiling and stirring and skinning, she scrubs them kids and shuts 'em up in the shack and when I come home with a fat possum for dinner you know what she says?"

"I don't hear no crates scraping," Ms. Glenda Mae calls from inside.

"I ain't lying. On the one day I get to sleep late, she gets me up before the sun is good and set in the sky and she says go get some more meat for supper. Like that, like it's easy. Like I can just walk down the road a piece with a sack and say excuse me, Mr. Possum, would you mind jumping into this here sack? Celebration or not, you know Sampson don't allow no slave to go that far without no pass anyhow and I swear those possums know just how far I can go cuz more than one leaped right cross the road and just sat and sort of looked at me: daring me to cross that road and scoop him up."

The loud clanging of pots and clinking of pans does little to stifle the men's laughter.

"Well, I fixed this here possum." John pauses, looking into the eyes of each member of his audience: the men lining up crates before covering them with cloth to make a long family table and the children barely off the porch about to light off to play in the woods. He points to the meat still steaming in the serving tin. "This possum ran right across the road in front of Old Johnson's buggy. Without so much as a warning, Johnson's boy veered a bit to the right, clipped the ol' possum, straightened up the reins, tipped his head in my direction and off he rode, horses, buggy, and all. I scooped the fat possum up and here he is."

The men applaud John's hunting skills. I laugh along with the children. The women moan. Tempe watches in silence.

"When I come home with this fat possum, you know what she says?"

"You got them crates ready?" Glenda Mae asks.

"That ain't what she says," John whispers loud enough for the ladies inside to hear. "She says, 'Hurry up and get cleaned up.' Now I ask you," John pauses to pull a splintered crate into place next to a lopsided box: "Is that a fine thank-you?"

"I think I can do you one better," Carter says with a laugh. "My woman gets up Sunday mornings and she bangs and clangs empty pots loud enough to wake the dead. When I'm up you know what she says?"

"What?"

"Did I wake you?"

"Empty?" a man asks.

"Empty," Carter confirms with a slow nod and a slow smile.

"I know they're empty cuz she gets me to drag each one round the side and pump 'em full of spring water. Then she dumps whole children—with their clothes still on—in the pots. She scrubs and scrubs till they're all wrinkled. Then she sews fasteners and darns socks, she starches long underwear and presses sacks. While this is going on, bread's rising and pies are cooling on the sill. When it's all done you know what she says?"

"What?" one of the children asks.

"Hurry up and sit down so the Lord don't catch us working. The Lord didn't see me pulling them tubs round the back and emptying them and filling them up again?"

"The Lord don't see plenty if you ask me," Tempe says.

"You children go run and play," Mama calls from the doorway.

Quickly, we gather the seven children and lead them across the yard to the edge of the garden. Most of them are Sampson's, some are from closer, some farther. We only have a few hours before sunset: before they all have to be back and counted. The sun is too bright. It's too hot for running games but running games keep little hands clean.

"What makes you the boss?" Franklin asks. He's about as tall and thick as Old Oak, the oldest tree on Walker land. That don't stop Tempe.

"You on my place, you bide by my rules."

"Last I checked this place and all y'all belong to Walker," Franklin says. He spreads his lips in what he thinks is a smile.

"Brother's right there," Buddy says between spits. He's taken to chewing on sweetgrass to make his breath sweet—just in case. He leans close to Tempe. "No cause to play children's games when you and me can go round yonder and play something"—he spits and leans in closer—"more becoming. Ain't that right, Sister."

What's Watson been telling him? "I ain't your sister," I say. "Only Tempe can call me that."

"What would I want to lay with you for when I can lay with Franklin here?" Tempe asks. "He's the smart one between the two of you. How many brothers and sisters y'all have now?"

"Four," Franklin answers. "Our mama has the widest birthing hips on Master's land. Pa says all Master has to do is say, 'Dessa, I need another pair of hands,' and Mama obliges."

"She sounds right fertile," Tempe says. She twists her lips and wiggles her hips.

"Ever since that old witch died, seem like everybody fertile, 'cept your mama," Buddy says.

Tempe balls up her fists.

"According to Mama," Franklin says, "your mama's mama made it so wouldn't no children grow anywhere around here."

"You a damned fool," I say. "If that was true, Tempe and me wouldn't be standing here, would we?"

"Maybe you one of them ghost babies too," Buddy says.

I'm not sure which is the bigger fool: Buddy or his brother.

"I guess you still saving yourself for your Master," Franklin says. "Ain't he gonna get you with child this year?"

Franklin. He's the bigger fool.

"You be careful," his brother says. "She'll put something on you that you won't be able to get off."

"You want to call me something?" Tempe asks. She steps closer to Franklin.

He moves back. "Nah, we all know you and your sister witches. Just like your mama."

Tempe springs. She wraps her legs around his chest and her arms around his neck.

"I knew you were my kind of gal," Franklin laughs. His laugh turns to coughing, then to heaving.

"She killing him!" someone screams.

"Franklin, leave that little gal alone!" his father yells from around front.

"But, Pa—" Buddy says.

"Don't make me …" The shuffling of crates finishes the sentence for him.

Tempe turns Franklin loose. Watson squeezes into the space between them. I'm not sure if he's protecting Tempe or Franklin.

"They don't mean nothing by it," he says. "You alright?"

That voice. I get to licking my lips imagining his salty skin on my tongue, picturing his hands along my back, his fingers tracing the curve of my neck. His lips, soft against mine. With his skilled hands and sharp mind, he's on Walker land more often than not. He belongs to the Kirks. Some nights, he belongs to me. If he sees half the money he makes from being hired out, he should be able to buy me in no time. His smooth hands rub Tempe's back. He leans his head so close to hers that his lips graze her ear.

"She'll be fine if you quit breathing on her," I say. My throat is tight. The words squeeze up and push out my mouth.

"You should take you a woman," Franklin says.

"Got one," Watson answers.

My heart stops. I'm licking my lips again.

"What's the matter with you? You got something?" Tempe asks.

Buddy, Franklin, and even Watson laugh.

"What you think about this talk about freedom coming?" I ask everybody except for Watson. Laugh at me? It'll be a long time before he gets to lie in the grass with me again.

Something like hate flashes across Watson's face. "I don't reckon I believe it until it gets here."

"Pa says if it comes down to a fight, he's ready to join the soldiers to set us all free," Buddy whispers.

"Ma don't want him to do it. She says he'll end up dead if he runs off," Franklin says.

"I'd rather be dead any day," Watson says.

If I had seen it, the light in his eyes, I would have been ready.

Only the porch is base. It has to be. Anyone fool enough to bound up the creaking wooden step, hop one-legged down the sagging porch, run around the shaky dinner table made up of splintering crates, and risk toppling tin plates and wooden bowls while yelling "Sanctuary" and skirting around a ring full of women who had spent hours baking, dusting, cleaning, and boiling, and now only wanted a minute to relax without someone underfoot deserves to be free from being tagged. Fair is fair.

"You know the rules," Tempe announces, "no hiding in the water."

"No hiding near the water," I add.

"No getting dirty," Tempe says.

"No getting anyone else dirty."

"No loud yelling."

"No roughhousing."

"What can we do?" Watson, always grinning, asks.

"Boy, with all those teeth in your mouth at one time, how do you have room for questions?" Tempe teases.

Watson flinches.

"Tempe's going to count to a hundred. You all run and hide. We'll find you," I say.

"What if you don't find us before supper?" Little Ivy asks.

"You won't eat," Tempe answers.

"We'll find you and if not, I won't eat until we do." I smooth the sprinkling of tears off Ivy's cheek.

"And if you reach Sanctuary," Tempe pauses, winding her arms in wide flourishing circles while I point to the porch, "you win."

"Has anyone ever reached Sanctuary?" Watson asks.

Tempe and I think it over. "Nope."

I close my eyes and hold a finger up as Tempe counts. "One ... two ... three ..."

The heavy padding of careless feet gives the little ones away. One hides in a nearby tree. One scampers to the edge of the wood, turns, and burrows beneath the canopy. Two hide in tall grass on the side of the house. One heavy-footed one, probably Franklin, stomps behind the house. Another one hides underneath a tin washtub. One shifts one foot to the other. There's always a runner.

Please just go hide behind the house. I'm sweaty and the thought of chasing one of 'em makes me hotter.

"What do you think they talk about in there?" Tempe asks somewhere between twenty-five and twenty-nine.

"Men."

"Why would they do that?"

"Well, you heard the men, they just talk about the women." I've been practicing my grown-up voice.

"The men only talk about the women when they want the women to know what they're talking about."

"How do you know that?"

"I've heard what men talk about when women ain't around."

"Are y'all even counting?" a little voice asks from behind the washbasin.

"Sixty-five!" Tempe yells.

Giggles, swishing grass, the curling and uncurling of little legs in tight places, and then silence: the silence of little children waiting for something good and terrible all at once. *Gotcha* makes little hearts beat faster.

"Well, what do they talk about?" I ask.

"Sex."

"Told ya."

"And politics and religion and war and freedom."

"All that?"

"And more when they get riled up."

"Is that what you do at night? Go down and listen to the hired hands talk?"

"Sometimes."

The words fall out and I can't do nothing to get them back. Tempe looks down when she answers. Tempe can't hold her lies any more than Old Missus can hold her liquor. Flash of brown skin and dingy denim.

"Ready or not, here we come!" Tempe shouts.

Watson, long brown legs and thin bony arms flailing, is already halfway to the porch. He's panting and sweating. His chest pumps hard. I just watch it, glistening.

Run.

Tempe's long, shapely legs carry her to within inches of Watson. It don't look like she's hardly breathing. She cuts through the yard with hardly no effort at all. It don't seem fair. Tempe can catch him anytime she wants. She knows the land and made the rules.

"Gotcha, gotcha, gotcha." I tap each little head quickly, dashing from one to the next so I can turn back to the race. There are no tears this time. The little hearts race along with Watson's.

Run.

Watson is just a few strides ahead of Tempe. If she leans forward just a little more she'll have him. If not, he'll reach the porch, Sanctuary, seconds before her. He slows, and even from the back of his head I know he's grinning. He zags sharply. You're running the wrong way! I can't get the words out fast enough. But then I see. He isn't running the wrong way at all.

The women must have heard the commotion. Armed with broomsticks they take to the porch in synchronized annoyance. They stand guard. Around back, the men have already stopped talking about the war, escape, and freedom. They're out front, gruff voices whispering: Run.

Tempe must have seen it then. We all do. Watson isn't running for the porch. Tempe stops. She stands still whispering: Run, run, run, along with everybody else. Watson never stops running. I wish he had taken me with him.

5:07 p.m.

"What do you mean you changed your mind?" Jacob asks.

The sound is a low whisper. Only, Jacob ain't here. His voice, his words, echo throughout the room. They come from Tempe's lips, the mouths of the patients otherwise asleep, from my own. "These men ain't playing. Don't you know they'll kill us?"

I hold my hand over my mouth but can't stop the words, the anger, the fear from tumbling out.

Jacob is everywhere. His heart races inside my chest. It vibrates within the walls, the floor, the beds. The patients sit up, stare forward with blank eyes. I turn to Edward. He's gone. Instead of lying in bed, Edward is at a workbench tinkering with a rusted tangle of metal. He is surrounded by cracked crates, busted boxes, soulless springs. The graveyard. We're in Edward's corner of the Yard. The place where he is expected to wring one more ride out of useless parts. His workshop. Drops of oil stain the floorboards. The space, cramped and dark, is otherwise tidy.

"What do you know about these people?" Edward asks.

"I know enough to know they do what they say they'll do," Jacob says.

"How do you know they won't kill us either way?"

"They honor words, Edward. You got to do it."

"The way I see it, hand me that," Edward points to a hammer, "these men don't have nothing to lose." The banging is melodic. The sound is musical, precise. The part slowly straightens under Edward's hands. "They don't have a stake in it. That bothers me."

"All they want is fair pay."

"For them."

"For us. After they get theirs, we get ours." Jacob scatters rusted nails on the bench.

"That's not right. If we all fight the same war, we should all win at the same time."

"What's right got to do with it? When do things work that way?"

Edward positions each of the nails along the metal. He carefully hammers them into place. When it's ready, Jacob takes the piece and sands it down. As they whisper, the rust disappears.

"Why do they need us? They drive the cars. All we do is clean them and fix them."

"We inside. Company's firing folks for even talking about wanting more money let alone striking."

"So all this, sabotaging the parts, is about them being mad because they can't do what they want to do?"

"Right."

"I want to be a driver."

"Man, you know you can't do that. The company don't allow no Negro to steer no streetcar."

"They know it too. Are they mad about that?"

"Man, one thing at a time."

"They want me to fight their fight. Put in faulty parts so a streetcar loses control, to show the company they need to rehire the workers and pay them more, but not one of them wants to be the one to do it."

"They'd be the first suspects. The company won't hire them to fix something they broke."

"And they don't want to fight my fight."

"It's not just your fight. It's ours, yours and mine. We fight together."

"I don't want to do it," Edward says. "I don't want to hurt innocent people for money."

"You ain't doing it for money."

"Now they aren't even going to pay us?"

"What difference does that make? You ain't doing it for money no how. You doing it for the principle. Right?"

"Right," Edward says.

"Principles have to eat," Jacob says. "They can't pay us right now. It would be suspicious. You and me walking around in new clothes, new shoes. Your mama, and Lord knows she can't keep no secret, in new dresses, store-bought hats. Wouldn't take long for two and two to equal four. What looked like an accident would look mighty intentional."

"Then let them do it. Let them kill one another."

"Nobody is going to die. We replace parts we already mended with broke-up parts. That's it. It's the 4:38 car. Nobody will be on it but the driver and conductor. Soon as they get the signal, they'll jump off. The car will just bump into a curb and stop on its own. Any investigation will prove what we already know. Gum don't hold nothing together for long. The company has to pay skilled drivers fair wages."

"They came up with this all on their own? And you agreed."

"That's why we gotta do it. If we don't they gonna say we did it. First thing out of their mouths will be we sabotaged the parts. We'll get hung."

"And if we sabotage the parts—"

"—We live."

"What kind of life is that?"

Sparks of metal and coal light the sky. We are out back. Jacob hands Edward a set of tongs. Edward heats the metal until it drips. Together, the two add chunks and scraps of metal. They work silently, breathing new life into unused things.

Chapter 14

Things ain't been the same since Dehaunting Day. The day ended well enough. The visitors ate, sang, celebrated. They knew it would take another miracle for them to step foot on Walker land and didn't know what it would take for any of us to get off it. When the celebrating was over, they gathered their belongings and hugged Mama and us tight. The men went to the back door to gather the passes and be counted. According to James, between men coming up twice and women sending kids up that ain't never been counted, some of them was counted two and three times. Wasn't until Master Kirk come back late that night talking about you one short, that they noticed Watson was gone. Dogs been barking for three days straight.

"Don't let on you sweet on him," Mama says.

"What you mean, sweet on him?" I ask.

I ain't never told nobody about Watson and me. I'm promised to him and nobody, including him, seem to know. Mama just looks at me and I know she knows exactly how I feel. She holds me. She smells like cinnamon, lilac, hyacinth, and jasmine. I breathe her in.

"I tried to tell you, you should be getting to know one of them hands," Tempe says, "least they free."

I wait for Mama to tell her it don't make no difference what he do as long as he can take care of me.

"Loving a slave is hard work," is all she says.

It seems like everything changes when Watson runs off. Walker starts sending for me or Tempe to come up to the house. Don't matter which one he sends for, Mama sends us both. Whether we're scrubbing floorboards, beating rugs, soaking drapes, or darning socks, it seems like he ain't never too far off. Watching. Since Old Missus passed, Missus been visiting with her sister up north. She took Ivy with her. The more she's away, the more Walker want me or Tempe around. As long as she can help it, Mama don't let that happen. When she can, she goes in our place. The more Walker send for us, the more Mama sends us down to help the hired hands instead. She says we need to learn a skill so we can make money. She works it out so we make little trinkets and the hired hands sell them for us in town.

The first time I get a silver coin I about die. Tempe and I add it to our collection: newspaper clippings, teeth, feathers, shells, and then coins of all shapes and colors. We need to find someplace to keep our treasures. The bundles are fraying. There's no telling how long they'll keep. Since we've been doing more around the place, Mama lets Tempe and me sleep in the tiny shack by the river. The floorboards underneath start to sink in but we don't mind. The dirt's a good hiding place until the river coughs it up.

It's been raining for weeks. The fields are flooding. The cabins are flooding. Even Walker House is flooding. Walker's got hands from three towns helping the slaves pick soggy berries, bloated cabbages, and anything worth saving. Even Old James and Old Samantha are out there slipping in mud, wrestling with limp branches. The whole place is underwater. Can't walk from one side to the next without being knee deep in it. That's why I don't notice the river swelling and spilling. It bleeds clear over the bank. It flows and flows like ain't no stopping it. Swallows the shack, the path. The river, the rain, or both, fills up the ditch all the way on the other side of Walker. We collect bones and bundles long after the river seeps back and the mud dries. We make up stories for each one. Each piece is remembered. Out of sweet cherrywood, we carve our very own book. The hands bring us paper. We stitch them together. Stuff the newspapers, like bookmarks, in between. Though neither one of us can read or write, each page holds a story. We remember.

Thanks to the flooding, Walker hires hands to help fix the place up while me and Tempe seem to be doing twice as much. They don't seem to be helping much. At least, not at first.

"Edward?" Buddy clears his throat, raises his voice and calls up to his friend's sweating back. "Seems to me you done developed one of them afflictions," he says. He wipes the sweat from his eyes with the back of one hand and holds the thick rope with the other. He lowers his voice. "What you think, Brother?"

"'Bout what?" Franklin asks.

I know he knows just what Buddy's talking about cuz I know it too and I'm clear on the other side of the barn. Without looking up, Franklin bundles four planks of wood together, ties the thick rope around them and tugs. On his signal, Buddy pulls the rope to send the pile up to Edward. I sure wish Tempe would hurry up. All she has to do is bring supper from the house. I've been sweeping and piling, lugging and listening to them speculate on which one Edward should take for his wife.

"Seem like Edward done caught something from round here," Buddy continues.

Every time we get there with supper, Buddy and Franklin get to teasing Edward about being sweet on Tempe.

"Don't think it's catching, do ya?" Franklin glances at his friend and back to his brother. "I don't want nothing from here I can't give back."

Edward unties the planks, halves two-by-fours, and gets to knocking them together.

"You might like what he done caught." Buddy unrigs the rope and throws it into a wheelbarrow stuffed with nails, debris, and rags. "'Cept it seem to make whoever catch it clumsier than a mule in a cane field."

"That don't make no kind of sense," Edward calls down.

"Can't seem to keep a shirt on neither," Buddy continues.

"Always walking around bare-chested. It must be something fierce. Soon's he step one foot on Walker land that shirt must get to itching and scratching cuz seem like he get to ripping it off, buttons popping everywhere."

"Too much starch probably," Franklin says. "Not saying nothing 'bout your mama, Edward."

"If you ask me," Buddy continues, "whatever he caught he got right here. Seems like the same thing you was trying to catch not too long ago, Brother."

"Don't seem likely," Franklin replies. "Although now that you mention it, he has been a mite bit clumsy. Wasn't you trying to catch the very same thing then too? That's how I remember it. Edward, don't you go bustin' up nothing up there again." Franklin runs inside the drafty barn and hoists himself up the repaired ladder.

"He break anything yet?"

"Nah, just fumbling with an old rickety piece of something he done made to look 'bout to fall apart, I swear before God."

"It ain't finished yet," Edward says. "I'm planning."

"Your planning got us mending and remending the same drafty holes for near two months since you been here," Buddy yells up. "Done seen more fixed up, broke, and fixed again now than ever before. New roof, near about, new hatch, new beams, and a window with a ledge for mice."

"It's for birds, for watching and feeding birds," Edward interrupts.

"Walker don't seem like the bird-feeding type, you ask me," Franklin says. "From here you can see clear cross the fields to the house. Man like Walker might like to come up here time and again to see what his people get up to. And what's that? You done made him a little bed for—" he stops.

The air in the barn seems to pop. I don't hear Edward's answer and I don't need to.

I been sweeping the same spot for the past hour. Still clutching the broom, I run to beneath the ladder. Mama will kill me if I go up there by myself. "Y'all need a broom up there?" I call. Thankfully, they laugh.

"How long you hired here for?" Buddy asks.

Edward has more talent than anyone, white or black, this side of the Chesapeake. Master said it at least a hundred times. Since he's been here he's patched and fixed the slave cabins, plugged leaks, patched walls, stained floors, and rebuilt the barn from the beams up. Don't seem to be anything that man can't do, except talk to Tempe.

"Till the work run out," he says.

"Sampson hired us out for two seasons before we go on home," Franklin says.

"I hire my own self out," Edward answers. "I says what I can do and what I can't and someone like Walker says what they can pay and what they can't and we strike up a sort of deal."

"And he pay you your money just like that?" Buddy's thick fingers snap.

"Don't usually have no trouble 'bout getting paid. I heard 'bout some workers doing all sorts of work and when it comes time to get paid, the person say they ain't gonna pay 'em."

"I do believe Sampson would kill Walker if he don't pay."

"Ain't that easy. I ain't got no Sampson or such. I'm free. I'm my own man. I can say I done the work. White man say 'I ain't gonna pay.' What can I do? If I take down all I put up the sheriff come around saying I destroyed something wasn't mine. I can't hardly take him to court. Alls I can do is wish real hard that something bad happen to him."

"That work? Cuz it don't work for me," Buddy says.

"I didn't say it works; just said that's all I can do. I can get mad but don't nobody care 'bout me getting mad. I got myself real good at a whole lot of things. Ain't much I can't do. People think twice before not paying me. Never know when they need me for something else."

"What you gonna do when the work dry up here? Sooner or later Walker's gonna realize on account of you he got more things that need doing than that's getting fixed," Buddy says.

"I been thinking on that."

"He ain't never gonna let Tempe go. It ain't his way. I can't think of no one that left this place that didn't leave dead or end up that way."

He can't be talking about my Watson. Buddy's just trying to rile me up.

"Maybe for enough money he'd have to," Edward says. Edward buy Tempe? What about me and Mama?

"You know it don't work like that," Franklin says. "How long did it take you to buy yourself free?"

"A long, long time. You planning on buying you and your brother free?"

"Don't know. Don't see no difference in the way they treat you and the way they treat me."

For a few minutes, alls I can hear is scraping. "Who this belong to?" Edward asks.

"It's yourn," Buddy says. "You made it."

"Right, that's being free. Buy your freedom. Don't matter how long it takes to get it."

A little something comes falling down. I snatch it up. Two strands of straw knotted together and braided into a tight ring. I slip it onto my finger. Finally, Tempe comes trudging in dripping a bucket of water and carrying a satchel around her chest. She smells of cornbread and Mama's greens. I slip the ring into my pocket.

"Y'all gonna have to come down if you want to eat!" Tempe yells.

The men scramble to their feet. Edward swears as he bumps into the ladder and nearly topples down.

"There's plenty to eat, no rush," Tempe says. "Mama made enough for all y'all." She nods her head toward the ladder as Buddy and Franklin make their way down.

"Tempe," they mumble.

"Boys."

Edward grunts and lifts the water bucket from her hands. He peers inside. I wait for him to ask where the rest of the water gone. He don't. He nods his head at Tempe, dips the drinking spoon in the bucket and drinks. Water slides down his chin. Tempe takes a long time deciding where to unwrap the satchel of food Mama sent.

"Why don't you take it upstairs?" Buddy suggests.

"Go on up there first," she says.

"Gal, ain't nothing up there gonna bite you," Franklin says.

"If it do I bet you I'll—"

"What you gonna do, Little Bit?" Buddy interrupts.

"I'll be sure to tell my mama you don't want none of her buttered biscuits, collard greens and neckbones, or fried chicken gizzards to cross your lips." Tempe snatches the bundle and turns to go.

"I didn't say that," Buddy says. He reaches for the kerchief as if he don't know better.

Tempe's thin foot shoots out and catches him in the knee. "Don't you put your dirty hands on nothing I got. I done told you that long time ago."

"And I done told you," Buddy begins. He lowers his eyes and steps toward Tempe. Franklin rushes from behind. I stand in between the two; both panting and staring holes through me. "I wouldn't say no to whatever you got in that bundle, Ms. Tempe," Edward says. His soft voice makes both Buddy and Tempe jump. He edges my body out of the way and stands in front of Tempe, his back to Buddy. "Can I carry that up to the loft for you?"

"I got it." The words barely push through Tempe's clenched lips.

"I can see that, ma'am, just wanting to help. I wouldn't want to miss none of your mama's cooking, good as it is." He licks his lips.

"I helped," Tempe lies.

The smell of supper trails behind her as she nears the steps. She hands the bundle to Edward before climbing the ladder. Edward, Buddy, and Franklin follow her upstairs. I count to five, waiting on her to get down like she got some sense. What's she doing up there with three grown men? Even if two are almost like brothers, they're grown men now. Heavy footsteps stomp above my head. Tempe's light feet flitter across the loft followed by her coos of delight as if the whole thing has been done up just for her. I sit on the bottom rung of the ladder, swirling my dirty finger in the water bucket. The ice had melted long ago. Fat drops of rain hit the dust outside the open barn door. Even with Buddy and Franklin there to look after her, Mama will kill me if I leave her alone.

"For me?" Tempe crows in surprise. As if we hadn't just last night crept up to the loft. There were little pictures scrawled in corners, in between crevices, in places most people—except Tempe—wouldn't bother looking. Tempe said they were flowers; they looked like legs to me.

"Sister, you really should come see what they've done up here. It looks like a little house. All that's missing is—"

"You want me to bring the bucket up there? You gotta go or something?"

The men whoop above. Their foot stomping and backslapping put an end to her sashaying and high stepping. She's downstairs faster than I would have thought. Seems like her feet don't hardly touch the ladder at all.

"You heifer." Her hot words scorch the back of my neck.

"I ain't jealous," I whisper between panting.

I'm out of breath. Tempe's too far ahead to hear me. I can't catch up even if I want to. She runs out of the barn leaving me to gather the empty wrappings and cloths, bucket, even one of Edward's ripped shirts for Mama to mend. For a while she stalks down the path swinging her arms in wide, angry circles, every so often chopping at the sky with her hand or punching with a clenched fist. "Hussy, wide-hipped heifer." Snatches of words drift behind her as if even the burden of holding her tongue is too much. As if she's the one gonna be left behind. She slows as she nears the river, allowing me to catch up. I walk slower. She stops walking when she reaches the deepest end, where the reeds are tall and thick in the air and tangled in a jumble of roots below the surface from what I've heard.

"Ain't got no sense at all, do you?" she hisses. How she can get words out of her mouth with her lips so tight shut I would never know.

With her hands on her bony hips, her feet planted on either side of the path, her cheeks puffed out and her mouth wide open, she blocks my way.

"Mama said not to go upstairs," I remind her.

Her eyes close into brown slits.

"She did."

Tempe steps toward me.

I take a step backward. "She just don't want you to be fast."

She takes a big step forward.

My heart jumps. I take a bigger step back. "Besides, Walker said he'll get you a baby. What you want with Edward?" My heart beats so loud she seems to hear it. She stares at my chest, mesmerized. I'm too close. Mud sucks at my feet. She pulls me close, like she's going to hug me, spins, and pushes me. I can't catch my breath or close my mouth or think of nothing but dying.

Chapter 15

"No!" I scream. I'm not ready to leave. The word echoes inside my chest.

"Stop that damn yelling," Tempe says. Her rough hands grab my waist. "It ain't nothing but knee deep and you acting like you 'bout to die."

I spit. Brush the hair out of my eyes. Shiver. "I did die," I say.

Tempe pulls me to my feet. She shakes her head. "How you have time to die? You ain't been in but a minute. You fell in, I walked in after you." She snaps her fingers. "It wasn't no longer than that."

"There were hands pulling me under the water."

Tempe laughs. "Course there were hands. How you think I pulled you out? With my teeth?"

"Not your hands." I bend down, press my face to the water. I can't see beneath the reddish murk. "There's somebody down there."

"What the devil are you doing? Come on, we gotta get back to Mama." She yanks me up by the back of my head. Her fingers catch in my hair. "I don't know if you got knocked in the head down there but if you don't stop this foolishness I'm gonna knock you in the head right here." With one hand still in my hair, she puts a fist up to my face.

"You gonna hit me before you leave me? Or after?"

"What you talking about?"

"You gonna marry Edward, he gonna buy you, and you gonna leave me and Mama right here."

She lets go of my head. My scalp tingles. Tempe just stands there watching snot and tears stream down my face. She stares for a full minute. "That what Edward say?" She ain't even trying to hide it. She's so excited she's doing a little dance right there in the river. It would serve her right if she slipped and fell right in.

"It's true, then. You'd leave us?"

"Ain't nobody leaving nobody. If he talking about marrying and buying my freedom, I can buy yours and Mama's too."

"How you gonna save enough? Walker ain't gonna hire you out."

"I don't know. Edward ain't even ask me yet. I got time to think on a way."

"What if he just up and leave, like Watson did?"

Tempe don't say nothing for a long time. She gets out the river. I follow.

"If he can, Watson will come back for you. If he can't, once we buy you free, you'll find him."

"Okay, Tempe," I say, like the world isn't much bigger than acres and acres of Walker land, like either of us has ever been off this property, like I'll ever see Watson again. Maybe it won't matter. As long as I got Mama and Tempe, what else do I need?

Tempe and me are sick in bed when Edward comes around a few days later with a wheelbarrow full of slates, nails, scraps of wood, and baubles to ask Mama if she needs any work done around the cabin before he leaves. He stands out on the porch, hat in hand, blocking a good view of the outside. Even after days of Mama's onion, lemon, and honey elixir, my chest is full of phlegm. Tempe's too. That don't stop her from jumping up, slipping something over her head, and running out to the porch faster than Mama can say no. She's too late. By the time she reaches the porch, Edward is gone.

"Oh, Mama," she wails without even trying to be respectful. "Why you go and run him away?"

"Child," Mama warns.

"Mama, there's plenty a man like Edward could fix around here."

"Tempe," Mama says.

Tempe keeps right on talking. "Look at this porch, you always saying it's rickety. You liable to fall clear off it one day. And what about this door?" She bangs it shut. It pops open. "See? No privacy at all. Some strange man wandering up the road could see all the good Lord," she slides her hands over her frame, "created right through this open door. The roof too. Between the rain and the squirrels dropping through the roof, it's a wonder we ain't all about to die!"

"Girl, if you would just listen!"

"There's plenty of work for a man like him."

"Excuse me," Edward interrupts, "I found the tools out where you said they was. I'll just start round back so as not to," he pauses, "interrupt you ladies' discussion."

The porch creaks. I turn my back to the door, shut my eyes, snore loud. Tempe flies inside. Her breath takes up the whole cabin.

"If you feeling good enough to run like that, you well enough to help out again. Go on out there and help Edward in the garden," Mama says. "I been meaning to fix up that fence back there for the longest."

Lilac. Tempe grabs a lilac-scented cloth from my things. I picture her wiping under her arms, around her neck, between her legs—just in case—scrubbing any bit of skin that Edward might see, touch, or smell.

"I know you ain't asleep," she calls before closing the door and leaving the scent of lilac behind.

It can't take no more than a minute for me to get up, pull a dress over my head, fix my side of the bed, and get to the door, but Tempe's already around back before I hit the porch. I haven't stepped one foot outside before Mama stops me.

"Might as well set out here with me. She's gonna be a while."

"Not if I help, she won't." I lean toward the step.

"Ain't no rush. Sit down a while," Mama says. She tucks her skirts, scooches over, and pats the space beside her.

"I won't be but a minute," I say. My heart's racing, my underarms itch. Sweat drips down my back. "I'll come right back when I finish helping Tempe and them with the chores."

"Tempe don't need no help, Spring."

Maybe Mama don't know how Edward watches Tempe when he thinks nobody's looking. Maybe she don't know how Tempe watches him back. I bet if she knew Edward was planning on

buying Tempe away she wouldn't be so quick to push them together. I inch closer to the edge of the porch. With Mama near
blocking the step, there isn't much sense in acting like I can't just
step clear off the edge if I want to.

"Mama, I been meaning to do some fixing up around here.
There's plenty I can do to help."

"I got some work you can do right here."

She pats the spot next to her again. I sit. My legs spill over the
porch. I tap my feet.

"How you doing? Been a while since Watson run off, hasn't it?"

"Yes, ma'am."

"I had someone run off too," Mama says.

She rubs my back in wide circles. I check to see that it ain't
Agnes staring back at me but it ain't. "Told me we was gonna run
away together. Guess time just seemed right and he run off."

"He ain't come back for you?"

Mama shook her head.

"Ever hear what happened to him?"

Mama shook her head, mouthed *no*.

"Something must have happened to him. He wouldn't have
just left you. Maybe he's dead. I hope that's what it is."

"That ain't nothing to hope for," Mama says. "I was angry
when he run off, hurt, disappointed. I wanted them to catch him,
drag him back. Until I learned what that means. You know what
would have happened to him if he come back for me?"

I want to say they would have run and kept on running till
they got to freedom. Like me and Watson will do. But it sounds
childish. I shake my head.

"They'd have killed him. His body or his spirit or both. He
wouldn't have been mine no more. Before I figured that out,

I just waited. I waited so long that when there was something needed doing, something I could have stopped, someone I could have helped, I didn't see it. I was too late. Don't spend your whole life waiting."

Mama don't seem in too much of a hurry to do anything this morning. Laughter drifts to the porch from around back. What kind of work can they be doing that's so funny? Their laughter makes Mama smile. I can just see it: Edward chasing Tempe through rows of fresh-planted vegetables. Her sashaying and side-stepping vines and roots I hadn't cleared yet. Both of them tripping over rocks and tumbling, her first and him on top, onto the ground. Ain't nothing to be smiling about. The laughter stops. Mama rocks back and forth on the porch, waiting.

"What you think they doing back there?" I ask. If she thinks they digging up turnips, she has another think coming.

"What you think they doing?" she asks.

Giggles. Tempe is too old to be giggling like that with a grown man.

"Not working," I say.

"Sound like work to me," Mama says. She scoots closer. We sit arm to arm, both of our feet tapping the ground. "I got a job in mind for Edward."

"What you need doing that I can't do?"

"Marrying."

Without wanting to, my breathing matches hers. My body rocks with hers. But my heart races.

"What's gonna happen once they get married?"

Mama looks at me full in the face. She gives me her mothering look. "Well, first Edward will—"

"Not that, Mama! I know all about that!"

Mama looks at me strange again.

"I mean," I say, "I heard all about that. Where she gonna live?"

"I suspect Edward will have to live here or visit her till he saves enough to buy her."

I about fall off the porch. "Buy her freedom, you mean?"

Mama stares at her feet. She wiggles her toes, buries them in the dirt. "I want to see both of my girls free before I die," she says. "Not runaways, free."

"That why you set on Edward marrying Tempe?"

"He bought his mama. He can buy my baby too."

"If he buy her, she be his slave?"

"When he buy her, she'll be his."

Chapter 16

May 17, 1864

Sunlight slips through the cracks of the cabin. It brightens the glimmer in Tempe's eyes, the shine on Mama's hairpins, the crooked stitch in the cloth between my fingers. We've been working through much of the night. I take the stitch out and start again.

"How do I look?" Tempe twirls slow; a pirouette of lace, lavender, and flowers. Flower petals in her hair, flower petals on her wrists, flower petals on her feet. Pink rose and lavender petals adorn her hair, her gown, her belly.

"Doesn't she look beautiful?"

"She sure does."

"I do, don't I?" Tempe laughs with her hands on her hips.

"Stop moving so much. I need to check a few things first," Mama says.

Tempe closes her eyes while Mama realigns pleats and smooths creases. Mama's shaking hands brush Tempe's belly. Tempe jumps.

"Tempe? There's something different about you."

"Maybe she's nervous about the wedding," I say.

"No," Mama shakes her head slowly, "that's not it."

"Maybe she ate something that don't agree with her."

Mama's lips twist like they do when she smells something rotting like a piece of meat, some curdling milk, or a lie. "You complaining about my cooking?"

"No, ma'am, ain't nothing wrong with your cooking."

"Is there something you want to tell me?"

Tempe shakes her head.

Mama raises a hand to Tempe's face, presses her forehead to Tempe's forehead and with her eyes closed she feels Tempe's belly. Tears roll down her cheeks. "It must really be a miracle," she says. "All them ointments and elixirs and you still with child." She puts her head to Tempe's belly.

Tempe's staring at me over Mama's head, daring me to say something. Without asking why, I drank every drop, rubbed every dollop. And I ain't never gonna have a baby of my own. Not one drop crossed Tempe's lips. Not one sliver slipped inside her. She's the one been lying for years. She'll have Edward and a baby and her freedom. What's left for me?

They so wrapped up in each other's arms that they don't notice me go. I don't want to but my feet lead me straight to the river. The cool grass cushions my feet. I sit on the bank, legs dangling. The river kisses my soles. Don't know how long I been crying when I feel a hand on my shoulder. He sits down next to me, quiet as a keep. Even though I don't expect to hear nothing but how everything's gonna turn out alright, I tell him everything. James listens in silence and after a few minutes, he does the same. He tells me things I won't believe until years later when Tempe tells me they true. By the time I get back to the cabin, Samantha and Rose are there. Mama and Tempe stand on the porch still fawning over one another.

"She's gonna have a baby," Mama says. "A free child."

"Half free," Samantha says. She's wearing a limp flower in her hair; her special occasions hat.

"Long as Tempe a slave, that baby's a slave," Rose says.

"Yep, a little free baby," Mama says. She nods her head like she and Rose said the exact same thing. "It's time to have a wedding!"

There are gifts: flowers with long stems, a thick homemade quilt, thin shells and words. One by one they lay hands on Tempe covering her in prayers.

"Lord, may this child know your undying love and unwavering mercy in her times of need," Rose says.

"Yahweh, may she never forget to praise your name," Samantha says.

"Lord, let this baby be born free," Mama says.

Before leading the women's march to the river, Tempe gives me a quick hug. I hold on too long. The sun shines but it's not warm. The air is cool; crisp enough to hurry our steps. Tempe's eyes are covered with a thick cloth. According to Samantha, slaves been getting married like this for generations. Can't nobody prove she's wrong. Samantha twirls Tempe round and round till she's about dizzy. She pushes her forward. "Your heart will lead the way," she says. "If Edward is the man for you, your heart will lead you to him." She covers all of our eyes with scraps of cloth.

We walk slowly behind, trusting Tempe will know the way. Blindfolded, the walk from the cabin to the river is a lot longer than I remember. Every so often Tempe hollers for us to duck down, watch our heads, move a bit to the side. Nettles stick to the bottoms of my feet. More than once she leads us straight through a briar patch or bed of pine needles. Over the years, our feet done worn paths all through the woods, the grass, around the fields.

She can't seem to find none of them. She stumbles and falls. We stumble and fall. She gets up and slips. We get up and slip. She seems to be able to find all the leftover slick mud. Gnats swarm around my head. My hair gets snagged in tree branches. Bushes prick my legs. We circle back twice before reaching the same long, spongy slick of grass leading to the mud we done slid in twice already. This time, Tempe leads us around it. I ain't the only one happy about that. Mama starts to hum. We all get to walking and humming and then Tempe stops.

There's a loud splash, followed by another. Chattering chipmunks, songs of wild birds and cheers of the men drown out Tempe's squeals and Edward's laughter. I uncover my eyes. Tempe jumps in the river. Edward in a pressed shirt and new dungarees runs to the edge and jumps in. He splashes through the river, running to her and her just about gliding to him. He holds her like it's forever. I believe it. Edward's gonna buy Tempe's freedom. They gonna save up and buy Mama and me. By the time the baby come we'll have a cottage and land, a mule. We'll be a family. Forever.

Chapter 17

Maryland E

November 1, 1864

The State of Maryland has A

Slavery Watch

While parts of the Union remain divided over the cause of slavery, Maryland has put quill to parchment and has abolished slavery in our great land. Last year's Emancipation Proclamation Slavery did not abolish slavery in the Union States.

While freedom is a slow process, sheriff's have deputized a group of men to carry out justice and let Maryland former slave owners know, slavery is dead.

Together, we will see Maryland and her faithful citizens, through the challenging times ahead.

Rer
foll
imp

The
that
rela
the
beh
of a
exp
in l
its

Things start turning up missing. First it's little things like doorknobs and cutlery from the main house and washtubs and fruit baskets from the slave cabins. Pretty soon it's cows and horses and people. The few field hands Walker had gone missing too. Walker sent down word that they'd run off—all of them at once. We don't believe it, though. Been so busy, ain't seen much of James, Rose, or Samantha.

"When you finish the washing, get out to the fields and see if there's anything needs picking." Mama starts each day with a list of work for Tempe and me. "Stay together. Check the barns, muck the stables."

"Ain't hardly nothing left to clean up after," Tempe says.

Every day I roll up the bed, do my business, get fresh water for Mama and Tempe, grind meal for the evening's supper, and wait. Some mornings I pick vegetables and weeds to pass the time. Mama can't stand to see us idle.

"Just do what I tell you," Mama says.

"Soon as Edward makes enough money I'm going to get away from here and ain't gonna be nobody here for you to boss around but her and I'm taking her with me!"

I'm out on the porch with a bucket of carrots, cabbage, and kale. "Why you always so mad?" I ask. She can't hear me, though. I set the bucket down and follow her. She's already down the river, hitching up her dress like I hadn't already hauled up a tub full of water for her to bathe in. I pull weeds nearby.

"I should be tending to my husband's house."

There ain't nothing I can say that won't make her mad. "You know, I ain't never even been there? Never set one foot in that door. Never slept one night on that bed. Never even met his mama. She's in there scraping Edward's pots, scrubbing Edward's floors, cooking Edward's food."

"You mad cuz Mama ask you to do chores round here and you want to be doing them around there?"

"Mama ain't ask me to do one thing for her since I been grown. Everything she tell me to do is for him." She waves her hand in the air.

I look up.

"Not him, *him*. Walker. Edward's been to see him twice since we been married. He ask for a price. Walker say not for sale. He ask for a pass for me to be with him. Walker say too much work round here for me to be running off playing free."

"What you got to go around there for anyhow? Edward's up here working more every day."

"Course he's working. Walker done sold off all the field slaves right after harvest. Edward says he's letting go of all he can, to hold on to what he got."

"How he just sell a body away?" Mama had talked about it. Auctions. Shackles. Down south. Bedtime stories to make Tempe and me mind.

"What? You thought Mama and them made them stories up like them stories about Gitche Goo-Goos?"

Slave cabins emptied. Cooking boxes, beds, people, all sold. "Why don't y'all run off?"

"Where we gonna run to? Edward's house? That's about the stupidest thing I heard yet."

"Edward should have saved up enough to get youse a good start up north."

"How we gonna get up north?"

"I can tell you how to get to—"

"You keep your runaway plans right to yourself, you hear? I don't want no part of no plan you and Watson cooked up."

"It worked for Watson."

"It ain't done you no favors and I ain't sure I believe it's done Watson any good neither."

"Buddy and Franklin would have told me if they'd heard something."

Tempe slips into the water. There's no sun to speak of that

woulda dried her but she stays in, knee deep. "I s'pect they would tell you if they'd heard something. What about his mama?"

"Watson ain't got no mama."

"Edward's mama. She's liable to meet the sheriff at the gate. Her boy running off with a slave, leaving her behind? She probably tell the law before we even get good and—"

"You couldn't just leave her, she's family."

"She's Edward's family."

"And Mama and me?"

"Youse family."

"Not Edward's family."

"What difference that make?" Her words are clipped. For a second, she don't sound like Tempe.

A few days later, Walker sends word not to go up to the house unless we called for. We tend our garden and the ones of the slaves who ain't been back. Walker hired Edward, Buddy, and Franklin to tear the cabins down and carry the wood to the soldiers—his effort for the war. One night after supper, Tempe drags me up to the house. With Old Missus and Old Walker dead and Young Missus sent away before the war got started good, we hoping to see Samantha and James tending the fire or stirring up something good. We peek in the kitchen window. Ain't nothing to see. No pots cooking, no fire burning, nothing.

A few days later, Walker sends for Mama.

"Keep yourselves and this place clean," Mama says. She keeps looking from Tempe to me, from me to Tempe. No matter where she is she keeps her eyes on both of us. And her hands. Her long fingers, cool to the touch, on our faces and eyelids, pressed against foreheads, wound around curly hair. "Take care of each other. There's enough people out there that want to hurt you, tear you down, don't you never do nothing but help each other up."

"Mama, you just gonna be up the house," Tempe says, like she believes it.

We hold each other tight. Squeeze till the breath almost run out right there and then.

"Can't we run?" I ask. "Go far away from here together. Don't matter where longs as we together."

"I don't know nobody that ever run that lived."

"Mama, if you run off would you come back? I sure wouldn't. Course you don't know nobody that run off and lived," Tempe says.

"I lost plenty that died running," Mama says. "Ain't gonna be no talk of running." She's pacing. "I don't want to hear no more about it. Tempe, Edward's gonna buy you. You two buy your sister."

"Walker done said he ain't gonna sell me, not ever."

"Maybe he just needs some convincing. Only way I know to save us is for me to go up to that house like I been called to do. I can't do nothing for you girls down here but from up there, I'll be watching over my gals—no matter what. As long as Walker got me up there, he won't bother with you two down here. If we ever get separated, if anything tear us apart, I'll find my way back to you both. No matter where." She stops, sinks to her knees and holds us tight. "As long as y'all don't ever forget me, I'll make my way back to you."

The sun sets same as it always do. Mama rips off a piece of her dress for each of us to hold on to. She wraps it around a handful of shells, some small rocks, a ribbon. By sunrise, before she can say I love you or whisper goodbye, Mama is gone.

Weeks later and we're inside the barn. It's cool and about empty. Animals are gone but it still smells like manure. Edward is standing with his head hanging low and his shoulders slouched, looking every bit like he wouldn't harm a nest full of bees. He looks down at Tempe's feet. "I says, 'Master Walker'—I tell you how much he like it when I call him that?"

Tempe and me nod yes. It's taken him thirty minutes to get to the good part of the story and he ain't there yet.

Edward clears his throat. "Master Walker, I been thinking on how I can help out in this war."

"What about Mama?" Tempe interrupts.

"I'm getting to that part," Edward says. He leans over, kisses Tempe's belly.

It's nearly time to get back to chores. Ain't nobody left to do them all except for Tempe, Edward, and me. Mostly Edward and me. Walker's given up on pretending to pay him but Edward comes around just the same. He mends, plants, weeds, harvests, and plows and does most of Tempe's work besides. Tempe can't reach over to pick up so much as a basket of clothes without Edward picking it up for her. If Tempe wants a hole dug, she just has to pick up a shovel and Edward will get to digging it. Don't seem to matter where she is, Edward finds her. You'd have thought she was the only woman to ever have a baby. He even has his mama doing Tempe's work. He carries home shirts with holes and scraps of fabric and brings back starched shirts and winter blankets. She sends buckets of biscuits and greens, hot yams, cornbread. Anything Tempe has a hankering for, Edward's mama can get her hands on it. Seems like everybody but maybe me and Walker waiting on Tempe. Only Walker's waiting too, I didn't know it then.

"Tempe, you want another piece of sugarcane to suck on?" I ask. I've been sucking on this cane since Edward brought it. I stripped the bark and whittled down the rough stalk. I'm near the sweet, juicy flesh and don't want to share. But, if it will keep her mouth busy. I offer my ripe piece of cane. She sniffs at it and turns her nose up. I can just about taste the sap on my lips. I must have smiled. She snatches it and shoves an end in her mouth. Don't savor it or nothing. She rubs her belly with one hand and wipes the juice from her mouth with the other. I never do get the rest of that cane back.

"So I say," Edward continues, "been thinking 'bout signing up to go fight alongside my brothers but then I get to thinking 'bout leaving Tempe. 'She be fine,' he says, 'don't I look after her?' And I get to worrying 'bout you, sir, and how you here with only those two little gals here to cook and fend and hoe. 'They strong enough to do all that need doing,' he say. ''Bout time they do more round here.' Yes, sir, but when them Yankees come tearing up the land, burning houses, killing up folks, who gonna protect y'all? I knows you sent Missus and Mama somewhere for safekeeping but what Tempe know about no gun? What Spring know about no hatchet. How they gonna keep them Yankee soldiers from killing you?"

Tempe laughs so hard I think she'll fall right off of the log Edward has set up for her. "Keep them from killing him?"

"I'd save him," I say. Edward and Tempe stare at me hard. "If he dead, how he gonna tell me how to find Mama?"

Tempe sucks her teeth. Edward nods.

"'What you make of all this fighting' he asks," Edward

continues. "I says, sir, I tell you the truth, this fighting got me scared. Yankees near burned up the whole town. Even the church been razed. They just running poor white folks, good ones too, out in the open and—well, no need to tell you what they do to them once they catch 'em. Ain't safe. With all the men and boys off fighting they done left the land and the womenfolk at the mercy of the Lord. 'No gentlemen would attack a lady.' These ain't gentlemen, sir. 'I'd have gone and fought,' he says, like he ain't paid a boy from town to take his place. I say, I hear the Yanks getting closer and closer everyday. Winning more and more. Killing up folks and tearing part families and leaving 'em every which way."

"The Yanks!" Tempe says. She beats me to it.

"Let me tell it," Edward says. He throws up his hands, pretending to be mad.

"Go on," I say.

"'Can't nobody beat our boys here on Southern soil, don't you worry about that,' he says. 'Before long this war will be all over and things will just be like they was in the good days.' But then I slip, The good days, sir? He gets to eyeing me up and down like he's weighing me. 'What you think it'll be like if those damned Yanks win? They stealing our land, taking our women. What you think they gonna do with you? You won't be safe, you know that. They ain't gonna take care of you and your family. Let you work for 'em, get you no safe place to live.' You sure right about that, sir. I was almost snatched up the other night on my way home. Streets no place to be. 'Didn't I tell you? Them Yankees, can't trust 'em.' No, sir. These were men from round here, I say. Said they would string me up if I even thought about joining the Yankee side. 'It's not fitting to turn your back on your home, boy. You ought to know that. South done born and raised you,' Walker says. 'We got to defend her. Streets ain't safe no how. A strong, able man like yourself ought to be out there fighting for our way of life. Got just as much right to defend the South as anybody. Don't you think?' Sir, I couldn't abide killing folks. Thought of it just turns my stomach something fierce. Walker smiles like that's what he been waiting on. 'Why don't you stay here awhile, until the war's over?' No thank you, sir, my ma's aging poorly and I wouldn't want her to need for nothing during the night. 'Can she cook?' he asks. He's getting excited. She think she can, sir. Sure do. Why the last thing my pa said, Lord have mercy on his soul, the last thing he said—before he met the good Lord—was, 'Woman, you sure is a mighty fine cook.' Least, that's what she says he said. By the time I came in to help, he was dead, a piece of cornbread still in his hand. No, sir, wasn't that much around the kitchen before she took sick but now, well, I just took to cooking for us both. 'Does she clean?' he asks. My mama's floors so clean you could eat clear off 'em. Strays come in off the streets just to eat offa my mama's floors, I tell him." I hold my sides in from laughing so hard. I ain't never met Edward's mama but from what he says, Ms. Lola Mae would kill him if he got her mixed up with Walker.

"'I been thinking on bringing Tempe or Spring up to the house,' he says. 'About time they start earning their keep around here. Maybe even pay them a little something.' Now I can tell he's still thinking about having my mama up there cooking and cleaning for free cuz he done forgot he ain't paid me nothing. 'She could buy her baby,' he says. 'Wouldn't she like that?' Can you believe it? Buy the baby? It ain't exactly how we planned but it's a start! First we buy the baby, then you."

He stops talking. He don't say and then we'll buy Spring. Just first the baby, then you.

Tempe stands up. She puts her hands on her hips. "Ain't planning on being here when the baby's born," she says.

"Don't see where you reckon you can hide with my baby 'bout to climb out any day now. It's too dangerous. Streets ain't safe. Woods ain't safe. Least if we wait till the baby's born and buy him, my child will be free."

"Baby ain't yourn."

Edward straightens. His hands clench. His jaw clenches. "This baby Walker's baby," she says. "You know that. Long as Walker got my papers, this baby his."

The cool April breeze stops. Edward moves to pass.

"You gonna kill him?" Tempe asks. "Cuz unless you feinin' to kill him, bury him, and send him straight to hell, ain't no reason to go up there. And if'n you kill him, you better make sure he dead before you get to running off and make sure he tell you where Mama is before that."

Edward bends down. He presses his face to her belly.

Tempe leans over, rests her head on his.

"I don't know what more I can do," he says.

"We'll think of something," Tempe says.

"Promise me you ain't gonna run away," Edward says.

"Promise," Tempe says.

Chapter 18

Tempe and me is all the time talking about running. The bigger her belly gets, the more we talk about it. Neither one of us wants you to be no slave. Your pa don't neither, but he's scared. Every plan we come up with he ends with, "Wait until after the baby." His eye gets to twitching every time we mention it. Pretty soon his wait turns into no: What if we? No. What about? No. How about? No.

Nothing is careful enough. Gets to the point Tempe and me wait on him to slip away for the night to talk about leaving. The longer the war lasts, the harder it is for Edward to get back. Days at a time go by before we see him. Any news we get come from Edward.

"How you gonna get Edward to come along?"

"With this baby," Tempe says.

We're lying out in the wet grass watching the clouds pass across the moon. The air is crisp. It's been months since we heard any but we listen for the familiar rumbling of faraway gunshots. I imagine thunder is the roar of a cannon. If I close my eyes tight and put my ear to the earth, I swear I can hear screams. Hoots, squeals, chirps, the night is noisy. All around the cabin, the garden, the wood, is thick with animals hunting, being hunted. The silence creeps up on us like a ghost. A loud, twig-breaking ghost. Tempe tenses beside me. A bird screeches. I want to jump but Tempe's nails digging into my arm pin me down.

"I said," a boy says, "is it safe to come out?" He repeats the screech. "It's a call, don't y'all got one?" He steps out from behind a row of trees.

Me and Tempe sit up. I reach around for a branch or rock or something, in case I need it.

"I didn't expect to run into nobody," the boy says. "What y'all doing here?"

"Living," Tempe says.

"Slaving's over," the boy says.

"What you talking about?" I ask. Poor thing. He can't be more than ten years old. Running around thinking he's free.

"Gal, y'all must be the last two slaves in the whole wide world. Maryland been free since last year and slaves all over been free for weeks."

"Then what you running around slipping through the woods for?" Tempe asks.

"Roads ain't safe," he says, "patrollers on the roads rounding people up."

"Didn't you just not one minute ago say slaving is over, we free?"

"They catching people up here, sending them to work houses, planting them on farms, selling them to folks. Y'all coming?"

Free? No running away, buying ourselves, just free. Mama will be home any day now.

"We waiting on our mama to get back," I say. "Soon's she get back, we'll be on our way."

"I got to get moving. My mama out there somewhere looking for me. I'm gonna find her."

"How you know where to look?"

The boy presses a splayed hand over his heart. "This right here."

"You ain't got no map? You end up dead just following that."

"I end up dead staying here too," he says. "Don't see the point of just waiting on being found. What if she hurt up? Some mean somebody might be keeping her and she can't get back to me. No, I ain't gonna wait here one more night. How long you gonna wait?"

I don't know. My whole body is shaking. Free? What if he's right? Should we just go and ask Walker? Wait on your pa? If this boy's running to find his mama, Watson could be making his way back to me.

"Whatchu gonna do if you don't find your mama?" Tempe asks.

"I'm gonna find her," he says.

"Your master just let you go?"

"I left. Soon as word came that we was free, we left. The master tried to convince us to stay. Said we was family and family don't just walk away. When that didn't work he said he'd pay us. I don't have no need for nothing. I have to get to my mama. Wasn't no price he could afford that could make me wait longer than I had to. I wasn't the only one felt like that. Some stayed. The rest of us packed up what we could but we didn't get to keep it. When he found out we were leaving, the crazy goat came chasing after us with shotguns. He was carrying on about us owing him and him collecting in blood. Good thing he can't see straight. I would be dead right now if someone hadn't already run off with his ammunition." We laugh along with him. I want to ask what it's like, freedom, if the stars don't look brighter, the water taste cooler, the berries sweeter, but I don't have time. He's caught his wind and is already edging back to the woods. "Y'all sure you ain't coming?" he asks.

I'm halfway up.

"We sure," Tempe says for the both of us.

He's already gone. The night settles as if he was never there.

Tempe lies back down. "We ain't free until Walker says we free," she says. Before long she's snoring.

I lay back down too but I don't sleep.

By morning we decide to wait for your pa to come back. Tempe don't want to leave without him. Between planning how to get Walker to tell us where Mama is, where she want to move, how she want the house to look and how she gonna act when she meets Edward's mama, Tempe don't hardly have time for me to talk about trying to find Watson. Soon as I bring him up, Tempe brings him down: need to find yourself a born-free man, she says. Like she done forgot your pa was born a slave just like we was. I don't argue with her. Soon as we get settled somewhere new, I'm gonna find Watson. I spend most of the days rolling last names around my mouth. Spring Kirk. What if Watson changed his name? I wouldn't blame him if he did. Who will I be then? Mrs. Watson. I can't get farther than that. River, Sanctuary, Grass. I think of all the places we shared. Would he choose one of those as a name? I just hope I like our new name. It would be awful to get saddled with a name that don't sound right but I won't complain, won't make a face or nothing. I won't let on that I don't like it, seeing as he worked hard to get us a name. At night I plan the wedding and the house we'll build between Tempe and Edward's and Mama's. I'll have to tell Watson there won't be no babies. But we'll have you. Won't need no babies of our own. I don't tell Tempe nothing. During the day I work harder than I ever done. Weeks pass.

"Ain't nothing wrong with your hands," I say. I spit.

Sweat and dirt are in my mouth. I been digging up all our treasures. Don't leave nothing behind, Tempe said, instead of helping. When I finish digging, Tempe gets to telling me what to put where and how to tie this bundle and that one. She got one more time to call me dim-witted. Before I can tell her, your pa come running through the woods. He quiets Tempe's fussing with kisses and hugs.

"Where you been?" I ask. "We been waiting on you."

Tempe gives me a look that could freeze the damned.

"I wasn't sure I'd find y'all here," he says. "I been worried something fierce bout where you two would be."

I can't help myself, I smile.

"Don't know what I would do if something happened to you and my baby," Edward continues. "Soon as I heard y'all was free, I go see Walker. I says, I'm here to take my family home. He says, 'You ain't taking nothing of mine nowhere.' I says, slavery done ended, Master Walker. He says, 'Not here.' I tell him, yes, sir, right here and all over Maryland. And he says, 'Then we moving down south, me, Tempe, Spring, and the baby.' I says, no, sir, no you ain't, slavery is dead all over. He says, 'You right, I be right back.' By the time he comes back to the porch waving that rifle, I'm already halfway across the field. Ain't stop him from shooting at me. I ran. I couldn't stay away no longer. I was worried he'd move you away before I could get back. I was praying you'd still be here. We gonna have to leave tonight. I got a friend who can get us on a train north. Done arranged everything. Further north we get, less chance of Walker following. Woods is getting as dangerous as the roads but I don't see no way around it."

"We'll leave first thing in the morning," Tempe says.

"We ain't got till morning," Edward says. "Got to be right now. I got us passage."

Tempe and Edward might have forgotten about Mama but not me. I'm not leaving without her.

"It's too dark, Edward, what about the baby?" Your ma pats her belly.

It's settled. No matter how well Edward knows his way, it's safer to leave in the morning. It's the tears that convince him. Least if we wait till morning, we can stop for help if we need it. I can see your pa don't want to but he agrees to see if he can't switch times with another family. He'll be back by sunrise. Soon as he leaves we get planning.

"We gonna have to get Walker to tell us where Mama is," Tempe says.

"How we know he even knows where she at?"

"Of course he knows. If he don't who do?"

"Alright, I'm gonna ask him."

"Why would he tell you anything?" Tempe asks. It's dark. No moon to speak of, but I know she's standing there with her hands on her hips.

"Cuz I'm a miracle."

"No you ain't. I am."

"And if he don't tell you?"

"He dies knowing something we don't."

Kill him. The more we talk on it, the easier it seems. Before long, don't seem to be no other way. We gonna wait till morning and give him a chance to save his life. It's only Christian. We'll ask him where Mama is. Least he can do for Tempe lifting the curse is tell us. If we right, we leave and go find her. If we wrong, he dies. He ain't gonna sell neither one of us. We too excited to sleep. We spend hours thinking how to do it. We'll go right up the front steps, up to the door, knock. He'll probably be expecting us to scrub the floors or get ironing or cooking. With nobody but him there, the place is bound to be knee-deep in dust. He'll let us in. We'll ask him then. We talk through turn after turn. Laughter, anger, begging; we got all his responses covered. If it comes to it, we got ours too.

Tempe's set on poison. If we're going to do it, I want something quick, painless. Shooting him seems easiest. Between cleaning them and using them to guard the Missus' garden from critters, Tempe and me been handling shotguns for years. Know just where to find them, too.

"What about the law?" Tempe asks. "If the Missus ever do come back, the first thing she'll see is Walker lying round with a big ol' hole in his head. The second thing is you and me gone. It won't be long before somebody's looking for us." If we drag him out the back door, through the fields and such, we can drop him in the ditch. But Tempe drags her foot along the dirt. I follow the trail she makes. Fire.

If Walker won't tell us where Mama is, we'll send him straight to hell. Won't even kill him first. Tempe will ask about Mama while I say it's chilly and get a fire going. The curtains will be first. I always hated washing and rewashing that brocade cloth. It made my fingers stiff. After the curtains, the rugs, the settee, Walker. Tempe's set on it if he don't tell. I try to picture Walker telling us where to find Mama and me and Tempe walking out the front door and down the path free.

I can't see it.

We're too excited to wait until morning. We set off for the house. Tempe lumbers behind me. I carry both of our bundles. She stops every few steps. We'd be there by now if she would just keep walking. She's breathing heavy. Just before we reach the river, her heavy breathing turns to moaning. A few more steps and she falls to her knees.

"The baby?" I don't need to ask. We waited too long. "Help me up."

The more I pull, the more her body seems to root to the spot. I heave her to her feet.

"Wanna go back?"

She don't bother to answer. We time our pace with her pains. Sweat drenches her body, making it hard to even hold on to her hand. She bites down on snapped-off pieces of bark to keep from screaming. She needs to rest. We sitting there swinging our feet at the edge of the river when Tempe's water come down. You won't be far behind it. Owls screech. Crickets chirp. Nightbirds call. Everything's waiting. The bark doesn't work, Tempe screams. To quiet her, I give her a twig to chew down on. It cracks between her teeth. She howls and I'm worried hounds will join in. I try to shush her but the look she gives me sends me scurrying to find her a clump of sweetgrass to grind. The words that come out of her mouth. When she opens her mouth to scream again, I shove a clump of grass, dirt and all, inside. I imagine her biting the heads off of fat worms. Sick moves up my throat. But you coming and I swallow it. I rub my hands over her belly making rhythmic circles on her skin. You squirm beneath my fingertips. You arch and stretch, Tempe screams. A few seconds later, you do too. Your cry is an angry wail. I take some scraps from my bundle, soak them. Tempe washes your little wrinkled body. It's the happiest I ever seen her. We slice the cord with a hunting knife. I bury the cord nearby.

She's rocking back and forth, singing to you while you nurse.

"What's his name?"

"Edward Jonah Freeman."

She's holding you so tight I'm worried you can't breathe. "Want me to hold him?"

"He don't deserve to be no slave," Tempe says.

"He ain't one. You heard that boy. Edward's born free."

"What if he's wrong? What if that boy was sent by Walker to poke fun, to get us riled up, just to see what we'd do?"

"Walker wouldn't do that. He would have just come down and said it himself. The boy was telling the truth. We free. The baby too."

"Free. And then what? Same people that slaved us still running around."

"Them running around don't stop us from moving none."

"Walker's free. Sheriff gonna haul him off for keeping us? For selling Mama?"

"We don't know if he sold Mama or not."

"These people decided we was gonna be slaves. You and me, Mama, her mama, her mama's mama. I don't want my baby growing up with their words in his mouth."

"Who gonna tell him? I ain't. Nobody's gonna call this baby a slave. Not you, not me."

"It ain't us I'm worried about."

Tempe has her mouth over yours. It ain't no kiss. It's like she's sucking the life from your body. You wiggle.

"Don't do it, Tempe," I say. My hand is on her shoulder. My breath's in her ear. "We'll keep him safe. You and me."

"We'll see," she says. She kisses your forehead. Squeezes my hand. She's bundling you up and already walking toward the house. I gather our belongings and hurry to catch up thinking, *We can't do this, we can't do this.* I don't say a word.

8:15 p.m.

We kept him safe, alright, Tempe says. Blaming me for his life, blaming me for his death, for the first time in a long while, I ignore her.

Walker's sitting on the porch rocking in that chair like he been up all night just waiting. "You put her up to this," he says, pointing at me. "You more like your mama than I thought. Ain't I done everything for you? I gave you a mama when your own up and killed herself."

James was right. I can't catch my breath. Don't seem like my body is working at all. My heart ain't beating. I can't swallow. Can't blink. All I can do is hear.

"Should have known you'd have had some of that devil in you," he says. "Nothing but the devil. First chance you get you run off and drag your sister and that baby through the woods. And why? Cuz somebody done told you you suppose to be free?" He spits a dark clump of tobacco that near hits me. I don't move. "Well, they done lied to y'all. The war done ended and they ain't set you free, did they? Ain't nobody come knocking on your door, door I provided, to give you no papers or nothing. I coulda told you wouldn't nothing change but you wouldn't have believed it, would you? How could you? Too full of your mama and her evil ways to know when somebody doing you right. It ain't your fault." He pauses, leans forward so far I think he'll fall clear out his chair. "Ain't Tempe's either. It's mine. I got my own self to blame. Treating you like family, like equals. I was going to let you all go right on working and I was going to go right on taking care of you all. No bad blood or nothing. But I see we can't do that. Can't be civil with animals. You want to be free. You free. There's your papers right there." He balls up a sheet of paper and tosses it by my feet. "Go on."

"What about Mama?" Tempe asks.

Walker gets to grinning. "That's what you come for? Agnes?" He laughs. "Why all you had to do was ask! I got the papers right there in the house. Come on in and help me get them," he says.

I step up on the porch and press my palm against the wood door. The smell of dust and mold hits me soon as I open the door. I hold my breath; don't get one foot across the threshold.

"Not you," Walker says, "you." He points to Tempe.

Your mama kisses you on the top of your head, squeezes you tight, and puts you in my arms.

"Just for safekeeping," she says.

She takes my place at the door. Walker closes it behind them. I'm out there rocking you when your pa comes. I put you in his arms. He's holding and kissing and loving on you. He's still holding you when we hear your mama screaming. Smoke's streaming from the roof. Windows get to popping. The house is on fire. A shot. More screaming. I run to the door to save Tempe. The door's already gone. Inside, the front room, parlor, sitting room is fire. What used to be furniture are melting balls of flames, the walls and floor are nearly gone. I'm calling, Tempe! Tempe! But there's no answer. She's the only thing on my mind. I can't live without her. She's all I have.

Your pa pulls me back, drops you in my arms.

"Run! Keep my boy safe!" he says.

The house is splintering, cracking in two. It's being eaten alive and taking Tempe with it. Your pa shoves me down what's left of the steps. Without looking back or knowing your name, he jumps into the flames. Two more shots, one more scream. I run.

You hungry, soiled, and angry. I don't know where we heading but I plan to stay in the woods most of the day. I ain't the only one. Freedom come alright. For most of us, it hasn't come on horses or with golden trumpets. Wasn't no angel going around saving all the slaves. Some owners turn people loose. Some slaves walk off. Far as I know, wasn't nobody going round checking if people had set slaves free. And don't seem like nobody's making sure we stay free either.

The woods overflow with people. They spill over paths forging ways where there were none. Even in sleep they seem to be moving. Some further south, others up north. A few of them wander, stumbling over rocks and people, silently staring straight ahead. Most people talking, singing, mumbling, laughing, moaning, crying, some of them all at the same time. Everybody's carrying some bit of news or looking for some. I can't rest at a log or sip along the river without somebody slipping behind me asking if I know their brother, sister, mother, father. If I can help them find their daughter, cousin, grandmama. Their stories keep me up. For that, I'm thankful. I can't close my eyes without seeing Tempe.

She's in Walker's parlor and I'm there with her. They don't see me. Walker's pointing a shotgun at Tempe's chest. Tempe's holding a hot poker above her head. He's about to pull the trigger. She's about to strike. I open my eyes.

I'm back in the woods. I can't catch my breath.

Keep moving. It's a whisper just above my ear.

I turn around but ain't nobody there.

Hurry up. The whisper surrounds me, blowing in both my ears at once.

"Tempe?" I whisper back. I know it ain't her but it's her voice. It feels like Tempe. I'm in the middle of the woods talking to myself. People walk right around me not paying me any mind.

You'll miss her.

"I don't have time for this foolishness," I say. "I ain't taking no parts in this."

Somebody's playing tricks on me. I'll stand right there until the rascal comes out. Ought to be ashamed. I'm tapping my foot, waiting. A hot breeze pushes against my back. The longer I stand, the hotter it blows. I'll just keep walking, I decide. "I ain't leaving on account of you," I say.

I'm not sure but I think I hear laughter.

I'm carrying you tight to my breasts. You mad about it and let me know it. I emptied one of them bundles and wrapped you up inside it. Left them shells, rocks, molded food behind. Memories scattered all over Maryland. From your smell won't be too long before I have to empty the other one. All I have left is this book, a few skins, a little bit of food, and you. Between screaming, you rooting around and biting on me. More than once I wonder if babies can drink blood cuz you sure seem fit to draw it.

"He's hungry," a woman says, like I don't know it. She slips up beside me. I been trying to mash anything I could find to settle you. "You ain't got no milk?" She puts out her arms. I undo the bundle. Hand you to her. She's shaking her head and clucking about how small you is and how lucky you is to be free. She nurses you till you fall asleep. "You ain't gonna get far with this baby and no milk."

I don't ask her why she got milk and no babies. She looks like she been running day and night since the war began. She fidgets when she sits, while she talks. She's itching to get on her way.

"Now we gonna have to watch out," she says. "Everybody ain't ready to stop slaving. They done set up so many rules and laws, the woods is the safest place to be right now. But won't be for long. So many soldiers marching, slipping, and running through the woods on the way to or from some battle, pretty soon we'll have to take the main road. The baby's likely to slow us down. Don't make no never mind, we'll head north at nightfall."

We? I don't even know this gal's name and she's already tied herself to us. You fall asleep in her arms. She ain't far behind you. Both of you snuggled up against a tree trunk, snoring. Soon as she wakes up I'll tell her we ain't going. What do I know about up north? How can I leave Tempe behind?

I can't sleep with the woods and my head filled with moaning, crying, and footsteps. I close my eyes and see your mama standing in the doorway burning. Each time I blink, my heart jumps. I hear crackling, popping, screaming. Before long it's like I'm in the house watching Tempe ask Walker about Mama. I can hear him laughing. Pushing up against her, whispering in her ear how he done sold Mama Lord knows where to God knows who. He grabs for her. She snatches up a poker. He reaches for it. She swings. The curtains catch afire, then the settee, then Walker. But he's got a shotgun. Shots splintering the sky like lighting splitting wood. Sometimes it's a shotgun in Walker's hand. Sometimes it's in Tempe's. It's always me pulling the trigger.

Get up.

I don't need no ad in the paper, no crow flying over my shadow, or no cock crowing to tell me Tempe's dead. I'm lying there holding my breath, one, two, three, thinking about her, Mama, Watson, Edward. Everybody gone. I'm thinking about the times I ain't never known that Samantha told us about. The things James said. The stories. Back when he was little, Watson, me, and the kids from the other plantations playing out back of the cabin, snatching crumbs of grown-folk talk, thinking we was grown. Mama teaching me to walk, to run, to be Spring and not Sister all the time. Not my mama? They wrong. All of them. The rumbling snores stop. There's no wind blowing. Nothing. I ain't breathing, ain't holding my breath no more and not bursting for air. It's pitch black. Something's moving. It's light-footed, graceful, close. It's right next to me, warm. It smells like cinnamon. Ain't no man, no animal either. I know it ain't nothing else but Tempe.

Seems like soon as I know it, I can see her. The only light comes from her. Her entire body smolders like burning coal. I feel like I should holler out or scream or pray but I don't do none of those things. I just wait. She kisses you all over. She can't get enough of you. I can't move, don't want to. She sits beside me. She holds my hands in her warm, smooth ones. We stay there, her sitting and rocking and humming and me just lying there not able to smile, to talk, to breathe. I can't open my lips, can't make the words come out. Can't tell her I love her. I feel a stinging sensation of love all around me, through me. She tells me everything she's seen since she been dead. How she flips through time like pages and sees whole lives. She tells me about Ella and Mama, Papa Jonah and Mama Skins. Remember, she says. She don't tell me everything but I don't know it then. She don't say it, but I know she wouldn't have done it if it weren't for me. She wouldn't have left you if there had been some other way. If I hadn't put it in her head that she could save us, that Walker would tell her where Mama was, she'd be alive today instead of me. My heart starts beating fast. I take a deep breath and hold it. I know by the time I let it out, she'll be gone. I hold it for as long as I can. Sooner or later I breathe.

I sleep for an hour, maybe more. It's still dark. You're bound to my bosom, full and happy. The girl is jumpy, ready to move. She's weaved some hides to make something you can hold on to. When we reach the river, she fills one with water, stitches it. We set off following the river. Twice as many folks out at night as during the day. She's asking folks about her kin: an old woman with eyes that twinkle when she laughs and nails as long and thick as fingers. A baby that ain't never opened her eyes.

"Ain't you got nobody to find?" she asks.

"You seen a woman called Agnes?" I ask the next person we see.

The woman stares at me, waits. "Agnes what?" she asks. "Walker, we belonged to Walker."

She purses her lips. "Who's your kin?"

"Just Mama and my sister, Tempe."

"What she look like?"

I get to describing her. Soon's as I say one thing, I remember another. "She's about this tall, no, this tall. About this wide, no," I picture her again, "this wide. She's got a laugh that could make the birds take notice. Her voice sounds like trickling rain, she moves like the river."

The woman grabs both of my hands in hers. "If I see her, I'll tell her you looking for her. God bless," she says.

"You ain't never gonna find your mama like that," my companion says after a few days.

I picture her twinkling-eyed, long-nailed mama. I'm not the only one, I think. We been walking for miles before I find out her name. We stopped a few minutes ago. She's nursing you for the umpteenth time.

"What's his name?"

You're suckling on one teat, already eyeing the other one. "Edward Freeman, just like his pa. What's yours?"

"Spinner, like my ma. She was the best spinner on the whole plantation. I'm gonna change my name, though. What they call you?"

Flames lick at the bottom of my feet, up my calves and thighs, to my belly, through my chest. They creep up my neck. Not Sister, not anymore. "Spring, my name's Spring."

Chapter 19

It's been days. Spinner tries names on and off as we travel. For a few miles she's Rose, she goes a whole day as Sunshine and a few steps as Tallulah. We've been practicing describing people. I've gone from asking about Mama to asking about Mama, Watson, James, and Samantha. The last time I described Watson as a flash of muscled-brown goodness, she stopped me: "Don't nobody care 'bout how he looks in your head. What's he look like for real?" Since then, my descriptions are more precise. It's my memories that fade. I lose count of how many people I describe them to. I interrupt a man in the middle of fishing. I'm halfway through describing Watson's long, brown arms.

"Does he have one of them grins that get people to smiling? Like this?" He demonstrates.

My body's shaking. He's asking about Watson's walk, the way he stands and leans to one leg, the way his arms swing just a little, the way his face don't tell nothing at all about what he's thinking. I'm swallowing hard, trying to keep what's inside in. I'm crying and shouting. You crying. By the time we get you settled down good it's night. We set out following the fisherman's directions at dawn. We don't have far to go but I'm out of breath by the time we get there. A post office / general store / fishery in the middle of a town just outside of Baltimore. The place reeks of fresh fish, crabs, and spices I ain't never smelled before. I know this is the place. It's no bigger than a slave shack but I'm the only one that seems to notice. People are lined up two-a-head from out the front door to clear around the corner. I ain't never seen so many folks in one place. I'm standing there with my mouth open. All them people. I see myself in their eyes. I'm sweating. My shift feels like rags. It clings to me. My bare feet are caked in mud, dirt, and animal droppings. I pat my hair. My tight curls are matted. I smell myself. I want to hide.

Spinner's looking like I feel. She swings her head from the front of the line to the back and back up again. Her mouth's wide open. She's jittery. I look back to the line. It's getting longer by the minute. All sorts of people wait in it. Old, young, men, women, poor, well-to-do, they got one thing in common: ain't none of them paying Spinner and me no mind. I hoist you up, straighten my shoulders, grab Spinner by the hand and lead us to the back of the line. The procession is mostly silent. Every so often a ripple of conversation moves through the crowd from lips to lips.

"Looking for a gal named Delilah, bout nine years old, chocolate-brown skin, this tall. Her folks are Antonia and Lewis Coleman from Salisbury," the man in front of me says. He starts shifting from foot to foot. His eyes are like large dark pools pulling me in. I know cuz he's staring at me. Seems like everyone in front of me turns too. You let out an angry cry. I'm squeezing you tight. Trying to find something to hold on to so I don't get lost in his eyes.

"We don't know her," Spinner says. She passes the message to the person behind us.

The man nods his head, turns ahead to await more news. News travels from one end of the line to the other for hours before we reach the shop door. Inside, fish hang from hooks, crabs scrabble around in buckets. The walls are plastered with pictures and newspaper ads. Lost, Lost, Lost. They all seem to say the same thing. Some got pictures. We shuffle past them. Can't neither of us read. I'm watching folks for signs of Watson. A familiar walk, gesture, shake of the head. Something. My heart's beating fast.

"What can I get you?" a man asks.

His apron is stained with blood. I can't seem to see nothing else but streaks of bloody handprints. Till I see a hole. Just like the hole that must be gaping from Walker's chest. Spinner is as jumpy as a cat in heat. She's grabbing on my arm and whispering in my ear but I can't make out a word she's saying. I'm about tired of her hot breath on the side of my face and spin around to tell her so when I catch a glimpse of something from the corner of my eye. His forehead's all creased up but I'd know that face anywhere. It ain't Watson. He don't look nothing like him. But Spinner's squealing about how I found him and how he looks exactly like I been describing and what a miracle it is. Before I can set her straight, he's around the counter grabbing me with thick arms. He pushes me back, looks me over from head to toe then hugs me again. He's crushing you to me. He don't notice until you scream to tell him about it.

"He yourn?" Franklin asks.

Well?

I'm about to say no. To explain that I let Tempe down. To tell him I should have been the one to die. That Tempe would be standing here, holding her boy, her husband by her side, if I had stood up to her for once. If I had believed I, and not her, was the special one. Each time I try to explain, she pinches me. She twists my skin in her hot fingers, leaving burned kisses on my arms. *Don't you abandon my boy.* Before I know it, I'm telling him you are. I let him hold you. He's staring at you. If he can see your pa in your long fingers and thin lips, he don't say nothing. His boss gives him a pack of sandwiches and five minutes to get back to work. Franklin leads us out back. I'm hungrier than I thought. Between gulps of tomato-and-cheese sandwiches, Spinner, me, and Franklin try to squeeze in all we got to say. Franklin's watching Spinner nurse. I'm waiting on him to ask about my milk.

"Y'all caught me just in time," he's saying, "me and Buddy heading up to Pennsylvania. He got a friend up there. Got jobs lined up and everything."

"You heard anything 'bout Watson?" I ask. My throat's dry. I try to picture him right. The color of his eyes, the shape of his head, anything. All I can make out for sure is his back.

He don't say nothing for about a minute. Then he smiles. "Last time I seen Watson, he was smoking past Tempe heading due north. Fast as he was running, I don't suspect he stopped till he got clear to Canada. You know they would have killed him if he came back, don't you? Kirk had a bounty out on him. Dead or alive, Kirk didn't care which. Between the patrollers and slave catchers, that boy couldn't slow down till he crossed the border and even then, with them pulling folks back and selling them further south, seems like there wasn't no time for him to stop running." Franklin closes his eyes like he can see Watson running.

I'm smiling right along with him, trying to make his memory mine.

Buddy strolls up thirty minutes later. Seeing him is better than I remember. He's quiet, almost gentle. Years in the service have made him think before speaking. We're late. Franklin's scrubbed down the shop and himself, said his goodbyes and got his last pay. Buddy's been telling us about the places he's been. Seems like he's seen the whole world.

"It ain't gonna be easy in Philadelphia," he says, "ain't none of us strangers to hard work. Long as we don't expect no handouts, won't be surprised when we don't get none. Between what me and Franklin's got saved, we be able to get a room for you two. Try to keep close as we can. Got jobs lined up for the both of us. There's farming outside the city. In the city there's domestic work and even factories. You two can take turns caring for the baby."

He's got it all figured out except Spinner's having second thoughts about leaving without finding her mama. Second thoughts turn to thirds. How will her mama know where to find her? She won't, we agree. Unless someone can get word to her. We can put an ad in the paper. Spinner's shaking her head, her mama can't read. What if her mama's up north? No, Spinner says, there ain't no reason to think her mother would be up north already set free and not send for her only girl-child. No, she ain't up north. The more Spinner talks about it, the more convinced she is that her mama is right there in Maryland looking for her. Don't have the heart to speculate on her being down south. None of us do. Spinner will stay behind. Buddy asks if I want to stay with her and have them send for me. I can't stop thinking about my own room. Making my own money. Picking and choosing my own work and being paid for it. Nobody telling me what needs doing or when to do it. Seem like everything about slaving is right here and freedom is right across that line.

Buddy's ready to go. He knows a place Spinner can stay until she's ready to join us in Philadelphia. He shows her how to get news to him through the shop where we found Franklin. Franklin will put in a good word for her so she can find work. It won't be long. Soon as she finds her mama, they can join us in Philadelphia.

"What about the baby, what will he eat?" Spinner asks. "Let him stay with me, till he's off the teat." She's reaching for you, her fingers opening and closing like claws.

You're all I have. Besides, your mama would kill me. I'm shaking my head no. You watching me with your mama's eyes just daring me to give you away. "We'll figure something out," I say. I swear you smile up at me and wink.

We have a minute to say goodbye and then a truck pulls up behind the shop. The back is full of furniture, mattresses, and people. Farm hands, travelers, and other workers take up each inch of space. Franklin goes around front to talk to the driver. Two men jump out the back. They exchange brief greetings before Buddy hops in. The driver's still fussing about numbers not adding up. After a bit of to and fro Franklin comes back, lifts you up to Buddy, hoists hisself up and puts his hand out to me. It's crowded but people make room.

"If anyone asks," he says, "you Buddy's wife, this his boy."

No one asks the entire ride but I'm rolling the words around my mouth just in case. We ride for miles, stopping every few feet for someone to jump off and a new somebody to jump on. Each person has a story. Your pa tells one about the war. By the time he's finished, he's made you a gourd and fashioned a nipple for you to chew on. Your uncle's tale is about the last time he saw his mama. Mine is about the last time I seen mine. It goes on like that for hours. Laughing, crying, whispering, singing, shouting, we swap stories in between bumping along the road. We're supposed to remember them, to pass them on to folks we meet. Everyone's looking for someone. Like a bucket, I'm carrying a head full of names and stories. Older ones spill out to make room for new ones.

After a while it's our turn to jump off. We're in the middle of a field. Somebody has given us milk for you and apples for each of us. If this is Philadelphia, it sure ain't what I pictured. It stinks of horse manure. Piles of it are just stacked on top of each other like crates. The air is so thick with flies I can't tell where the dirt ends. But it's free thick air and though I can't hardly breathe, I'll make do. Tracks run through the fields. On either side of them, rickety shacks rattle and shake every time the wind blows good. Don't look like they big enough to hold all of us but if we take turns, one inside, one out, we'll be alright. I just hope we don't have to walk too far to use the pot. Buddy and Franklin start walking beside the train tracks. I'm right alongside them. You're in Buddy's arms, sleep-smiling up at him like you know he's family now. The sun's bright but it's cold. It's winter. We're walking farther away from the smell of dung. Grass crunches beneath our feet. Birds sing. The air is crisp with the smell of snow. Fat flakes begin falling. A train whistles from far off. Smoke billows across the sky.

"I thought there'd be more people in Philadelphia," I say.

They laugh, mouths open, heads back, laughter. Even though they laughing at me, it sounds good.

"If this was Philadelphia, these railroad tracks would be dollar bills. And them shacks would be grand houses. Them horses and cows over there would be Misters and Missus lined up with trays of fish eggs and frog legs and champagne just waiting to serve someone like me."

"Franklin's just funning. In Philadelphia, all the buildings this high, and the men are this tall and the women right up there, this tall. You short. People will know straight away you ain't from there. But me and Brother will fit right in, we'll tell them you're with us. You'll be fine. They got roads and streets bigger than any you seen before. The sun shines longer, brighter cuz it's bigger there."

"You been there?" I ask. Your father nods, yes. "Then why you come back?"

"I come back for what's mine."

His eyes get dark. Franklin smiles but I don't think Buddy's talking about him and I don't ask.

"What kind of work they got there in Philadelphia?" I ask.

"Bud and me got factory jobs lined up. All sorts of steel work for train parts, buildings, automobiles, you name it, they need it. They got factories for factories. Buttons, shoes, dresses, rugs, anything you can think of come in or out of a factory."

"Maybe I'll get me one of them factory jobs."

"You could get a job as a domestic like this," Franklin snaps his fingers, "cooking, cleaning, baking, washing, mending, or farm work."

"And I'd get paid for it, right?"

"Sure enough, gal! This ain't slaving, this working," he says.

"We have to get you fixed up, of course," Buddy says. "Can't have you out there looking like no slave."

Before I know it, I'm walking faster. They huffing to keep up.

"You beautiful all cleaned up," he continues. "Don't see why the world shouldn't see how pretty my woman is."

Now, between you and me, I ain't have no intentions on slowing down. But my legs start to thinking it's a good time to stop moving. Buddy and Franklin speed right on past me before they notice I ain't coming. I gather my common sense and catch up. Buddy puts his hand in mine. We talking about how we gonna save money to buy a big house. Each of us will have a room and there will be a room for our mamas, Spinner and her mama, anybody else that need a room. We'll charge for dinners, have rent parties. Between all us working and making money doing odd jobs, we'll be rich. I don't know how long we walk. The train whistles again. It's loud and close. It's barreling down the tracks. A flash of yellow, purple, red, black.

"Hop on," Franklin calls. He's halfway in.

Your father hands you to your uncle and leaps in beside him. All that smoke and noise and y'all rolling right out of my life on a fast-moving monstrous beast. My feet scramble every which way. I'm close enough to touch the side. I lift my arms up to try to slow it down or grab hold of something. Buddy grabs one hand, Franklin takes the other, and they hoist me up and into the car. We all huffing and puffing. I'm loud-laughing so they don't hear my heart.

After a while we settle down and I can look good around the car. It's a freight train. We ain't the only ones in there. Skeletons of machines, stacks of crates, and people cram just about every inch of that car. Outdoors races by. Inside we rock and shake as we rumble across the country. Smoke and whistles. I jump at each wail of the train. My stomach lurches with each dip and bump. I busy myself with you. But soon as you fed, you fall asleep like the loud noise suits you just fine. I clear off a little patch of floor that isn't covered in hay and whatnot and set out supper. I can't eat none of it. With all this rocking, don't expect it would stay down no how. I make the mistake of taking a deep breath. I like to choke. Sweat, bodies, manure, dirt. Going up north sure better be worth it.

People hop on and off all the way to Philadelphia. Some of them don't hardly say a word. Some won't stop talking. To pass the time I pull out the book me and Tempe made. After a while I get folks to write their name or make their mark in it. Some write a few lines. Some draw pictures. Some give me clippings to add to it. Newspaper headlines, pages from books, Wanted posters, receipts. The longer we rattle on, the more I collect. I tell stories. Grand ones about escapes and revolts and little ones about people holding on to treasures. The whole world races pass.

By the time I finally get to sleep, Buddy's shaking me. Franklin's hollering, "This our stop!" like the train ain't still moving. If I was awake good, no telling when we'd have got off. I must be still half asleep. The train's moving through a station. We're going slow enough that I can see the wooden platform, the yellow-and-green station house, the looks on people's faces. Franklin's at the opening, folks lined up beside him. Buddy's still shaking me. He pulls me up, gathers my bundle, pulls us toward Franklin. Before I can say a word, Franklin leap-steps right off the train. The others follow. It's our turn and I'm saying, "I can't do it."

You sure is gonna do it.

My whole body leaps into the air. Tempe's pushing me. My feet hit the wood and don't stop moving till I feel a hand pulling me back.

"Slow down there," Buddy says. He's laughing and wiping sweat from his forehead. "We got a while to travel before we home. You plan on running all the way?"

The station ain't but a little thing. We in it and out it in one step. It's nice, though. Shiny wood benches, wood doors; my back aches for whoever's got to scrub all that. I know right then I was born to be in Philadelphia. Smells of baked bread, fried fish, and smoked meats hit me as soon as I'm outdoors. Right in front of the station, women braid and sell warm pretzels. Boys roast chestnuts, sell newspapers. Men sell shoe shines, information, and rides. The street is a ball of bees and they all buying or selling something. Franklin gets directions and we're on our way. Whole hogs glare at me through plate-glass windows, merchants yell prices, housewives haggle over discounts. People rush through the streets, work clothes starched and pressed. Trolleys drawn by horses trip up and down Chestnut Street. I feel eyes watching us like we're some picture show. I feel myself shrinking. Head down, shoulders slumped, body folded inward to make myself smaller, to disappear, I shuffle between the two brothers. I don't look back but I know Tempe ain't far behind.

Franklin pinches me. "Stop walking like that," he says. His back is straight, so is Buddy's. They fit in with the crowd of folk going and coming. Out the corner of my eye I see Tempe. She's wearing a clean dress, her hair is neat, she's wearing shoes. She belongs. I clutch you tight, straighten my shoulders, hold my head up and do my best to look like I belong too.

We reach the church before nightfall. It's a stone building with a wooden cross on the front. I want to touch it. Men and women rush in and out of the door carrying slips of paper, pressed uniforms, bags of food. Little kids play outside while older children learn their lessons. "A, B, C," they repeat. I want to stay and listen but Buddy's got his hand pressed against my back pushing me across the threshold. Inside, music plays, a choir sings, people laugh, argue, pray. For a little while, it feels like home.

The woman, Mrs. Leyland, rolls her eyes for what has to be the umpteenth time. She sucks her teeth. Crosses herself. Whispers a prayer under her breath and tries again. "What did you do before you got here?" She holds the pencil poised over the form.

"I done told you," I answer, "I was a slave." I have told her no less than five times. "I done everything."

She drops the pencil to the desk. Rubs her eyes. She closes them, then peeks from under her long lashes. I'm still there. She stares at me like she wishes I wasn't. Her eyes liked to burn holes through mine.

"I told you, I can't write that. People don't want to hire ex-slaves."

"It's the truth. All of us," I point to Buddy and Franklin, "born slaves."

"That may be true, but I can't write that on this form. Ms. Spring, no one wants to be reminded you were a slave. Is that what you want people to think of when they look at you? When they look at your boy?"

"Well, I ain't lying," I say. I cross my arms. The wooden chair creaks as I lean forward. "I did the planting, plowing, harvesting, washing, mending, baking, cooking, smoking—" She holds up a slim, manicured hand. I hide mine, nails bit short, skin calloused, beneath me. She snatches up the pencil, scrawls on the page. "Do-mestic," she says. "It means you good at everything. I have quite a few domestic positions. Once we get you cleaned up, you'll be good for any one of them. Got to get someone to care for the baby." She taps her nails on the tip of her desk. "I got just the place!"

"I ain't giving up my boy." I'm ready to go.

"Of course not," she says. "We have to get you set up with a place to live and I have something in mind for you and the baby." Barely looking up, she glances at Buddy and Franklin. "You two come with fine references. One of you will be working at the shipyard, the other at a steel factory." She shuffles papers in her hands. She looks Buddy over, then Franklin, reads the forms again. "Here." She gives them each a sheet.

They look them over, switch the papers and fold them carefully in their pockets. Franklin gives her a wink. Mrs. Leyland don't say nothing. She goes back to filling out the form. Race, religion, age, she asks. Don't seem to matter what I say. She's half writing before I open my mouth. She pushes away the stack of papers and pulls out a thick book. She thumbs through listings of rooms for rent. Some have photos; others are just markings and checks in boxes. "You two have been set up on the even side of Grammercy and it just so happens that we have an opening across the street for your wife and boy."

Your father thanks her.

"I'll put you on the family list so when a spot opens you can live together. Do you know what date it was when you got married?"

No women praying over me, no splashing through the river, no love. Married and not even a pretty dress.

"Wasn't too long ago, ma'am," Buddy says.

She fills out a paper. "We'll just set it for today. Pastor will sign that. He doesn't place much stock in jumping the broom weddings. Did you have one of those?"

I close my eyes. I can see your mother flitting through the woods searching for Edward.

"It doesn't matter," she says. "It doesn't seem likely a slave owner would allow time for much more than that anyhow. We just need to get a few more papers filled out. What's the baby's name?"

Just as I open my mouth to tell her, your father answers Bud. Like that's a name.

What?

A rush of hot air. Mrs. Leyland's papers get to trembling. She don't notice cuz she's busy fanning herself. She starts writing like she can't see me shaking my head.

"It's Edward, ma'am," I say.

"Bud Edward? Or Edward Bud?" she asks.

"Just Edward."

Tempe stops throwing a fit. The hot air winds down. "Now, that's an interesting name." Leyland's smiling and nodding. "Short for Justice? One of them powerful names. People need strong names to live up to."

I don't understand city folk. Franklin's smiling and flirting and smoothing corners. He's saying your name is Edward and how youse named after a friend of the family. Every so often she smiles and nods. She's shuffling papers and asks, casual like, "What's the family name?"

We standing there inventing whole lives and got five minutes to do it. Walker? Too much tied up to that place. Everything I had, I got and lost right there on Walker land. Walker wasn't family. No matter what happened before, Buddy, Franklin, and you are the only family I got. Right now I can choose a different me. Free from years of slaving. Free from being a second-best miracle. Seem like everybody I met was shedding theyselves in the woods, in the truck, on the train, right here. I can let loose the past. I'm rolling names around on my tongue. It's got to be a name with a future. One that's strong and proud and free.

"Well, ma'am," Buddy's saying, "we all free men, all of us."

"That's fine, Mr. Freeman," she says as she writes.

Chapter 20

1866

Grammercy don't look nothing like it do now. Rows and rows of houses line both sides of the streets. Each brick house is shoulder to shoulder with the next one. Scrubbed walkways lead up to spick-and-span steps and fresh-painted doors.

When we finally get to Twentieth Street, we're tired. I'll be at 117 Twentieth Street. Buddy and Franklin at 120, across the street. We stand out front for a good while. It's neat, cared for. My first three-story house. The door is painted red, the steps damp and freshly scrubbed. It smells of honeysuckle and lemon and fresh bread. I'm hoping it's the right place. The house next door looks empty. Flower petals litter the front of sagging, dirty steps leading up to a peeling door. It's staring at me through gaping holes where windows should be. I can see clear through. Cross the threshold through the dining room, sitting room, kitchen, and out back to the gardenless yard. I can picture it, though. With your father fixing the roof and your uncle fixing the floors, and the rest up to God, it could be a home.

"You ain't near as ornery looking as I heard you was," a woman says. She introduces herself, laughs. "Ain't that just the prettiest little baby?"

I turn fast, almost spinning right into the prettiest woman I have ever seen, Sable. Her voice is sweet like music. She's smiling. Her black hair is pinned up into tight curls that bounce when she talks. She don't look much older than us. Since this is a rooming house, she must be one of the boarders. She studies my face, hands, body, feet. "Etta Mae got you signed up for all sorts of classes, don't she?" She laughs. "You and the baby will be staying here. I got a boy of my own. One big as you." She points to Buddy and Franklin. "His name's Christian. He's on his way back. Fought in the war."

"Now, you look too good to have a boy grown as me," Franklin says.

"Etta Mae already has a line of gals in mind for you to meet," Sable says. "Eligible ones."

He winks.

"For marrying," she continues.

Your uncle does a pretend shiver. "I'd just as soon wait on you to marry me, thank you."

"I done married and buried men twice your age," she says. She reaches her arms out and you wiggle like a pig at a fair. You two always been thick as honey. "You'll work during the day and go to classes at night." She sways side to side while she speaks. Before long you give in and sleep. "I'll mind the baby while you work, study, or go to church. Seeing as you're married, I'll make an exception on male visitors but no single ones. One other boarder shares the house. We share the kitchen, outhouse, and dayroom. We all do the cooking, can you cook?" She don't wait for an answer. "Good, this ain't no hotel so we all got to do." She edges us up the path and closer to the steps while she talks. "I own the house next door too.

Getting it fixed up for when my boy gets back. You girls will move there soon as it's ready. You two should get going." She waves your father and uncle off. "You'll be staying with Mr. Johnson. If you need someplace quiet to think, just go right next door, let yourself in, and while you're there, pick up a hammer, some nails, and put your hands to use. Your backs too," she laughs.

Buddy and Franklin wave and head across the street. Your pa rushes back and kisses you on the head, brushes his dry lips against my cheek. They stroll over to a group of men.

"Next time that husband of yours sees you you'll be looking like a wife," Sable says.

Tempe laughs.

Before I can say nothing to either one of them, Sable's push-pulling me up the stairs into the house. Up one flight of stairs to another, there's a room for everything. Up another few stairs, across a landing it's room six, our room. I ain't never had my own anything. As long as I can pay the rent, this is our home. She unlocks the door and fresh air smacks me in the face. The window is wide open. Thin lacy curtains snap and blow on the breeze. I can't wait until we're alone. I put the bundle down by the door and hold my arms out for her to hand you over.

She's inside the room pointing out back. "The outhouse is right there next to the washhouse," she says.

Over the top of her head I see two wooden shacks, side by side. There ain't no fence but I can tell where the backyard ends. The grass is bright green, soft looking. I can't wait to run barefoot out there.

"I'm gonna get this little one fed while you get yourself settled. What's he—a month?"

I nod. The milk's curdled. I know before I check but I give it to her anyway. I'm ready to tell her why I ain't got no milk, how

I'm the mama you got now but not the mama that birthed you.

"I'll dig up something I had from when my boy was his age," she says. "I kept just about everything, you know, for grand-babies." Then she's telling me what time dinner is, and not to eat in my room. That reminds her to tell me there's no smoking or drinking or gambling except when there's a party. She's talking about how she can't wait until I meet the girls and chattering as she closes the door behind her.

All the sound goes with her. I ain't never sat on no real bed before. I press it with both hands just to feel it push up against my fingertips. I practice sitting on it, crossing and uncrossing my legs like I'm Mrs. Leyland. I lay back slow. The bed squeaks. The mattress is firm beneath me. I lay flat on my back, then on my stomach, on one side, then the other. It squishes and bounces. I love it more than anything until I feel the pillow and I love that even more. I'm never getting up.

Across from the bed, there's a big bureau full of drawers and cabinets. I start imagining it's full of treasures: dresses and shoes, coats and just maybe, in one of the little ones, something pretty like a necklace, a ring, or a shell. I run over and open each drawer. Other than scattered, dried flowers, there ain't nothing in them. I empty the bag of clothes the church gave us. I hang up two dresses and put one thing in each drawer. There's a door on one side of the cabinet and inside, there's a mirror. I'm staring back at me. My dress is stained. It looks like I haven't washed in months. Mama would kill me for walking around looking like this. I shut the door quick. I put the book on the top of the bureau.

I'm sitting on the edge of the bed, bouncing up and down soft-like. It starts feeling good. I'm smiling and giggling and before I know it, I'm standing on the bed jumping up and down trying to touch the ceiling. I'm laughing. There's a sharp knock on the door. I get down quick and answer it.

"You got somebody in there?" Sable asks. We both know ain't nobody up here but me.

I hear giggling and shushing from just below the steps. I'm out of breath but I answer, "Why, no," in my best Missus's voice. She peeks her head around me. She's staring so hard I look too. Black footprints all over her white linens. She's mumbling about grown-up children playing while babies trying to sleep. She strips the bed. She don't seem mad but I don't never jump on her furniture again.

I'm back sitting on the edge of the bed waiting till the laughter dies down when the room gets hot. I got the book on my lap. I'm fingering the grooves in the skin. I look up and Tempe's watching me.

You sure got a way of messing things up, Tempe says.

I jump.

You look just like pa when you do that.

We ain't never had no pa, I'm about to tell her, but she's already shaking her head.

Did too. Who you know born whole without no mama or papa? Tempe sits down on the bed. *This is nice.* Smoke comes out her mouth when she talks. I'm worried Sable will charge me for smoking in the room. She won't believe I ain't. By now the room smells of charred wood. Tempe's laughing so hard she can't hardly tell me. But she's talking about how our father, Little James, escaped Walker's. He almost got North when he got caught by patrollers and sent South. He run off again and joined a rebellion group. Lived off a little patch of swamp. By now she's wiping her eyes even though I don't see no tears. *All that and know how he died?*

I don't even know how he lived. How would I know? I shrug.

I'm getting used to her sitting next to me. Wispy and thin. You been eating? I want to ask. She's beautiful, even now. Her body is like one long question mark. Her neck curves slightly when she leans down to talk to me. I don't remember her being so much taller than me. The rest of her body pulses in time with her heart. I know it's rude to, but I'm staring at her heart bump-bumping in her chest and watching her skin blow like air: in and out, in and out. She don't seem to mind. Always did like being the center of attention.

He fell in a ditch, broke his neck and snap, *he died.*

It takes me a second to get what she's saying. We had a father and now we don't but I ain't had no father before now either and I won't. I'm crying. She's tickled. She's laughing again and smacking her thigh. I'm waiting for a knock on the door, wiping snot and tears from my face and trying to catch my breath and wondering: Are we both crazy? She's cackling like death is about the funniest thing she can imagine. Will they put me away in one of them asylums? What will happen to Edward?

She stops laughing just like that. She's staring at me. *He and I laugh about it but I can see why you wouldn't think it was funny.* She says it like she's feeling sorry for me for not being dead.

Here I am free and don't have to be dead to be it. I got a family, a husband, a baby. And she's feeling sorry for me? Then because she's all in my head and it don't matter no how I tell her, "You ain't nothing but a haint and there ain't no such a thing. You ain't even here. I'm here, that baby here. And he's mine. Like it or no, I'm his mama and he ain't gonna know nothing about you. I mean it." I get up and put the book way back in a drawer. I slam it shut. She's gone when I finish but I'm holding my breath, waiting for her to hit me or set me on fire. Do something. I'm setting here shaking when Lillian comes in.

"You better not let Sable catch you smoking in here, she'll double your rent," she says.

By the time we get to the back door, Lillian's telling me to act surprised. She swings open the door and there's you in a dressing gown in Sable's arms with at least half a dozen women gathered around you.

"It's your welcome party," Lillian says. She grabs my hands and leads me to the group.

There's musicians playing and somebody singing. Someone's frying up fish, another's turning a corncake. I'm trying to make my way over to you but each time I get close, somebody stops me. You look just like so-and-so, one says. You sure you not related to the Jones or Watsons or Smiths or Fowlers? I hear it all. I ain't sure about none of it. I tell them I don't know who my people are or where to find them. They look at me like they know what that's like. So many of them are lost too. They ask who's looking for me.

I don't know what to say. What's the newspaper say about Walker? How do folks back home think he, Tempe, and Edward died? What they think happened to me? They think I done it? Got 'em all shot and set the place on fire? Are they looking for me? Patrolling the woods, lanterns shining, dogs barking, sniffing me out? How long until they lose my scent? Do they think I'm dead? Think it's Tempe running around with her feet in this soft, Philadelphia grass? Did they bury me? Go around the house separating soot from bone and throw me in a ditch out back? What if the whole house is gone? Burst into fire like a dry piece of wood. Or swallowed whole and sent straight down to hell. Is that where Tempe is? Is that why she's burning? Next time she comes, I'll ask her. Lillian plucks me free from the women and delivers me to the washhouse. She hands me a bucket of water, some soap, and a scrubber. "These yours," she says. She's pushing me inside. "Scrub your hair too. Take your time." Can't be but a few minutes later when she's banging on the door talking about it's time to get dressed. I ain't bring no clothes down with me. She pops the door open and hands me a towel. I got about a minute to dry off before she opens the door again and trades me the towel for some undergarments and what feels like a soft piece of fabric. It's too dark to make nothing so I'm not sure what she's expecting me to do.

"You got it on yet?" she whispers through the peephole.

I know I don't have long before she throws the door wide open with me buck-naked standing in a washhouse for the whole world to see. I feel for the holes and slip it over my head. It's a dress. It moves when I twirl and kisses the back of my legs. I open the door and step out.

"Looks good on you," she says.

She winds the towel around my hair and leads me to a woman on a stool. I don't catch her name but she's pushing me down, so I sit between her legs with my back to her. "It's May-Belle," she repeats her name loud, in case I can't hear her. I feel like a child. She pats my hair dry, then she's twisting and oiling. My scalp tingles and soaks up the moisture it's been missing. My head smells like lavender. I reach up to touch. Maybelle swats my hand and giggles. Out the corner of my eye I see you passed around and kissed, cooed at and cooing. You're laughing. For a second I'm jealous till I remember, youse mine.

Sable pulls up a chair to sit next to Maybelle. "Your boy still looking for work?" she asks.

Maybelle snatches up some strands of my hair. She's pulling too tight. "Still looking," Maybelle says. "He can't seem to find nothing. With all these country folk coming to town, there's no way for decent folk to make a living. Sorry, honey."

I don't know if she's sorry for talking bad about country folks, cuz I'm country folk, or for pulling on my hair so tight my head hurts.

"Maybelle, ain't nobody coming here taking no job your boy wants. He mop floors, muck stables, clean outhouses? Work seven days and seven nights for pennies? Until he's ready to do that, he can't say nothing about nobody taking no job from his bony little hands. There's work enough for everybody, everybody who want to work."

"Who gonna hire him? They making all sorts of laws and regulations against hiring colored folks. I ain't saying it's cuz of them. I'm just saying it wasn't like that before them."

"My boy got a job lined up before he left, a good job," Sable says. "A nice factory job working two shifts a day, six days a week, just waiting on him to come home and fill it."

Maybelle's twisting my head down in a way I'm not sure it's supposed to go. I'm thinking my neck's about to give way. Even if my neck snaps she'll still be holding on to the braid of hair she's been pulling on for the past minute. Finally she releases it. I just about got my head where I want it when she turns me to the side, my head on her lap. She's wetting a fingertip in her mouth. She aims it at the side of my hair, smooths down baby hairs around my ears.

"What makes you think Christian's gonna come back to Philadelphia after he done seen the world? He ain't come back yet. Maybe he found himself a wife and they settling somewhere down south near her people."

"Don't be spiteful, Maybelle, it ain't becoming."

"By the time he gets back, one of them old slaves will have

snapped up his job. Wait and see. Everybody wanna hire a 'yes-sir-er.' Any job you set them to, them fresh-out-the-fields Negroes will do it. They be so happy to get a job, probably end up paying the bossman for giving it to them."

Lillian rescues me. "The baby needs his mama," she says. She's standing there grinning and you laying in Lillian's arms just sleeping.

"Just a second," Maybelle says. Another finger in her mouth, she smooths the other side of my face. "Done."

"Maybe she don't mean no harm," I say.

You're asleep in my arms. We're sitting in the grass under the apple tree, sharing hot fried fish and a steaming slab of corncake.

Lillian starts tapping her feet to the music. "Oh yes she does," she says. "She just don't know half of what comes out of her mouth. I blame the drink. Not that she touches it. But if anybody could use a stiff drink, it's her."

We're laughing when Mrs. Leyland sets down. "You girls ready for class?"

Don't know how long we sit there reciting sounds and words. By the time Sable comes to collect you, we tracing numbers and letters. Lillian's faster than me. Tempe too. She sits real close to Mrs. Leyland, shouting out answers nobody but me can hear. Mrs. Leyland says I'll catch up in no time. The party's over. We blow out the lanterns and clean up the backyard. The women leave me with presents: combs for my hair, my first bracelet, a scarf. You sleeping with Sable since she "got the little dumpling washed and fed and can't stand to wake you." I let her get away with it. There's a candle in my room when I get there. I light it and lay on the bed watching shapes creep up the wall. I can't sleep none. I sit by the window. Bats fly through the night. The city's as loud as the country. Across Sable's yard, there's a whole other row of houses. Beyond them another row and another. We all shut up tight.

I climb back in bed and just lay there thinking about watching you grow up and wondering will you look like your mama and praying you don't hate me for making you mine. I wake to the smell of coffee. It's Sunday morning.

Your pa's already downstairs with you in his arms. We sit in the parlor a spell; you, me, and Buddy. He's been talking to Sable about fixing up the house next door. I ask him if we a family for real.

"Don't see why not," he says.

I want to love him. He's reliable, a good provider, and a good man. Sable brings us eggs and toast and lets us sit in the parlor and eat it. She takes you after breakfast so we can get started next door. We standing in the doorway, with one hammer between us, wondering how we gonna fix all this with four hands.

"Gonna take a whole lot of Sundays," your pa says.

He gets started. He's pulling at nails. I'm piling moldy bed things and curtains in the middle of the parlor. While we busy working, folk just start turning up. Franklin's first. Next, men carrying tools tip their hats to me and look for Buddy or Franklin, whichever's closest. After brief discussions, some go on up to the roof, some to different parts of the house. Some get to banging on walls, others are pulling up floorboards. It's a choir of sawing and hammering and talking and laughing. It's a wonder they get anything done at all. After the men get a good rhythm going, women come with buckets, scrub brushes, and washtubs. Some drop off children next door, some set them to work.

Above the scraping and scrubbing, clipping and cutting, sweeping and digging, they talk.

"You got work lined up?" someone asks.

I tell them I think so.

"Keep your head about you," a woman says.

"Don't look none of them in the eye," someone warns.

"Just keep your mouth shut, your head down, get your work done, and make sure they pay you," someone else says.

"How am I supposed to do that?" I ask.

There's plenty of advice.

"If somebody don't pay you, don't complain about it," a woman says. "Go right next door to the neighbor and do a better job there than you did for the first. Get them to start competing with each other. Sooner or later they'll be paying you more than you ask for."

It sounds like a lot of work to me. How am I supposed to get two jobs when it's hard enough to get one? It's even harder to keep one. A few of the women had been slaves from further south. They swap stories over soapsuds. Every so often somebody shares a tale of whippings and lynchings. There was one about slaves getting up to whip the overseers, another about bodies swinging down from trees and chasing the would-be murderers. I keep my stories to myself. Once in a while, a story bubbles too close to the truth. Tempe helps me push it back down. She watches me work, pointing out specks of dirt and chasing off broken spirits only she can see.

"I ain't never gonna find my baby," a woman cries.

I want to say she might, to tell her stories about folks finding one another in the same town, on the same train, through newspaper ads and church grapevines, but I don't know any. I could tell her about Buddy finding Franklin and me finding him or about men in the woods with names on their tongues waiting on people to ask about them. About women staying behind, searching for their mothers. It don't seem like enough. I can't look her in the eyes and tell her to hope or pray or wish harder than she hoping or praying or wishing right now. And with Tempe standing there shaking her head no, I know that woman's baby is gone. Because there is nothing I can say, I say nothing.

The silent ones scare me the most. They scrub floors, beat carpets, chip at old wallpapers, and I can tell they doing more than just fixing this house. It's almost dark when warm hands lift me up from the floor. My knees ache, my back hurts, but that floor sparkles. By the looks of the sky we've been at it for hours.

"Time to head to church," Sable says. She's got you in a different nightdress. It matches hers. "Took longer than a day for this place to get run down. Gonna take more than one to set it right again."

"I'll just do one more room," I say.

She waves her hand around. I follow the movement with my eyes. All around floors and walls have been patched and scrubbed, rooms that had doors are flung open wide, aired out. There's a window where there wasn't one before. The men are already outside. The women finish packing up. They leave their supplies in the house for next weekend.

"Everybody's looking forward to meeting y'all," Sable says. It's almost gentle, one minute we in the house, the next we out. We walk to church together. Lillian strides ahead of us with a group of young girls. Buddy and Franklin walk behind us with the rest of the men. Sable and I are in a cluster of women. We march down the sidewalks of Grammercy like soldiers. I watch the women wave to old folks and ignore, like a herd, a girl digging through trash.

"Why they ain't say hello to that girl?" I ask.

"Who?"

I don't say nothing. I know she knows who I'm talking about. I walk slow-footed.

Without turning her head, Sable says, "She ain't one of them."

"One of them what?"

"One of us."

"They treat her like that cuz she don't believe in their god?"

"She don't believe in nothing far as I can tell. She's lost."

"How she gonna get found if y'all don't help her?"

"She can follow behind. We're leading the way, ain't we?"

I look back, wave. The girl stares like she don't see me. She turns away, goes back to rooting through garbage.

"She's gonna be a mama," I say.

"Yep."

Mama. I'm staring at that girl so hard I see her. Mama's shaking her head, looking like she raised me better than this. She's ashamed of me. Then she does it, she slips into Agnes. It's so quick, I can't breathe. She turns away, turns her back on me and I'm running. Before she's gone I wrap my arms around her, hold her, I tell her I'm sorry and I love her. It's a whisper, nothing more than a hot word pressed against my ear. "Remember," she says but it sounds like I love you and it fills me and I'm holding and holding but she's slipping away. Then Agnes is gone and that girl's pushing me away, sharp nails and bony fingers.

"I'll be back," I'm saying, but I don't touch her no more. I catch up with Sable. I'm waiting on her to say something. She squeezes my hand. I look back. There's Tempe, her arm around that girl's shoulders. Tempe nods her head. That girl, that baby neither, won't make it through the night.

Chapter 21

Music shakes the foundation of the stone church. It's the same one we were at just yesterday but it seems bigger. The ceilings look higher. Thanks to the candles, I notice the windows are painted over in bright watercolors. The walls are bold red and rich gold. It isn't like any church I could have imagined and none I seen since. If there's one, there are hundreds of painted Jesuses. Jesus with milky white, bronze, or mahogany skin, staring down from brown, blue, or black eyes hang from the ceiling, the walls, the backs of pews. He's everywhere.

So is everyone else. Seems like all of Grammercy is packed inside them four walls. The children are sent to the corner for Children's Service. There they are greeted by stern-faced teachers dressed in starched-white uniforms. Their fussing and chattering quickly settles into reciting psalms. A nurse comes to take you to the baby room where you won't be "disturbed" but I know it's so you don't get to crying. The baby room is in another corner, hidden behind a thin wall of books that only half covers the nurse when she sits down to rock you. You ain't but a month old. Don't seem to care who holding you as long as they singing, talking, or feeding you.

The men head over to another corner of the church so they can talk in private. We pretend not to hear them whisper about the Klan and lynchings. Every once in a while one tells of a new job opening or warns about somebody who won't pay. The women mostly seem to talk about whose kid is doing what, what employer to watch out for, and where to get bargain stew meat. For a time, talk turns to good work, shoes, and hair. It gets crowded when the Leylands enter the room. The women, married and single, start fanning themselves like the room done gone hot. Mrs. Leyland greets me, only it's Etta Mae tonight, Sister Etta Mae, she tells me. She's telling me how pretty I look and kissing me on the cheek. I'm sure there's a splotch of lipstick where the wet mark is but I leave it till I get home. With one eye on her husband, she talks with each woman a second before standing beside him. He introduces himself, the Reverend Justice Leyland, and kisses my hand. I don't want to but I know I'm blushing.

"And her husband, Buddy Freeman, is just over there, dear. You met him last night," Etta Mae says. She's got her hand on his shoulder and her head leaning toward him.

With his arm wrapped around her waist and the way he's watching the words tumble out her mouth, I see like everyone else, this is love. Ten minutes later and Reverend Leyland is transformed into the man standing in the middle of the room, sweat dripping down his forehead, veins popping from his neck as he clutches the Bible in front of him. "Brothers and sisters," he says, "I say the Grace of God has let loose the chains and set our brothers and sisters free from bondage. Ain't that right?"

"Lord have mercy!" the crowd responds.

"Now the Lord has fulfilled his part. Today, the heathens walk amongst us and the Mighty Lord has said to me, them heathens sinners, every last one of them!"

"Amen!"

Heathen? Sweat drips down my back. I'm looking toward the door wishing I was on the other side. Some fresh air will feel good right about now.

"Ain't their fault, oh no! The white man kept the Good Book from them!"

"Bring 'em low!" the congregation responds on cue.

"Kept it for himself! Kept our brothers and sisters in ignorance so they would go straight to ..." He pauses, mops his forehead. "Now I'm just gonna say it, cuz we all know, brothers and sisters, they going straight to Hell!" he roars. Sweat drips down his face, his voice shakes. His body don't move one inch. Only his eyes slide round the room. "God only knows what the white man had our brothers and sisters doing. Fornicating! Drinking! Lying! Working on the Sabbath! God seen it all!"

From above his head, baby Jesus glares straight at me. Working on Sunday.

"Why he let them keep us slaves?" a woman near me asks.

"The Lord works in mysterious ways," the reverend responds.

"Where was he when they sold my babies?" another woman asks.

"Right there, keeping you safe," the reverend says.

A nurse swoops in. Shushes her, holds her while she cries. "Was he in the war?" someone asks.

"Right there beside you on the battlefield," the reverend says.

"And when my mama died rather than stay a slave?" a man asks.

"Right there, guiding her way to Him." The reverend wipes his brow. He shifts his weight from foot to foot.

"That ain't God," a familiar voice whispers. It sounds old, tired, hurt, sad, and so afraid I weep for it. It's me. "All that stealing and selling folks and chaining them, that ain't no parts of God."

"The heathen speaks the truth!" the reverend says. He launches into a sermon about forgiveness and sin. I'm edging closer to the door when the choir starts. Only thing keeping me from that door is their sweet voices. The words wash over every ache of my body. They heal every cut and stitch every wound. Too quick they finish.

"We got a whole lot of new faces in the community," the reverend says. He's looking pleased with himself. "Ain't none of you alone. Would all the newcomers please gather around me? We're going to make a nice big circle with the newcomers up front and a ring around them."

It takes a while to get settled. The women make up one side, the men the other. The closer I edge toward the door, the more the circle draws me in. It closes in on me.

"This'll do," he says. "Now we're going to start at the outside and work our way in as we confess our sins. Brother Ezekiel, we'll start with you."

Brother Ezekiel stole socks off a line, someone else let food go to waste, someone else used the Lord's name in vain. The confessions go quick, like people can't wait to get them out their mouths. Not working hard enough, sassing an elder; no matter what sins they confess, the circle says nothing. It's nearly my turn. I imagine my confession. Which one do I say first? What will they think of me? It's my turn. Words jumble around in my head. I take so long to answer that someone squeezes my elbow, someone else pats my back. I'm looking around for Tempe. She ain't here.

I open my mouth. "I'm not sure I believe," I say.

Silence. They gonna push me out like they did that girl.

I don't care. I don't need none of them. As long as I got you, Buddy, and Franklin, I don't need nothing else. Will Sable kick me out? She'll have to. She'll turn her back on me and walk away. Only, I'll be the one walking. First thing in the morning we'll set off, if she gives me till morning. Won't give her the satisfaction of putting us out. We'll set out tonight. Won't have nowhere to sleep, but it'll be alright. I been through worse. We'll sleep outdoors. You'll be in my arms, safe.

The reverend nods, moves on to the next. My heart's beating loud. Then there's an organ playing and the choir's singing. Etta Mae slips beside me. She's smiling like she feels sorry for me, like she didn't expect nothing less. I'm mad and I'm hurting and I don't know why.

"We got Bible classes twice a week," she says. "I signed you up for both. You got reading on Monday nights and arithmetic on Tuesdays. There's Celebration Committee, Sick and Shut-In Committee, Sewing and Darning Committee, Cooking Committee, Cleaning Committee, Worship Team, and the Mourning Group. I'm on the Education Team. All of us on the Welcome Committee. You can try them all out and see which you good at."

Over the years, the groups roll into one.

A week or so later, Sable takes you in to sleep with her so Buddy and I can talk. We in the backyard laying in the grass pretending we in love. He's holding my hand and stroking my face and telling me how beautiful I am. I'm telling him how strong he is and how handsome he looks all grown-up. I'm trying to get the words I love you to come out my mouth. He must be trying too, cuz he opens his mouth and instead of words, his tongue pops out. Then it's in my mouth and I don't mean to but I jump. We laugh and let loose our hands.

"I would have loved you before the war," he says.

I'm looking up at the stars and practicing counting. One, two, three. The moon's bright. Far across the city, train whistles blow. Gas lights burn in the houses across the backyard. "I seen people willing to kill people they love, just to keep us slaves," he says. "I fought beside people in the same uniform who wouldn't sit beside me and eat. I buried men who were like brothers. Men who would die for me. For you, too, without even knowing you. Make sure that boy knows that."

"Where you going?"

"I can't stay here," he says. Your pa's watching me watch the sky. I know he wants me to look at him. To tell him it's alright, to go on. "I can't sleep at night without waking up screaming." I put my head on his chest and listen to the beat of his heart, the sound of his voice vibrating before it hits the night air. "In the day I see ghosts. I can't hardly look at you without seeing Tempe beside you. I'm losing my mind."

I tell him about your mama. He don't say nothing for a long time.

"When it's time, teach that boy where he come from. Ain't no running from it. You ain't no slave. But no sense running from what you was." His hand's in my hair. "I been fired from the factory cuz my hands start shaking every time I hold metal. I got me a job out on the ocean. A big old fishing rig. Get to travel for a bit, let the sea soothe my soul. The house next door is all fixed up for you and the baby. Soon as you ready, you move in. I done put down a deposit. I told Sable I'll pay on the rest once a month. It'll take a while but the place will be yours."

We sleep out in the yard side by side like brother and sister. In the morning, he kisses you on the head, me on the cheek, and sets off. It's years before he makes his way back home.

2:30 a.m.

"Mama," Edward whispers.

It's yesterday morning. We're in my bedroom. My covers are scattered half on the bed, half off. I'm snoring loud enough to call hogs. And he's sitting there, at the edge of my bed, calling my name.

"Wake up," I whisper. But I don't. I'm lying there asleep like nothing else matters. Like it ain't the last time I'm going to see my baby. "Wake up!" I shout.

Listen, Tempe says, but she's crying too.

"I'm about to head out to work," he whispers. His voice is gentle, soft. "I won't be coming back." His eyes are red. His cheeks are streaked with tears. "You're going to hear a lot of stories after I'm gone. They'll say I did it to help get rights for union workers. They will say I did it because I was scared not to do it. But they don't know the truth." He pulls the covers off the floor, tucks me in tight. "If I don't do this, I'm a dead man. They'll string me up from a tree and nothing will ever happen to them. Mama, they've decided how I'm going to live. I'm going to decide how I'm going to die. I'm going to stop them from crashing that car. I don't know how. I just know I won't be coming back home. I love you, Mama." He kisses me on the forehead, backs away from the bed, closes the door behind him, and he's gone.

Chapter 22

It's been a year since we moved into the house next door. Franklin still lives across the street. I moved in a few weeks after Buddy's first check arrived. Between his pay and what I make working shifts down the factory, doing odd domestic work and sweeping up hair at the salon, we do alright. Still, soon as she hears Christian's coming back, Sable sends Lillian over too.

When she gets word he's coming, Sable sends for the Welcome Committee. The lawn is cut, the house scrubbed from floor to floor. Cracks filled, joints oiled. She gets a whole hog. The whole thing, even the head, is slow roasting in a pit for a full day before Christian even gets home. Women drop off cakes and pies. There's fresh ice and gutted fish. Lillian and me scrub and bake right along with the rest of them. That's how I notice she's gonna have a baby. We sitting alone in Sable's kitchen ripping out sharp fish bones and soft innards. I'm scooping 'em out and setting them on a newspaper next to their heads like Sable told us to.

"You sure you feeling alright?" I ask for the third time.

She's bent over a pot spilling out breakfast she ain't but just ate.

"My cooking don't agree with you?"

She's coughing up more and more. I run to get Sable. She takes Lillian to a friend's. Someone fetches a doctor. Lillian don't come back for a few hours. By the time she does, I got the heads wrapped in paper so she don't have to look at them. She's smiling and holding her belly.

"I'm with child," she says.

That don't explain the coughing but we all too happy to notice, and when she dies nine months later, we don't remember her being sick at all.

Sable's just settled Lillian in the back room, propped her feet up and the window too. I'm sure she can hear us. "So you just gonna let her stay here till the baby come?" she asks.

At least that's what I think she says. With her mouth full of laundry pins I can't be sure. The food is all cooked, the table's just about set, when Sable notices a spot on the tablecloth. Instead of putting something on top of it to cover it like Lillian had suggested, Sable strips down the table. She scrubs the tiny spot until it's three times as wide but clean. We go out back, hanging it to dry in the sun. She saying she hope it don't rain but I'm hoping it do. Not a lot, just enough to make her wish she hadn't put up such a fuss about that little thumbprint of a spot. The crisp, white cloth flaps in the wind. Sometimes I pretend not to hear her.

"Don't think I set no time to how long she can stay," I say.

"What will the church say?"

"I reckon they gonna ask how they can help and if they should have the committee make the baby some bonnets."

Sable sucks her teeth. I only go on special occasions: welcomes and funerals. What difference do it make what they say?

"What about me? Don't you care about what I think?"

I don't say nothing for a while. Out of the corner of my eye I watch Sable wringing a rag like it's a little neck. You over a year old. You toddling round on unsteady legs trying to catch rolling apples.

"Course I do," I say. "I spend lots of time thinking 'bout what you want. I say, Spring, and I put my hand on my hip like this," I show her. "Spring, now what you think Sable gonna say when you let Lillian stay with you in her condition? A woman in the family way with no family to speak of? And I say, Hush, gal, if Sable wants her out, she'll put her out. This is her house, cuz it is, so it's up to her who lives here or no. Don't matter if you paying on the house month by month. If Sable wants to keep that whole house empty, it'll stay empty. And if she gives a room to someone that's been like a daughter to her, someone who now more than ever needs a place for her and her child, who am I to speak on it?"

"I ain't known you to not speak on something since you been here," Sable says.

"Sure nice to have a celebration," I say to get her mind off Lillian. "A baby and your boy coming back all in the same day."

"You think Franklin's in love with her?"

I don't think no such thing. "Sure, why not?"

She's cooking up some idea. I go back to the kitchen.

"She putting me out?" Lillian asks.

"Not if I can help it."

I make her some tea to stop her from shivering. It's late when he comes. Christian is bigger than Sable said. He looks just like her, acts like her too. He dotes on her. Can't seem to get enough of her. He's hugging and kissing on her, picking her up, twirling her around. She's laughing and entertaining. The committee does the rest. Someone sets the table; someone piles it high with food. Someone else organizes a line: men first, then women. Someone keeps the punch flowing. There's music and singing, dancing. While Sable eats, Christian tells stories about places he's been. When that's done, he sings with the band. Then he takes turns dancing with all the women. He's got his mama's knack for socializing.

The dancing is just getting good when Etta Mae and Justice show up. They work their way around the yard. Before long, Etta Mae's got Lillian cornered in the kitchen and Justice got Franklin hemmed up in the backyard.

"There's gonna be a wedding," Sable says. Her voice is giddy and I'm about to ask her what's in that jar she's been sipping out of when Etta Mae asks the musicians to stop playing for a spell.

"Folks, we about to have a wedding," Justice says, but he ain't Justice no more. He's the reverend.

Folks are whispering, we're all wondering who's getting married. Franklin's standing with his hands in his pockets rocking back and forth on his heels like he's wondering too. He's surrounded by a group of men. I can't tell if they're holding him up or holding him in. Is he here for the wedding? Etta Mae's leading Lillian by the arm. At least she'll be up front, get to see the whole thing. Instead of sitting her down, Etta Mae delivers her up front to Franklin, only it looks like he's stepping backward. They're standing about as far away as they can from one another when the reverend says something over the air in between them. Before either of them can say a word, they married. Poor things, ain't even near no river for a proper wedding. The men are slapping him on the back and pushing Franklin so before long he's kissing Lillian full on the lips. Except for me, everyone's clapping and cheering.

Sable's grinning. They'll take the front room so Lillian can be close to the outhouse. You and me got the whole second floor to ourselves.

You run yourself tired. Somebody takes you in to lie down. I'm setting in the grass thinking 'bout nothing much at all when Christian sets beside me.

"My mama says you used to be a slave. That right?" he asks.

I nod my head yes.

"Whereabouts?"

I tell him near as I know.

"Who your people?"

Something in his voice makes me want to make something up. Lay claim to kin with names I don't know in places I can't even imagine. I try to think of all the people I met these past few months. They were from all over. I can see their faces, hear the sounds of their voices, but the names of their people and the places they call home sound like one long moan. Snatches of my own life flick off my tongue. River, Fire, Farmer, Story, Freedom, Present. None of them sounds like much of a name. He's watching my lips like he's just waiting for a lie to drop out so he can scoop it up and eat it. I can't help myself. "Walker," I say.

"Sure 'nough?"

"I ought to go check on the baby." I'm halfway up.

"Shame what they done to your sister."

I know that I'm shaking cuz he's helping me sit back down and his hand is holding tight to my arm.

"Like killing her once wasn't enough," he says.

I look around for Tempe. I know she's nearby. I hope she can't hear him. I don't want to hear him neither but I can't hear nothing but him. The band is still playing even though I can't hear no more music. The choir's still singing but ain't no songs coming out of their mouths. There's crickets aplenty but none of them chirping. The only thing there is is his voice. I want to call him a liar. But he's talking about a band of farmers seeing the house all blazed up and running in to save Walker and instead finding Tempe bleeding to death with a hole in her chest and what looked like two men dead beside her. Between the fire and smoke, couldn't make out what parts was Walker's and what wasn't so they mixed them both up and buried them. They figured she done it. Took hours to cool her body down enough to grab hold of.

"Truth is," he's saying, "she's probably dead long before it but they don't want to let her get away with killing two men so they string her up to a tree and hang her. Cut her down and scatter her body parts every which way. She'll be forever tied to this Earth, wandering."

I should have asked her what happened after I'd gone. She never seemed to want to talk about it. I'm laying in the grass now. My eyes are closed. I'm watching my sister burning when I feel my insides swell up. My whole body's burning from the inside. I'm shaking. Feel like I need to be somewhere else. To do something.

He's lying beside me just watching me cry without tears. When he gets tired of that he starts making things out of grass. Rips it up from the ground and makes little nooses for my fingers. He slides three of them on. "Seems you ought to be thanking me for setting you free." He's puckering up his lips for a kiss.

I open my eyes and see Tempe, her hands just about wrapped around Christian's neck.

"Tempe!" I yell.

She drops her hands, puts them on her hips.

"Tempe what?" Christian asks.

She disappears.

"Tempe set me free," I say.

"Nah," he says. "If it wasn't for my troop, y'all still be slaves." He's tilting his face close to mine, pointing to his mouth.

"And now, I gotta be thankful to you for giving me something that shoulda always been mine?"

"Fine, don't thank me," he says. He's pretend-pouting. "You could at least be thankful I made your life easier."

I laugh. Can't even help myself. "This is easy? Why if you ain't told me, I wouldn't have recognized it for myself. I got four jobs," I say. I hold up four fingers.

"Ought to be thankful you got one," Sable interrupts.

"I'm thankful for every little penny I get. I scrub, cook, bake, mend," I say. I don't know how long she been standing there. I sit up.

"You get more jobs than anyone I know. Just can't seem to keep them," she says. She's shaking her head at me.

Christian winks and slips away. He's out by what's left of the pig, singing with a group of men.

"Don't know how you keep getting them and losing them, sometimes in the same day," Lillian says. She plops down onto a nearby seat.

"Oh, I can tell you how," Sable says, like somebody asks her. "She gets there when the sun comes up, talks to the wife. You got work you need help doing? She sings in that sing-song voice."

"I don't talk like that." Nobody's paying me no attention.

"You know how she do," she continues. Lillian's bobbing her head like they done solved a crime. "She gets to scrubbing with one hand, baking with the other, mopping with one foot, sewing with the other, and the lady of the house gets to thinking, damn, if she can do all that, what more can she do? Why, little Spring here shows her. She's inside doing housework and outside harvesting potatoes ain't even been planted yet. If she can do all that, the lady thinks, she can mind the kids."

"Well, ain't that right where she messes up?" Lillian interrupts.

"Sure enough it is! So she there supervising the doing and the minding and the husband get home and they sit there talking about how good the wife is at supervising and minding and how tired she must be. His poor wife needs a rest, would Spring mind putting the kids to bed and telling them a story? Why'd he go and ask that for? Spring go on and bathe 'em and put them to bed and blow out the candles and she get to telling them a story. Them kids get to wailing, the parents come a-running. Mama, the oldest one says, Spring told a story about men in sheets coming round and snatching up folk, the boy cries. Then the girl, who's always adding her two cents says, Mama, she said if we don't go to sleep, we get snatched up and sold down south! That ain't never gonna happen, the father say. Tell them ain't no such thing as being sold away from your family, the mother says. Kids just a boohooing by then. The husband red-faced with his hand on his wife's shoulder daring Spring to tell them that someone could come up in their house and steal their children and sell them off. Like such a thing is possible."

"It happened to my mama," I say. "Stole right from her family. Why couldn't it happen again? It ain't like everybody give up on slaving. Why it make sense for my folk to be stole but not them?"

"Your folk ain't white," Lillian says.

She says it like it's logical. One and one is two. Black and black is slave. We done had this conversation a hundred times or more. She says it like I should know better.

"Now, Spring, get to humming 'stead of talking," Sable says. "You know how that riles folks up. They get to telling her she's ungrateful for not thanking them for giving her a job and that they aren't paying her since she spoiled their family by bringing slave stories and besides, she don't bake that good nohow!"

"Now that ain't nothing but a lie," I say. "I'm a darn good baker!"

They right, though. My mouth has cost me many a job. To hear them tell it, if I ain't humming slave songs or hanging my head like an old dog, I'm working slower than I can, working faster than I should, ungrateful, dim-witted, and angry for no good reason. Most of the jobs I get, I get cuz I was a slave. People expect there ain't nothing I can't do, nothing I won't do. More than a few times a supervisor or some other boss put his hand somewhere it didn't belong. I ain't say nothing about it, though. Just slipped a bit of ground tobacco in his tea or coffee, some ground leaves in a meat stew. Not enough to kill nobody, just enough to make them run to the pot and pray to God they'd make it. Sometimes they did, sometimes they didn't. Depended on what they done and what I remembered from Mama's old scrawlings. Her notes are more pictures than anything else. Most of them look like blueberry bushes or things that don't grow here in the city. I don't expect no harm to come from it but doing it makes me feel good for a little while. Makes me stop feeling like I'm burning up each time somebody ask me something they don't want to know about anyway.

Most of the jobs I lost, I lost for telling the truth. A wife would corner me and ask while I was busy scrubbing out her dirty sheets, if I didn't like it a little bit when the master showed me some attention. She'd giggle and ask if she should be worried about her husband, if she should trust me alone. It wasn't nothing for a grown man to ask to see the scars he imagined ran up and down my back, to ask how the whip felt on my skin. They want to be close up to pain, until they are. When I get mad about them telling me all they think they know about my life, they call me angry. They say it like I ain't got no cause at all to be upset, sad. Can't hardly feel nothing without somebody telling me how I should feel instead. I can fall down a whole flight of stairs and won't there be somebody at the bottom telling me I should be grateful to be alive?

If I'm tired of being accused of working too fast or too slow, of being called a whore cuz somebody's husband done watched me walk away, I should work slower or faster and not be a temptation. If I'm sick from carrying loads of laundry and smashing rocks and planting crops, I'm a "lazy little ungrateful heifer lucky I can't be whipped no more but who needs to be reminded of how good things are now." And when I can't seem to stay two steps ahead or just really want somebody who don't want or need something from me to wrap their arms around me, I should smile, laugh, sing more and not look so sad sometimes because Lord knows I ain't got nothing to be sad about. With all these people telling me how to feel, it's a wonder I feel anything at all. But I feel everything all at once. Happy, sad, scared, lonely, disappointed, mad, lost. Who can I tell? Everybody's so busy making up their minds about me, nobody wants to hear me tell them nothing different.

We clean up the backyard. Wrap the bones up to send to the butcher, put the tables in the cellar, blow out the lanterns. Everyone's said their goodbyes. I know Sable's in there pretending to be asleep so I don't come take you home. So, I'm heading home empty-handed. I'm almost to the back door when Christian whispers.

"You ready to stop burning?"

His hands are on my wrist and his mouth is so close to my ear that I feel the words go straight to my brain. I nod my head, yes. His hand is on my back and before I know it, we make love in the grass and I don't mean no harm but inside I'm still burning.

"Ready?" he asks.

He's halfway up, putting his clothes on in the dark before I'm standing. I get dressed too. He grabs my hand. We slip out of the yard into an alley. We run through the alley like school kids. We're giggling and knocking over trash cans. Each clatter of metal on concrete is like music. Scattered piles of spilled garbage with rotting food and broken bottles are like paintings. We dance through the streets. He's always a few steps ahead. It's a game of Gotcha. I'm it. He's slipping in and out of alleys, behind buildings, through yards. Maybe he's my Edward. I'm trying to make my way to him. If I love him, I'll be able to find him. He's getting farther away. Now, he's nothing more than a shadow beneath dim streetlights, a stone tripping down an empty street. I'm on fire. I can't stop moving. I don't even know where I'm going. But there's a brick in my hand and the first window shatters. He makes his way back to me. He's grinning, proud. We bust out five shop windows before the chill sets in.

The river. We've run through so many alleys I don't know where I am. There are no streetlights here. There's little light at all but the stars and a sliver of moon. I don't need light to see it. It's small, like a trickle, and muddy but I recognize it by the way it moves like breath. It's been here all along, waiting on me. His footsteps are soft splashes. He's laughing and sliding his way to the other side. It ain't no wider than a front room. He holds out his hand. I see Tempe splashing and running her way to Edward, him rushing to her. I reach out my hand but he's gone. Tiptoeing up the bank. Hands on hips, head cocked, impatient.

"Well, come on!" he yells. "Ain't nobody gonna carry you over."

I slide down the soft grass. Mud kisses my shoes, sucks and pulls. I fall. He's on the other side, laughing. I could die here. In the middle of this dirty stream. It's nothing like the water back home. The word sinks into the sludge. This is home now. I could follow this little bit of river all the way back to Walker's and it wouldn't carry me home. Wherever my family is, that's home. I'm on my hands and knees in the mud in the middle of the night. I won't die here. You waiting on me. I got a family, I got a home. I stand up, brush the mud and leaves off my dress. I'll wash it in the morning before anyone's up. Without looking at him, I head home.

He drips along behind me. I'm pretending he's not there until he puts his shirt over my shoulders. It's damp and spattered but I thank him. We hold hands as if they aren't caked with mud. Our palms flake as we press them tight. I'm walking lopsided. My soles are thick with dirt, one more than the other. I'm stomping, trying to bang the dirt from beneath my feet and keep up with him both. How does he manage? I look to see if his shoes aren't covered in mud too. His toes, swaddled in mud, wiggle when he walks. Behind him he leaves a trail, like manure. I laugh. The more he asks me what I'm laughing for, the harder I laugh. I laugh till my sides hurt, till I'm empty.

"I love you." He whispers it in the air above me.

I'm still laughing when I say it back. I know it won't last when he kisses me on the forehead but I slip in the house. It doesn't matter. Not yet.

Chapter 23

Grammercy

October 31, 1867

Race fuels fire as Grammerc

After days of questioning suspects, the police have found that the two bodies recovered in last week's fire that cost a total of five lives, were those of the culprits.

The string of vandalism that has plagued our community's streets, fueling tensions between neighbors and causing contention in an otherwise friendly Philadelphia neighborhood has abruptly died down.

Police credit neighbor's vigilance and cooperation.

Rer foll imp

The that rela the beh of a

I don't like him. Tempe's watching me get ready to go out.

"Why not?"

He won't be around long.

"He's gonna die soon? Ain't there no better way to say that? Maybe sit me down? Hold my hand and say, Spring, don't fall in love with this one. This one's going to die."

I didn't say he's dying. I said he won't be around long. She shrugs. "Why you jealous? You had everything. A husband, a baby." She's gone before I finish.

Christian and me terrorize the folks of Grammercy for months. Some nights we don't even make love. Just get right to making havoc. I spend less time being angry during the day. I'm even singing more. Tempe won't talk to me. I see less of you, Lillian and Franklin, so it's a while before I notice her getting sicker and bigger and you calling her mama.

I work every day. Get fired from one job and pick up another one. I don't mind what I'm doing, what hours I'm keeping. I set my life by the sun, slip in the house when it rises, slip out when it sets. As long as I'm bringing in money, shouldn't matter none. But of course it do. One morning I'm about to slip in the door, I'm taking off my shoes so I don't clip-clop across the floor, got one hand on the knob and it don't turn. It must be stuck. I rattle and shake but it don't budge. I run around to the back, hot as it is the windows are closed. I tap on a window. No answer. Tap on another one, no answer. I'm getting mad now. I'm locked out my own house. I'm back around front, my tapping turns to banging. I'm looking around for something to bust out a window. I got a rock in my hand but I can't throw it. By the time Franklin opens the door, I'm slumped in the doorway, cradling the rock like it's my baby.

"You want to act like a stranger, we treat you like one," he says.

For a few nights I'm home by dark. A week passes, then another one. Even Tempe's back. She don't mention Christian. She mostly talks to you while you sleeping, watches me, or hangs over Lillian's shoulder. Before the month ends I'm back at it. Me and Christian get more and more reckless. We get closer and closer to the imaginary line dividing the black folks from the white ones. Only, it ain't really imaginary. There's a thick row of trees keeping us apart. I done been on the other side. Worked in some of them grand houses where I had to walk past a city block full of trees just to get to the other side and then up some slope to a house where I had to come in through the back door. I hate those damned trees. Don't seem able to stop hating them. Some nights, when Tempe ain't around, Christian and me flip through the book. He laughs and makes faces when I tell him the truth so I make up stories about running away, rebellions.

"Your master ever take you?" he asks. He's angry, mad at me for something I couldn't have kept from happening in the first place.

I shake my head no.

"You sure?"

His mind's already made up so I don't bother trying to change it. I don't answer no more. I don't share the book with him no more neither. When he asks me about it, I tell him the past makes me sad. Pretty soon he stops asking.

Over time we make friends with a few other folks who ready to take charge anyway we can. It's time we take what's ours, they say. To hear them tell it, the only thing keeping us down is the white man and the only thing he got that we don't is them trees. We sit around in basements talking about sawing them down. Sometimes we talking about the trees, sometimes we ain't. I ain't never heard of no quiet saw. "How you gonna down something with nobody noticing?" I ask.

The point ain't for nobody not to notice, the point is just to cut them down, they say. I don't see how we gonna get close enough to cut one down let alone all of them. The closer we get to that line, the closer the police get to us. As long as we causing trouble on our own streets, don't seem to matter none. But bust a window down on Main Street and it makes the news.

"I'm gonna make the front page," Christian says.

I tell myself I'm doing it for you and for Tempe and Mama, for all of us. We been talking for hours about not taking this and not doing that, setting boundaries. I'm tired of talking. "I got an idea," I say.

In less than an hour, we in front of them trees and they burning. The thick trunks and branches are lit up, pure fire. Burning branches catch the grass and soon the grass is on fire too. We stand back. The wind picks up. Burning leaves kiss dry flowers and soon all of Grammercy, white and black, is burning.

We run. Christian and me make it almost all the way home before we realize we the only two running.

"They must have gone another way," he says.

In the morning we hear how people was pulled from their houses for all-night questioning. How they was beaten and broken even if they didn't know nothing. I'm waiting for a knock on the door. Tempe's pacing back and forth. She stops every few steps to shake her head at me.

You better not leave my boy. She says like I got a choice in it.

"I'll run and take him with me."

Run where?

"Take me with you. Take me where you go when you ain't with me." I'm begging her.

I don't want my boy to end up like me.

"Dead?" I ask.

With no place to go. Only thing keeping me alive is you.

"I don't know what to do," I say. I'm crying.

I'll take care of it. Just stay here.

I don't go nowhere for weeks. Lose my jobs. I take in washing. Between shifts, Franklin delivers it for me. I'm there when Lillian's throwing up blood. I need to get Sable to keep you and to send Christian for a doctor.

"Mama?" you ask. You looking straight at Lillian. I'm about to correct you.

"I'm alright, baby," she says. "He calls me that. I don't mind." Blood's bubbling up through her mouth.

I'm banging on the front door with you in my arms.

"He's been gone for weeks," Sable says, "left for New York looking for work. Coulda sworn he would have told you."

She don't say nothing about it but I know she knows about us. "Can the baby stay with you?" I ask.

She opens her arms. "Mama!" you squeal.

"Say bye to your mama," Sable says.

"Bye, Spring," you say.

The door closes. I'm knocking on another door asking somebody to send for a doctor. I get back and Lillian's passed out on the floor. Tempe's sitting beside her, holding her hand.

"What you doing?" I ask.

Waiting.

By the time the doctor gets there, Franklin's home and Lillian's sitting up saying she feels so silly to have fell out and how a little bit of blood ain't cause for alarm. The doctor talks to Franklin in private. I'm holding her other hand, making plans for when the baby come. I'm telling her I'm gonna be home more.

"Stop all that busting stuff up," she says. "Please. That baby needs you. This one too."

For a few weeks everything's fine. We have a routine. You and me get up early, just after Franklin sets off for work for the day. I get a nice bath ready for Lillian while you and Tempe sit with her. Sable comes over with breakfast. I teach you shapes and colors. When she's up to it, Lillian recites songs for you. Sable teaches you stories. After supper we sit out on the front steps. After dinner we go out back. I do Lillian's hair while you play in the yard. I bathe you, feed you, and put you to bed. You fall asleep in my arms.

"Night, Mama," you say one night.

That night, the fire stops burning. All I have, I have for you. I ain't just Sister or Spring no more. Seems like that night, I become a mother. You don't stop calling Lillian and Sable mama but at least you calling me mama too.

It's a few nights later and we already in bed when Lillian's screams wake us. The baby. Franklin's yelling he'll be back and running out the front door. You and me run down to her room and Lillian's laying on the floor sweating and moaning. I'm holding one hand, Tempe's holding the other. I can tell you can see her too from the way you smiling up at her.

You ain't afraid. Don't seem odd to you that you can see through her body, assuming you can. She running a hand through your hair, patting you on the head, she can't stop touching you.

Just this once, she says.

I know that if Lillian wasn't dying, she wouldn't be able to touch Tempe and Tempe wouldn't be able to touch you. Tempe scoops you up in her arms. She holds you for a second before you slip through her. I catch you before you fall. The midwife comes in saying this ain't no place for a baby. She hands you to Franklin and shuts you both out.

"We ain't got much time," she says.

The baby pushes out. The midwife puts her to Lillian's blue lips for "a kiss for safekeeping."

The Mourning Committee makes burial arrangements, does the baking and cooking and the washing. Takes weeks to get them out of my house. They trying to help but they always underfoot. They set up a schedule for them to take turns caring for you and your sister so I can take in more work. For a few weeks, we're a cause. They spinning clothes, creating pamphlets, organizing bake sales. They got bags full of baby clothes, blankets, and books. All donated from the folks of Grammercy. I'm starting to get used to them cooking and praying and dusting and singing till somebody round the corner dies and they gone.

I'm surprised to find that I miss them. Christian is back with a wife taking up Sable's time. We don't see much of her. Some nights I can hear her laughing through the living-room wall. If I set out in the hall, I can hear whole conversations. I don't do it often, but I'm there getting ready to go out and sweep the front steps when Christian tells her he's moving to Canada where a black man can make a "decent living." She's fussing about not seeing him or his wife. She's telling him to wait and see, things will get better here. She'll give him that whole house if only he'll stay. She'll move in next door and he won't have to see no more of her than he wants to. He'll be the man of his own house and for a year he is.

I can't stand to listen no more, so I creep back inside. The next morning she lets herself in. She takes the back room of the second floor. I take on more jobs and with Buddy and Franklin working and saving too, we buy the house in a few years. She cooks the breakfast, I cook supper, we both fix dinner. She takes care of Franklin like he's her son, he lets her do it. From time to time when Buddy comes, she don't ask why he sleeps in the front room if I'm all the way up on the third floor. She don't say nothing about creaks on the stairs, the smell of cinnamon burning, my talking to Tempe, Tempe talking back to me. And a year later when she slips out of my house for the last time, after Christian is buried and her daughter-in-law moves back to her people, Sable locks herself in where no one can hurt her but ghosts.

Chapter 24

4:00 a.m.

The glow from the streetlamps below casts shadows against the walls. A pitchfork here, a sinister-looking ghost in a pointed hat there. I can hardly trust my eyes. The bed creaks. The other beds are empty now. Patients must have moved on some way or the other. Edward's the only one left.

Hush.

It's Jacob. He's wearing shoes but I recognize his shuffle. "I hope you don't mind, ma'am," he says. "But I was in the room next door and thought I'd pay Edward a visit." His lip is split. He smells of blood, sweat, and sweet mint.

"How you get busted up like that in the hospital?" I ask.

He looks at me like I don't know more people get broken up in here than outside of here. "Officers had some questions they wanted to ask me."

He's close now. Breathing up all my good air. Wasting the little time I got left.

"Did you have answers?" I ask.

"That's the thing. Seems like ain't nothing I have to say, nothing they want to hear. All they want to know is if Edward is working with the railway to bust up the strike or if he's working with the unions to strengthen it."

I sit there rubbing the wood of the book. Tempe's standing behind him. Can he smell her burning?

"Don't you want to know?" he asks.

"I don't see how it would make much difference either way," I say. "He's my boy, no matter what side he was on. And you can take the opportunity to remind me that my boy ain't no boy like I don't see he's a full-grown man and I'll take the time to remind you that no matter how old he is, he's my boy."

"Ma'am, I just meant, Edward's made some decisions that only a man can make."

"Like what?"

"Like changing his future."

I look from him to the bandages they tell me is my boy. He's under there somewhere, waiting.

"Changing his future? Or changing yours? See, if you or somebody put him up to some sort of plan to break the strike or start one, if he come up with it or didn't, if he's working for the union or against it, if he was aiming for the store or swerving away from it, my boy's still going to die for it."

"Then let him die a hero."

"The death of a hero is no different than the death of an average man."

"Average men are forgotten. Heroes aren't."

"I'm going to make the headlines." It's like sitting here all these years ago with Christian talking about spilling fire like blood through the streets. I'm blinking but I can't stop seeing his face. If Sable hadn't convinced him to stay in Grammercy, he wouldn't have ended up lynched, swinging from some tree. He'd be alive now, laughing about hot-blooded men and the women that love them. Would he look at my boy and say, Just like his mama? Hot-headed. Would he be down there holding Lil's hand, patting Gideon on the shoulder, staring into silence with Buddy and Franklin? Or out there raising hell with the police and the protesters? Maybe he would have led Edward into the riots.

Either way, we here now.

"Can I talk to him, alone?" Jacob's asking. Tempe's nodding yes.

I lean over and kiss Edward's forehead. Tears stain the bandage. "I love you, son. Always will," I say.

Jacob's sliding the curtain behind me. I'm in Tempe's arms. I feel her holding me up before I realize what it means. I'm holding her tight.

"Man," he says, "you right about your mama. She's a bird and a half. I see why you want to do right by her. I don't know why you don't want to let her in on nothing, though. Seems like she can handle the truth. If you want her to think this got something to do with the riots, I'll go right on letting her think it. Police sure don't seem to have no problem with it. Neither side do either. The union all riled up calling for the police to round up all the scabs, railways calling for blood and legislation, strikers going wild. They stealing trolleys and setting them on fire. This is the start of something big and there you are in the middle of it. You ought to see it. You in the papers and everything. Couldn't have been me. You a hero, man, no matter how you want me to tell it."

Tempe's looking excited. She's all lit up.

"No," I say. "Not yet. Please." I pull the screen away, push

Jacob aside. I hold Edward's hands tight. I'm thinking, *Don't go, don't leave me,* but I don't say it. "Remember," I say. I got my head to his mouth listening for breathing, words, something.

I'm still holding his hand when the doctor declares the time of death: 4:37 a.m. Lil's there when I get back down to the waiting room. They all are: her, Gideon, Buddy, and Franklin, even Sable and the Mourning Committee. Picketers are gone to another march. The police decided Edward can't cause no trouble, they're off to another emergency. Other than us, there are only a few people on the streets this time of morning. I'm burning. I'm so angry that I'm surprised when I look down and see my feet don't leave scorch marks on the road. There's a high-pitch sound in my head, wailing. I cover my mouth but it ain't coming from me. The chorus. They singing about saviors and warriors and heroes and wanderers. Somewhere, Edward and Tempe are singing together, arm in arm, all the way home.

The Gramm

February 21, 1910

Philadelphia Riots Heat Up

A series of arrests, crack downs and investigations have led to the arrests of dozens of union agitators across the streets of Philadelphia.

According to officials, the police's prime suspect, Edward Freeman, was posthumously acquitted of all charges.

Protesters hit the streets chanting "Murders end in 1910!"

Though the Chief of Police says he will lead an investigation into the tactics employed to gather information and question witnesses, he "remains of strong supporter of the Department and their commitment to justice for all communities."

He is calling for calm and has called on help from the military to ensure our fair citizens are safe from more riots and destruction.

Rer
foll
imp

The
that
rela
the
beh
of a
exp
in l
its
beh
con
or v

Acknowledgments

My life has been made richer in part thanks to the stories that have come before mine. I can only hope to do the same for those who come after me. Thank you to all the writers, storytellers, and dreamers for making it possible for my book to be published. I would like to thank Gran for leading by example and loving me fiercely. Special thanks to my mother and sister for listening to my stories when I was a child, feeding my imagination always, and supporting my pursuit of me. My heartfelt thanks to my children, Amira, Marat, and Noah for traveling across the world in pursuit of my dreams, for your inexhaustible support and love, and for providing beacons of hope for the future that will always lead me home. Thank you all for inspiring me to be a better me. You three are my joy.

Remembered began with a series of questions. Thank you to Lancaster University Faculty of Arts and Social Sciences for funding my research and allowing me the space, resources, and time for practice-based research so that I could explore where the questions led. Thank you, Jenn Ashworth, thesis supervisor, colleague, and friend, for challenging me to write painful stories, crying as I cried, and for your support, editorial and otherwise. Thank you to the Department of English Literature and Creative Writing for years of supporting my creativity, research, and projects, and for the many colleagues who were generous with time, information, and feedback. Thank you, Jonathan Taylor and George Green, for carefully reading my thesis and believing it should be published. Thank you to my dear friend Naomi Kruger for your close reading, for answering questions late in the night, and for your translations. Thank you, Wanda Sosa Hawkins, Peace Toleito, and Candace Hantouche for years of friendship and support no matter where I am in the world. Thank you to the Society of Authors. The Authors' Foundation Grant awarded me precious support and space to write when I needed it most.

As I prepared for life post-PhD, thank you, New Writing North. The Northern Writers' Award for fiction provided me with support to buy time to edit the novel and afforded me opportunities to engage in the wider writing community. Thanks to you, I met my wonderful agent, Elise Dillsworth. Thank you, Elise, for championing my writing even before you read the complete manuscript, for your editorial eye, and for your patience in the face of my impatience. Special thanks for walking first in front of the world's largest canine and putting your life at risk. And a warm thank-you for knowing *Remembered* would be at home with Dialogue Books in the UK and in hands of the lovely Sharmaine Lovegrove.

Thank you to Caskie Mushens and to Jenny Bent of the Bent Agency for helping *Remembered* find a home with Blackstone.

Thank you to the team at Blackstone for welcoming me as

one of your authors and for bringing *Remembered* to readers in the US and Canada. It means so much to me. Thank you to my editor, Deirdre Curley, for your eye for detail and close reading.

Finally, a warm thank-you to readers everywhere for spending time with my characters and their stories. May all of us find our way home.